Shooting Stars

Leslie Hodgson

Horse on Cover by: Valerie Haverfield

To my mom and dad,
Wade and Laura Cook,
who have taught me to believe
in myself, follow my dreams
and never give up.

CHAPTER 1

"Every accomplishment starts with the decision to try." -
Anonymous

Isaac

Isaac jumped out of his chair and banged his knees on his desk. Like someone had flipped a switch inside of him, he was instantly done with feeling like a crazy person. Things were going to change—today. His questions and frustration burned inside of him, overpowering the pain in his knees. Why did they live in a house way up in the mountains and barely saw any other people? Why did his parents seem so sulky and sometimes sorrowful? And why did they spend the whole fifteen years of his life doing the same routine with no break ever in sight?

Isaac thought that if his parents didn't want him to ask questions, they shouldn't have had so many books in the house. Isaac knew just by reading fiction and non-fiction books alike that their lifestyle was far from normal. He couldn't find anything about this secret, code-language his parents taught to him and his older sister, Stella.

However, he did find mention of something he could do... but only in fiction books. That's why he kept it a secret from his family. He could move things without touching them. But the other thing he could do was not in any books at all, not even fiction books.

Every day, his parents thought he was just being a boy, playing out in the woods building stuff and exploring. But that's not what he was doing at all. He was making plants grow out of the ground with the touch of his finger.

Isaac strode across his room. He was so fed up with keeping secrets and being bored out of his mind. Not even his parents' constant educating of them could help anymore. He had to get out! Letting his determination feed his pace, he opened the door and tromped down the stairs.

At the bottom of the stairs, he saw his dad at the coffee table fiddling with Isaac's telescope. Looking at his dad was like looking at a large version of himself: dark, coarse hair, blue eyes, olive skin. And for some reason, looking at his dad also slowed down his fiery energy. He asked in a regular tone, "Dad?"

"Yes, my son," he answered without looking up.

"C . . . could we get out of this house tonight? It's been a really, really long time since we left and . . ."

"And you feel like you're going crazy?"

"Well, yeah."

"Me too. Yes, we'll pull out the car and get out of here tonight."

His dad definitely was a large version of himself and that made Isaac feel less lonely, and maybe even more confident. He watched his dad for a moment tinkering with the telescope.

"What are you doing with my telescope?"

"Just checking to . . . make sure everything is operational."

"Oh. Hey dad?"

This time his dad looked directly at him, which almost made him back out of asking, but he knew it was time. "Then, when we get home, can I talk to you about some things?"

His dad didn't answer immediately, just stared back at him with soft eyes. Again, Isaac saw sorrow there. After a moment, he answered, "Of course, son. We can talk about anything you'd like."

Isaac smiled at him.

"Now, go get your mom and sister and let's get out of here."

CHAPTER 2

"The vibrations of mental forces are the finest and consequently the most powerful in existence."

Stella

One thing was certain—Stella had no idea what was going on. It seemed to be awfully loud, like her brain was a radio that could only pick up static. It was dark and she was laying her head back on the seat of the car with her eyes closed trying to figure out why she felt like she was trying to wake from a drugged sleep. A blip of clear vision came into her mind . . . her dad was driving the car. It was late at night and the car swerved. She remembered seeing a tree before she blacked out and now, opening her eyes, she saw that tree directly in front of their smashed car. Outside the windows, Stella saw lights flashing around and thought maybe an ambulance was there... but the lights were green, and though she was struggling to think clearly, she knew green wasn't a color on an ambulance. And these lights were zooming across the sky like a shooting star—only much closer.

She jerked with panic when she remembered she had been sitting next to her younger brother.

"Isaac! Where are you?"

Stella flung her arm to the other side of the car to grab her brother and only felt the seat. He was gone. The still unidentified lights stopped zooming around and left everything in darkness and at that moment, someone seized the front of her shirt. Adrenaline surged forward like a tsunami racing through a city. She was ripped out of the car to the ground and she kicked and fought like a wild animal in a battle for its life.

"Stella, Stella! Stop! It's me sweetheart, its mom!"

"Mom! What's going on? Are you hurt? Where's dad? Where's Isaac?"

"Listen to me Stella, listen!" Her mom sounded panicked, which made the hair on the back of her neck stand up.

"Mom, what's wrong? Where's Isaac?"

Isaac spoke somewhere near her, "I'm here Stella." Stella felt Isaac touch her and she was flooded with relief.

The green light returned and all three of them looked up and watched as it arched across the sky. Shooting stars usually make you feel hopeful—why did this one make Stella feel as if she should start running quickly the other direction? The light disappeared behind a nearby hill and all was darkness again.

"Mom, what was that? Where's dad?" asked Stella.

"I can't explain everything to you now. I have to go help your father. I must send you both away. Someone is trying to find you. You must go. Stay hidden. Don't come back here."

Another light appeared—not green, but a bright bluish white that was outlining a tree. To Stella's shock, the tree was lifted out of the ground and was now hovering horizontally in the air. In the glow of the floating tree, Stella saw her father with his arms stretched up.

"Dad!" What the heck was going on? Did her dad do that to the tree? Stella watched her dad make a throwing motion and the tree soared swiftly through the air and went back behind the same hill the green light went behind. As it too disappeared behind the hill, no crash was heard, and the green light was back, and it was going fast. It catapulted straight for Stella's father. She saw her dad transform into what looked like the same bluish white glow that was on the tree and then he shot upwards like a rocket. But the green. . . whatever it was, hit the white lights and created a huge explosion.

There were more sources of light now, this time constant, orange, and flickering . . . *fire*. There were several trees now lit up with it, making the ambiance of a war zone. The white light was gone and from the ground, Stella saw the green light zoom overhead then land gently. What? What was going on? The green light faded and she thought she saw a large man appear.

An unexpected wave of fear and panic swept through Stella. Before she could react, her mother grabbed her chin and forced her to look at her. Isaac was down on his stomach on the other side of their mother. He too was trying to lift his head and see the man, but her mother held the collar of his shirt tightly in her hand.

In the light of the fire, Stella's mother said hurriedly, "He's seen us Stella. You must go now. I will not see you again. Not for a very long time. I love you both. Listen to me... your Father and I were just trying to protect you—that's why you didn't know."

"Mom, what are you—"

"Shh, Stella! No time. Remember the beach I always showed you the pictures of? With the lighthouse? Picture it now, both of you. Do you have it?"

Isaac nodded his head. Stella said "Yes, but mom—"

"Stella, do as I say. Think of the sand, the ocean, the lighthouse. Good-bye, my darlings."

Stella watched her mother and felt a warmness sweep through her body as she saw they were being consumed by that same white glow they saw on the tree. Stella started to think it was a dream. She watched as her mom let go, then repeated to her, "think of the beach!" She couldn't see anything but white light, and judging by the warmness she felt, she must look like that tree and her dad.

"WHERE DID YOU SEND HER?! WHO WAS THE OTHER STAR?!" was the last thing Stella heard before she felt herself being jerked upwards and the air was speeding by her like she was a bullet no one could catch. She had no choice but to surrender to unconsciousness.

"Maximus... what we feared most has just happened."

"All of them? Please say no."

"Isolde managed to transport Isaac and Stella before the Minion could reach them."

"But Isolde... Eli?"

"Killed."

"Where are the children? Did the Minion find out about Isaac?"

"He did see Isolde send two Stars away, but he did not know who it was."

Maximus spun around and started down the spiral stairs.

"Maximus!"

He stopped and looked back.

"The time has come. They will want to know everything, and it will be up to you to begin their training."

"Yes — I understand. I must go find them before they wake up."

CHAPTER 3

"You believe easily that which you hope for earnestly."

Stella

Stella's head was floating—but her body felt stuck to the ground as if she had been turned into lead and welded to the spot and her eyes felt glued shut.

A gamut of questions and thoughts were floating through her mind but it was difficult to grasp any of them. It was just night wasn't it? Why was the sun now searing her eyelids? What was this gritty dirt she was laying in?

Stella thought of Isaac and her eyes flew open. She tried to sit up but she almost blacked out again, so she laid back down and closed her eyes.

Stella saw a shadow come over her, blocking the sun from assaulting her eyes from behind her eyelids and then she heard, "It's ok, don't try and sit up. You'll feel better in a minute."

She jerked again and opened her eyes to see a man who looked very much like he spent a lot of time in the sun. He was dressed in cotton beige pants that were rolled up to his mid-calf, and a white button-up shirt that was made of a very light material. His skin was exceptionally tan, and his hair looked like it had been bleached blonde in the sun. And the eyes… they reminded her of someone… or were they just the kind of eyes that you envied whenever you saw a pair of them? He spoke to her now in a voice placed perfectly on the pitch scale, "When you are ready I need to take you both inside."

She looked over and saw Isaac a few feet from her. He was still unconscious but breathing deep and slow like he was sleeping.

She looked back at the man. Even though he was a stranger he did not scare her for some reason. "Who are you?" she asked. She managed to lift her head an inch and then bent her knees to get her feet in the sand, but her neck decided her head was too heavy to hold up by itself and it let go, causing her head to fall back down.

'That's ok," said the man "I'll help you." He slid a hand behind her neck and lifted her forward until she was sitting up on her own.

"So, who are you again? Where are we?"

"My name is Maximus—more to be explained once you and your brother are inside and rested."

Maximus walked over to Isaac and lifted him into his arms like he was a small child, not a teenage boy.

"Is he alright?" she asked.

"Just unconscious," Maximus answered. "Can you stand?" he asked her, "Unfortunately I can't carry two teenagers."

Looking up at him Stella replied, "Yes, but *where are we? What happened? Where are my parents?*" She somehow knew Maximus had all the answers she needed.

Stella stood, still feeling sore and dizzy, but now fueled by a desire to get her questions answered.

"I will answer all your questions—but let's get inside to my home and you can rest first." Maximus started walking away. Stella saw he followed a set of footprints that were faced in the opposite direction from which they were now headed. She concluded they must have been from Maximus coming to get them. Following the footprints with her eyes up the beach she saw they lead straight to... a lighthouse? Her mind reeled because the lighthouse in front of her was the lighthouse her mom had told them to visualize last night.

Calling out to Maximus she said, "Wait! Wait, you live here? You live here in this lighthouse?"

CHAPTER 4

"Every thought of yours is a real thing – a force."

Isolde
(ĭ-ZŌLD)

"If you don't tell me where you sent your daughter, I will take you to Gershon himself. That, my lady, is worse than death."

The man who was the green light now held Isolde's neck tightly in his hands. Isolde recognized him when she saw the green glowing flames. His name was Dreold and he was the most powerful of Gershon's minion. The minion were twelve men that had once been loyal to Orel as stewards. But now they were the 'minion' and did Gershon's evil bidding. They gathered followers and enforced the rules in exchange for the promise of worlds of their own to rule once Orel was dethroned. Anyone who appreciated a safe, quiet environment with freedom to do as they pleased had all the reasons in the universe to hate and fear Gershon's minion.

Isolde glared back at Dreold like his hands on her neck weren't hurting her at all. "Take me to him then. I'll never tell you."

Dreold let out an angry yell. In his rage, he tightened his hands on Isolde's neck. With his face only an inch from hers he shouted, "Don't you understand? I was supposed to kill you ALL! I will shorten your misery if you just TELL ME! WHERE IS YOUR CHILD?"

"Stella has the ability to undo Gershon's damage and rule the Zodiacs if she so chooses. Maybe you should change your allegiance if you want to be left alive."

"The offspring of Eli and Isolde will *never* rule! Gershon's law is already spreading through the Zodiacs faster than a raging wildfire. Orel never had this amount of control over his people, which lead to his downfall. My allegiance is with the right man. I will be rewarded."

"We won't waste time talking politics," Isolde said. "Obviously your views are distorted. You can do whatever you want to me and I will never tell you nor Gershon what you want to know."

Dreold tightened his grip even more and Isolde struggled to breathe. "Who else did you send with her?" he asked, voice shaking with anger.

"I only sent away my daughter, why do you think you saw two?"

Isolde knew how to get Dreold to kill her instead of torturing her for answers she would never give about her second child. She knew it was death either way—now or later—might as well be now.

Her goal was always to keep her children out of danger. It was difficult for her and her husband to conceal the powers they held and the energy force they created, but they had done it for several years while raising their kids on Earth—a place away from the Zodiacs and all the turmoil and danger there. They chose Earth because Gershon would think it insignificant because of the low intelligence. Where did she and Eli err? How did he find them? Would Maximus keep them hidden with him, or would he take them back to the Zodiacs?

She was racked with guilt, thinking how she should have prepared her children. They had no idea. They only knew life on Earth—in a Solar System.

"I will give you one more chance!" yelled Dreold in her face. "Give me answers and I will spare your life!"

"No," Isolde said calmly.

"Fine," he said in a low growl, "then you are coming with me." He took one hand off her neck and pressed and squeezed a round charm he had on a necklace. He was starting to light up in a green glow again, and Isolde knew he was taking her back to Gershon. She couldn't let that happen.

She couldn't do what Dreold could, or what her husband could, but she did have her own powers. She could counter darkness and evil with light and goodness. That was the gift of the people of the Summer Triangle — three of the brightest Stars in the sky: Vega, Deneb and Altair — to counter dark and evil forces.

Though Isolde faced an unfair predicament in which evil would seem to win, she knew that her killer would ultimately suffer a lot longer for his crime than her momentary physical pain. Her belief was that in the end, it would be she who 'won', because justice would deal harshly with iniquitous men.

She focused all her thoughts and strength on anything positive she could conjure, and then pushed them out of her which sent a visible shockwave through Dreold and beyond. The evil that was touching her and the good she electrified out from her body couldn't abide each other so they burnt apart in a searing flash.

CHAPTER 5

". . . you can't have a Universe without mind entering into it . . . the mind is actually shaping the very thing that is being perceived."

Stella

Stella stood in the doorway of the lighthouse in utter amazement. From the outside, the lighthouse looked hundreds of years old. She thought that she would find nothing inside but cement walls, stairs and a few rats.

She watched Maximus lay Isaac down on a plush leather couch. The walls were made of horizontal tongue-in-groove wood stained a beautiful maple color. The circular room looked like an elongated octagon with the way the wood walls were placed on the circular structure.

The light from the windows made the wood gleam so everything was bathed in a warm, orange glow.

The stairs spiraled and jutted out of the walls. There was no handrail, so they almost looked like they were hovering there. Underneath the stairs in four different places were big squares that emerged from the walls. Stella thought they must be rooms because there were windows on them.

All the furniture, rugs, lamps and interesting science trinkets made Stella feel comfortable and at peace for the first time since... the car accident! The panic was back, and all her questions were swelling up inside her to the bursting level. She rushed to Maximus who was putting Isaac on a couch.

"I need to take Isaac and go find my parents. We need to go now. They're in danger."

"Your mom sent you both here to me, Stella. Please, just rest for a minute; stay next to Isaac. I must go to talk t—"

"How did she SEND us here? Where is she? I don't even know you. How does she know you?"

"Stella, I promise you will learn all the answers you want.

Please, just for a minute sit here with Isaac so he is not alone when he wakes."

Stella opened her mouth to protest but Maximus put his hands on her shoulders, and without hurting her squeezed them firmly and said "Stay here. I am just going upstairs. I must send a message." He walked her backwards, made her sit on the couch, then let her go and said "stay" while motioning to her like she was a puppy. As she looked over at Isaac, she heard Maximus run up the stairs.

"She wants answers," said Maximus.

"Of course she does."

Maximus was in the uppermost room of the lighthouse, where the spotlight for the ships was usually operated. There stood a magnificent golden telescope. If he were to stand it on end it would be about as tall as a grown man and the magnifying glass end was about the size of a basketball.

He didn't have it turned towards the sky, but toward a wall, where a sheet of silvery white liquid cascaded down from the top of the wall to the floor.

Like a projector, the telescope cast an image of a man, life size, onto the sheet of liquid. Maximus talked to him as if he'd seen him every day of his life, and needed him in his life very much. "How do I even begin to explain things to them?"

"There is no easy way."

"Must I be the one to tell them of their parents?"

"There is no other person on Earth who can, Maximus. I think it best they stay here until they learn their basic defenses. The protection I have put on the lighthouse should hide the energy force of them using their powers. It would be unwise to risk alerting Gershon of their whereabouts by moving them to the Zodiacs."

"There is another option. May I bring them up here and have you tell them?"

"They aren't ready to know me yet. We don't want to put too

much on them all at once."

"If I were experiencing what the children are, I would think it comforting to know you."

"Yes, but let it be their choice. There is already so much that will be forced onto them because of what happened tonight. It was Eli and Isolde's choice for them to remain without knowledge of their heritage and home. It was also Isolde's choice to send them to you. Obviously she realized she could not hide them anymore."

"Alright," said Maximus with a deep sigh, "I will tell them about their parents so they can begin healing . . ." he paused as his voice choked up, "from their loss," he finished.

"You will do well, Maximus. Give them time and they will heal."

Maximus nodded and bent his body in a gentle bow, then descended the stairs slowly, sadness making each step more difficult than the last.

CHAPTER 6

"Creation is always happening. Every time an individual has a thought, or a prolonged chronic way of thinking, they're in the creation process. Something is going to manifest out of these thoughts."

Stella

Isaac was waking up. Stella was gently trying to straighten his dark and thick hair with her fingers, but her attempts were futile. Even now at fifteen, he still had a boyish quality about him.

He looked like their dad with skin an olive complexion that tanned really well in the sun. His eyes were the same as Stella's though—all different shades of green—from hazel-green to emerald-green and bluish-green depending on what they were wearing and the mood they were in. That's about the only thing they had in common.

Stella had potential to look like their mother . . . which was her deepest hope. Stella, now seventeen, had very light strawberry-blonde hair with matching eyelashes and eyebrows, and fair skin that was "sun-kissed" with a smattering of freckles over her nose and cheeks.

Stella often heard her parents tell her how she got her name. It meant 'star'. They would say, "Because you are bright and beautiful like the brightest star in the sky." They taught her to love the way she looked because she usually envied Isaac with his sun-tanned skin and dark lashes. Stella had her mother to look to and she knew what it meant to appear bright as a star. Her mother glowed like a bright summer day.

Finally, Isaac opened his eyes. He looked confused and started looking around the room. Suddenly he jumped off the couch as if it burnt him. He was on his feet, knees bent and poised to run. He started talking very fast, "What happened? Where's mom and dad?"

"Isaac, calm down. Sit," Stella said pointing to the couch next to her.

Isaac sat down, but was on the edge of the couch and breathing very fast. Stella told him the only answer she knew, "This man named Maximus found us on a beach and brought us here. He lives here I think."

"Maximus? But who is he? A BEACH? What's going on Stella? What happened?" There was a little pleading in Isaac's voice. He was obviously scared, but as always tried not to show it.

Behind them, Stella heard, "Hello Isaac. I am Maximus."

Isaac jumped off the couch, spun around to face him and instantly started putting questions to him.

Turning to Stella, Maximus smiled and chuckled, then said, "between the two of you asking so many questions I might not be able to get an opening to actually answer any of them!"

Stella, trying to be like her diplomatic mother calmly said, "We're scared and confused. I can tell somehow you know the answers. Please tell us."

"Alright, I will try," he said. "I am going to make a few guesses and you can tell me if I'm right or wrong. Then we can move to some answers, agreed?"

With skepticism, Stella answered, "Alright . . ."

He continued, "I am going to guess that your parents taught you much about the night sky... names of stars, planets, and galaxies. Am I correct?"

"Yes," replied Isaac, "we each had our own telescopes and every clear night we'd go and look for a little while before bed."

Stella asked, "How did you know that?"

"Let me make a few more guesses and then I will explain to you how I might know these things."

"Go on," she replied.

"I have another guess that you have both been reading since you were two years old."

"Yes . . ." said Stella.

"Well, most children don't start reading until they are five to seven years of age."

"Sure they do!"

"No, Stella, they don't... which leads me to my next guess: you were home-schooled and lived very far up on a mountain or tucked deep in the woods."

"We lived on a mountain, *and* in the woods," said Isaac.

"And," Maximus continued, "you know two different languages. The one we're speaking now, and then a different one you could only speak with your parents . . . one they might have told you was a code language."

He switched to the language and said, "You know how to speak the language Zeego."

Stella's mouth dropped open, and she looked over to an equally shocked Isaac. "Could you please explain to me how you know all of this?" asked Stella.

"I know all of this because I knew your parents. They didn't home-school you because you lived too far away on a mountain. They lived on a mountain, far away from everyone else so they *could* home-school you. They had to, because you were very different from the Earth children."

Ever perceptive of each word someone says she asked, "Don't you mean from OTHER Earth children? And what do you mean *knew* my parents?"

She watched Maximus take a deep breath, then he answered, "I am about to tell you both some things that will be hard for you to believe. You will want to tell me that I am lying, but I promise you I am not. Your mother chose me for you, she sent you here to me."

Stella had her eyes locked on him. Her body was tense and she could feel Isaac's tension as well.

Maximus said, "Last night, your parents were in a battle to protect you... last night, they gave their lives for you."

Stella heard but she could not process it. After a few moments she stuttered, "But... what? .....why? ..... what do you mean?"

In monotone, Maximus said, "They died."

Stella instantly flared with anger and shouted, "How do *you* know? You don't know anything! How could you know? You weren't even there!"

Maximus, with a calm voice, said, "I know because there is no other reason you would be here at this lighthouse without them."

Stella's anger crumbled into anguish. She slid off the couch, covered her face in her hands and wept. Sobbing over her words, she asked "What... happened? How... do you know... all this? Oh... Isaac!"

Isaac remained rigid as a board, staring straight ahead. Stiffly, he said, "Mom said she wouldn't see us again. Not for a long time. She knew she was going to . . ."

There was silence but for Stella's sniffling. Then Isaac asked, "So, when that green light crashed into the white light... was my dad that white light? Is that when he died?"

Maximus swallowed then answered, "I wasn't there, however I've been informed of what transpired, and I believe that is what happened."

"And mother?"

"Your attacker took her life after she sent you two away."

There was a palpable feeling of grief felt in the silence.

Maximus said, "I will leave you two alone for a while. I will be back with a hot drink and some food."

After he left, Isaac finally turned to look at her and she saw tears spilling down his cheeks. He came to sit next to her and they cried together and talked quietly.

The weight of what had happened pressed down on Stella. She only knew life with at least one of her parents always in yelling-distance. Where were they to live? Who would take care of them? She wiped a tear to dry her cheek, but another came quickly to keep it rightfully wet.

Maximus came back after a while holding a tray with steaming mugs and toast. The smell of the food didn't entice her, but rather made her stomach queasy.

Maximus said, "I know you don't want this, but your body is lacking strength of any kind, so try to at least take a sip."

Because arguing took too much effort, she took the mug from him, and so did Isaac. The warmth on her hands was soothing. Under his gaze, she took a sip. She felt the warmth go down through her body, and it made her aware of just how cold she really was. The soothing effect it had on her was bringing more tears. "Toast?" asked Maximus.

Stella cleared her throat, "No, thank you. I'm fine."

Isaac took one then slumped back on the couch without eating it.

Maximus sighed heavily. He was sitting in a chair on the other side of the coffee table. He said, "I have learned what you saw last night, and you have seen enough to probably believe what I am about to tell you. I am assuming you both want more answers?"

They both nodded.

He sighed again then said, "Last night, you saw your father performing some of his abilities. He possessed the ability to move objects without physically touching them, and he could transform himself into matter that looks most like a star, and travel as such a 'Star'.

"Your mother's abilities are more difficult to explain. It is simply that she could send out waves of bliss—or happiness, pleasure, optimism, joy—whichever word you want to use, and she could send them through the universe as a physical force. The warmth that you felt when she touched you... that was her gift. But then, when you felt yourself flying through the air and found yourself here... your mom did not do that. You did; and you could do that because of your dad, and the gifts that you were born with because of him."

Stella and Isaac stared at him in silence. Stella felt like she was watching this scene from the outside and it almost felt like she was being tricked—but she did see what she saw.

Maximus said, "Should I continue?"

They nodded again.

He went on by looking at Stella and saying, "Stella, you were not born here on this Earth."

Stella swallowed so her voice wouldn't sound like she was nervous or choked-up then spoke, "Where was I born?"

"You were born on Vega."

"Vega.... oh, do you mean, *in* Vegas, like Las Vegas, Nevada?"

"No, Stella. Vega, the *world* . . . or the *Star.* Your mother's home."

Stella's heart started thumping in her chest. Of course Stella knew of Vega. Her parents had taught them much about the night sky. It was the fifth brightest star in the sky—now she was to believe that it was a world, possibly like this one? She asked, "The world? People can't live on a star. They are just rock and gases."

Maximus spoke in a quiet, soft voice, "You only think that because that is what the scientists on Earth see with their probes and telescopes. But what they see is a veil of sort, or in other words, a shield that covers up the truth from them."

Stella's thumping heart went even more wild. "What's the truth?"

"The truth is, you live in a universe where almost every star you see is a world, with life in abundance."

This news was met with yet another span of silence, and then it was Isaac who asked a question. Stella was a little startled to hear some anger in his voice. *"Why didn't our parents tell us this?"*

CHAPTER 7

*"To have ideas is to gather flowers; to think is to weave them
into gardens."*

Isaac

Isaac's anger didn't "come out of nowhere" as Stella and
Maximus might think. Isaac had been harboring a secret for
quite a while. All this time he thought his parents and Stella
would think he was some sort of 'freak' if they knew the
things he could do. When he was out playing on his own, he
made things move and zoom through the trees. The first
discovery of it was when he was lying flat on his back in the
woods and looking up at the bottom of the trees. He imagined
them moving aside so he could see the sky and the branches
shifted and parted for him!

Isaac had read stories of others being able to move things
with their minds, but they were always fiction. He could also
do something else as well, and he had never read of anybody
else being able to do such a thing.

There was a day when Isaac was wandering around
outside and stopped to kneel next to a flower bud in the
ground. It was only two inches tall, and was still tightly
closed keeping its final shape, color and size a secret.

With nothing else to do, Isaac laid down next to it for a
while and see if he could see it grow. He imagined it being a
flower no one had ever seen before. It was to have eight
petals of bright blue and the middle of the flower would be a
vibrant purple square.

Isaac closed his eyes and smiled with the vision of being
able to take the flower home to show it to his family. When
Isaac opened his eyes to look at the little bud, he jumped up
onto his feet, startled! Where the green bud had just been
stood the very same flower he had imagined! He was

completely baffled as to how this flower grew that fast in the first place, and then to grow into the flower he had in his mind? To him it seemed unreal and impossible. Yet, there it was—seeming to stretch its petals and smile at him as if saying, "Here I am!"

After much deliberation on whether he should tell anyone about this, he finally decided to keep it a secret. Isaac ran back to his house and returned to the flower with a spade and a box.

He dug all around the flower, careful not to sever roots and then lifted it gently out of the ground and into the box. Isaac snuck back to a special clearing of thick green grass he had previously found for himself and planted his flower there. Then he returned home and told his parents all about his completely normal day exploring the woods.

The next day, Isaac thought he might try it again, and to his surprise created another flower from his imagination. It was three, five pointed stars stacked and rotated on top of each other so you could see each of their points.

Both of his flowers smelled like any other flower. Isaac thought maybe because he had never smelt a flower that didn't smell like anything other than a flower. He tried it again. This time he imagined the same flower he had just made, but he imagined it smelling like the rotten garbage he had to take out this morning. He laughed at the image of Stella smelling it and flinging it like a dirty rag.

Isaac brought the third flower that had just materialized to his nose. He was a genius. The rotten-garbage flower. Oh, how many little brothers would praise his invention? Isaac had laughed with the thought of all the grossed-out big sisters.

Now, Isaac thought of his meadow, and the many flowers and strange plants he had created there. He thought about all the struggles he faced having to hide his gifts from his parents and sister. He felt like an alien, so he distanced himself from them. Despite Stella's efforts to try and discover what he did all day, he still managed to keep his secret from her. Isaac knew she would tell their parents. He didn't want all the worried attention. He just wanted to be their son and brother, completely 'normal'.

He realized that what his parents did last night and all that Maximus was telling him meant maybe he wasn't so different after all. His parents had gifts too, and apparently Stella as well. Isaac guessed that normally, a kid might feel comforted to know others were like him. He admitted that it probably did make him feel better, but at that moment, he felt a strong irritation at his parents for not telling him. He lied to them for a long time and struggled to keep his secret—now to find out that he wasn't so strange after all. Unless they were ashamed of who they were? Should Isaac be ashamed too?

Maximus answered Isaac, "Why they didn't tell you was a choice your parents made for themselves. I cannot tell you why, I can only guess. When I teach you more, you might come to understand their reasoning."

"Were they ashamed?" Isaac asked.

"No, Isaac. They were proud of who they were, and of who you are. Your future is larger than you know."

Isaac had an unexplained urge to tell Maximus about his secret, but suppressed it quickly.

Maximus said, "You haven't seen outside Isaac—why don't you have your sister show you around?"

"But I still have a lot of questions, and I want t—"

"Yes, I understand Isaac, we will continue talking. I want us to all move around a little first, and I think it important that you have a look outside."

Shrugging, still irritated, Isaac stood up off of the couch and pulled his sister up with him. They walked to the door, and went outside as the sun was setting. What Stella had told him was true, they were at a beach! Isaac ripped his shoes off and walked a straight line to stand in the wet sand. Calming down now, he looked at Stella who had followed him and asked, "How did we get to this beach again?"

She answered, "I'm not sure, but look back at the house."

Isaac did and . . . it wasn't a "house" at all, but a *light*house — *the* lighthouse his parents had so many pictures of.

CHAPTER 8

*"Is your inclination to run away from this truth or to face it,
learn from it and be better?"*

Maximus

Maximus stayed on the chair. His mind was whirling
with all that had to happen within the next couple weeks. He
knew Isaac and Stella might ask to return to the Zodiacs soon
to see their homes.

To do this however, they would need to understand the
danger. They had much to learn and the timing had to be
right.

Isaac and Stella entered and walked directly to him. He
stayed in the chair as they stood before him.

"Ok," said Stella, "we think our mom always planned to
send us here because she has shown us pictures of this beach
and this lighthouse all our lives."

Isaac said, "We believe you Maximus, because we know
our mom sent us here to you because you have the knowledge
we need."

"We also want to know if there is a way we can have a
funeral for our parents?" asked Stella.

Maximus knew this question would arise. He had
contemplated already how to answer. He stood up and
kindly said, "There is no body to bury for your dad, and your
mother has already been transported to Vega to be buried in
her homeland." He also knew which question was coming
next. Just as he had played this out in this mind before, Stella
asked, "Well, then may we go to Vega to be there when they
bury her?"

How could Maximus tell her 'no'? It is their mother after
all, and they have the right to be there. But exposing them
this early would be too dangerous. There was much they had
to learn before they could leave this beach. With that

inescapable circumstance, he had to do what he must, "No Stella, I cannot take you there yet. The dangers are too many."

Maximus expected nothing less than anger, confusion and hurt from the children, and that is what he received. Stella's well-blocked tears found their way down her pale and beautifully freckled cheeks again, and Isaac was asking why they couldn't go and explaining all the reasons why they should, and had every right too.

Maximus, not knowing how the children could physically handle all he was telling them, tried to stop Isaac gently by saying, "Remember your mother sent you here. Remember she told you to stay hidden."

The kids were both looking at him with pleading in their eyes. Maximus couldn't recall ever seeing anyone so lost and confused.

"Stella, your parents moved here to Earth when you were just a toddler. They did it because there were many who threatened to kill you."

"Why?"

"Because, your parents' marriage formed a powerful alliance between otherwise separate worlds. It was anticipated by the people of the Zodiacs that the child (or children) of this alliance would have the power and influence to overthrow Gershon."

"Who is Gershon?" Stella asked.

"Gershon is an evil man who has overthrown the true ruler of the Zodiacs."

"What are the Zodiacs?"

"I am sure you know them. They are twelve constellations in which the Solar System travels through every year. Your parents taught you their names and shapes didn't they? Aries, Taurus, Sagittarius, Cancer . . ."

Isaac finished, "Libra, Aquarius, Scorpio, Virgo, Gemini, Leo, Capricornus, Pisces."

"Yes, I knew you'd know them," said Maximus.

"Yes, but they are *worlds*?" asked Stella.

"Yes. Worlds we call Stars—capitalized in the Zodiac language."

Isaac asked, "Was I born on a different World . . . or Star?"

"No, you were born on Earth—but your heritage is also in the Stars. If Gershon, the enemy, were to know of your existence, he would do all in his power to destroy you. A male heir of Eli and Isolde would be the biggest threat to his quest for complete control. Your parents hid you both to save your lives. Why they didn't tell you of these things, I am still uncertain. I do know they wanted you both to be old enough to choose if you wanted the throne and to be able to withstand the physical dangers of what taking the throne would bring."

Maximus saw Stella sink to the floor like the shock of all this information was squishing her. "More tomorrow," he said. "I'll show you to your rooms."

Isaac said, "I'll wait here so we can keep talking."

"Tomorrow, Isaac. You both need rest. We can spend all of tomorrow with questions and answers."

Stella stood with Maximus' help and walked with guidance to her room.

CHAPTER 9

"Our thoughts, or in other words our state of mind,
is ever at work 'fixing up' things good or bad in advance."

Stella

Once again, Stella found herself waking up and having to reorient herself to where she was. Though she felt mostly exhausted, she also felt something that motivated her to sit up and swing her feet to the floor. It was like she had this small circle inside of her that felt peaceful and confident, and it was that small circle that kept her entire body from being taken over by stress, grief and tiredness — it kept her moving and breathing; even though the rest of her body and mind would like to shut down and become a blank void.

Last night, Maximus had stopped above the first step which had the solid room underneath the stairs and pushed a gold button on the wall. Stella watched as the staircase moved downwards all the way into the room.

Inside was a large bed, with a silk-thread comforter of navy blue and copper-penny pin stripes. One wall had windows overlooking the inside of the lighthouse and a beautiful mural of winged horses of all colors galloping together in a lush green pasture during a bright, starry night. The painted stars were large and reminded Stella of many little moons.

Now that it was morning she could see more details of the room, like a desk with a few materials and books placed on it. On a tall, skinny table stood a globe that looked like it was made of painted glass. There was the largest bean-bag she had ever seen, covered with a baby-blue suede material. Stella felt as if she had been in this room before . . . and felt as if someone had made it specifically for her. She loved all shades of blue, loved horses and had always imagined herself flying away on one. The night-time 'dreamy' comfort of the room made her feel strangely inspired and happy.

Stella looked at the mural again, and though there was sunshine beaming in through the windows, the horses looked protected from the sun in their night-time dream world. They lived constantly under glistening starlight. Stella wished to join the horses and be with stars so close she could feel as if she were one of them.

She decided to find out if Isaac was awake. She walked over to the little gold button that would bring the stairs back down for her to climb out. Next to it was something that wasn't there last night when Maximus had shown her how to work the stairs. There was a square shape on the wall that looked like it had transformed into plasma, and it glowed white. Then words in black appeared on it: There are clothes in the dresser for you. Isaac is awake; we will meet you out on the beach with breakfast when you want to join us. ~Maximus

Marveling, Stella walked to the dresser and opened the drawers. There were clothes just like ones she would find in her dresser at home! Had this been another teenage girl's room?

CHAPTER 10

"Whatever the mind of man can conceive it can achieve."

Isaac

Isaac was enjoying the beach. Soft, cool sand; sounds of crashing waves on the rocks and seagulls calling out to each other; and best of all: the smell of salty ocean air. He felt as if he might wake-up from all of this at any time. What happened to his parents seemed unreal. It was inconceivable that he was here on this beach within seconds of being in the woods. When he thought about his parents being dead, his insides hurt like someone was gripping and squeezing them, and it made him feel nauseous. Really, he had no physical proof they were dead. But he felt it. He knew what Maximus told them was true.

The beach did a great job of calming him despite the strength of the storm that raged inside of him. He thought to himself that the only thing he could do for his parents, was to find out more about them, and about himself, so he could do all he could to avenge their deaths.

Maximus was sitting next to Isaac on the beach, eating fruit and cheese with him. Isaac felt comforted by his presence as he was maybe the only man who might be able to tell him why he could do special things. Isaac had kept his secrets pent up for so long — he had to talk to somebody, or he might detonate so he said, "Maximus, can I tell you something?"

"Of course, Isaac."

"Could my parents do many things that nobody else on Earth could do?"

Maximus didn't answer right away. He was still looking out over the ocean, the breeze making his sun-bleached hair ripple like the water.

Isaac's question had required a yes or no answer, but

instead Maximus said, "It is expected that the children of Eli and Isolde would be born exceptionally gifted and talented . . . do you have unique gifts and talents Isaac?"

With excitement building quickly, Isaac responded to Maximus' question by scrambling to his feet and saying, "Follow me!" He started running quickly in the opposite direction of the ocean, toward the green vegetation in the middle of the island.

Isaac knelt down next to a tree which had a few feet of smooth, damp dirt all around it. He was panting slightly, and heard Maximus catch up to him and stop in front of where he had knelt. "Ok, Isaac. What am I here to see?"

Isaac touched the ground with the pointer finger of his right hand. He closed his eyes and imagined the rotten-garbage flower he had made before. Smirking, Isaac pictured Maximus pulling a grotesque face after smelling the flower. Isaac took his finger off of the spot of ground, and opened his eyes to watch. Within a second, a poke of green pushed out of the ground, and at an unnatural speed grew the rotten-garbage flower.

Isaac plucked it and gave it to Maximus. Maximus looked surprised but he took the flower.

Isaac said, "Smell it!"

The second Maximus took the flower to his nose he ripped it away and scrunched his face. Isaac was not disappointed by Maximus' repulsion and laughed heartily.

Smiling now, Maximus looked at Isaac and said, "You think you're pretty funny, eh?"

Isaac laughed more.

Then they both heard Stella's voice calling Isaac and they turned and jogged out of the trees toward the beach. Stella was standing where they had been sitting with the basket and the food. Maximus walked when they reached the sand, and Isaac continued to run all the way to his sister.

"Sorry, Stella! We were . . . trying to find some more fruit for you to eat when you woke up." Isaac hated to admit it, but he had become skilled at thinking of excuses to cover up his secrets.

Maximus had joined them then. Isaac saw him still carrying the flower, and before he could distract Stella, she saw it too. "Oh wow! That flower is gorgeous! I have never seen one like it! Can I see it?"

Isaac started, "No, it has nasty little thorns on it that will hurt your—"

"Sure," interrupted Maximus and handed her the flower.

Stella took the flower straight to her nose and had a predictable response.

"What on Earth—?!" she said.

Maximus said, "That's exactly right, there has never been another flower on Earth like this one."

Stella just stared at him for an explanation.

Isaac was getting nervous. He wasn't sure if he wanted Stella to know yet or not.

Maximus was looking back and forth from Isaac to Stella, then continued to look at Isaac and Isaac knew it was time to tell Stella but he didn't know how she would take the news.

"Stell, I'm going to show you something, and you have to promise to tell me what you are thinking right when I am done showing you, deal?"

"Isaac, I'm really confused. Why are you so nervous right now?" asked Stella.

"Because, I have been keeping a secret. I am about to show you something that I can do, and I am nervous about what you will think."

"I am your sister—we're best friends, remember?"

Sighing, Isaac said, "Follow me."

"Isaac," said Maximus, "you can show her here."

"No, I need to find the right kind of ground."

"You only think that, because you've only ever seen flowers grown out of soil, but you can do it here too. Just believe in yourself, do exactly what you did back in the trees."

Contemplating for a moment, Isaac decided to trust Maximus and dropped to his knees in the sand. He touched the ground again with his pointer finger, and tried to imagine a new flower. Stella loved blue, so he imagined a flower that had a big center like a sunflower, and instead of brown, was flecked with all different shades of blue. The petals would be heart shaped, and white. As for a smell, the only thing that came to his mind was the smell of his mother. Isaac took his finger off the ground and opened his eyes. He waited but nothing was happening. He looked up at Maximus.

Maximus asked him, "Did you imagine what you would do with it? Did you imagine yourself or someone using it?"

Isaac shook his head.

Maximus motioned for him to try it again.

Isaac put his finger back in the sand and closed his eyes. He imagined Stella's flower—the different flecks of blue all through the middle and the heart-shaped white petals. This time, he imagined Stella touching it and smelling it.

Holding that image in his mind, he took his finger out of the sand and opened his eyes. Out bloomed the flower, just as he imagined it. He stood up and looked at Stella.

She stammered, "I . . . wow, Isaac. How did you . . . how long have you . . . it is gorgeous!" and she knelt down and touched a heart-shaped petal.

Isaac took an inward sigh because she obviously didn't think he was a freak.

CHAPTER 11

"Man is made or unmade by himself; in the armory of thoughts
he forges the weapons by which he destroys himself, he also fashions
the tools with which he builds for himself heavenly mansions of joy
and strength and peace."

Stella

The sun had set on the beautiful beach, and Stella was in her room, looking out the window at the moon and stars. She had not 'stumbled' onto any secret about herself the way Isaac had. She wasn't upset with him for not telling her. In fact, she understood completely why he didn't. She probably would have felt the same way. What upset her was that Maximus kept telling her she had great powers as well. Stella knew of none, and did not believe him.

She thought of Isaac and the motherly affection she felt toward him—especially now that she was the only family he had—and visa-versa. *At least . . . I think he is the only family I have,* she thought. Stella remembered what Maximus told her about being born on Vega, and felt a thrill of excitement in thinking she might still have family! Thinking of the possibilities of relatives on another world, she tried to imagine how different they were, and if she had anything in common with them.

Stella heard a thumping sound. Since her door was on the ceiling and also underneath her visitor's feet, they had to stomp their foot to knock on her "door".

Stella got out of the bean bag which sat next to a window overlooking the beach and went over to the gold button, and twisted it slightly to the left. The stairs descended and Maximus walked in wearing a pair of his cotton-beige pants (not rolled up this time), and a white, zip-up sweatshirt and shoes. He'd only been barefoot since they'd been there.

"Are you going somewhere?" she asked.

Maximus looked down at his feet, and laughing said, "Oh . . . you don't miss out on a thing, do you? No, I was just going to gather some more firewood."

"Oh."

Stella didn't like awkward pauses, so she asked, "Is there something I can do for you?"

"Yes . . ." Maximus looked over at her window, "I just wanted to check on you, you've been in here most of the day by yourself."

"I know. I'm only tired and trying to rest."

"Why don't I believe you?" he asked, looking back at her.

Jokingly Stella said, "Probably because you know everything."

Maximus laughed and Stella smiled.

"Can I tell you something you don't know?" he asked.

"Go for it."

"Making people feel good is one of your talents inherited from your gifted mother."

"Many people can make others feel good. You can too — you make Isaac and me feel better."

"I'm glad. My number one wish is that you and Isaac will be happy, and that you will like me."

"Well, we do."

Smiling, Maximus said, "You know, this room is quite something."

"Yes, it is. I love it in here. Any shade of blue is my favorite color."

"That must be why the room is all blue!"

"What do you mean?"

"Sometime in your life, you had probably visualized a room all made in blue, with a bean bag looking out a window, and a desk full of books, and all the comfortable, beautiful things you have in here. I am guessing you like Horses as well . . . and have imagined Winged Horses a time or two."

"Yes . . . so?"

"So . . . this room wasn't like this before you arrived. Your mind is very powerful, and by imagining a room like this often, it materialized for you. The room doesn't have special powers—you do."

"I knew it . . . you're a mad man."

"I speak the truth, young-lady. I came up here to bring to your attention that Isaac is not the only one with powers. I know it probably bothered you a little bit to think he was."

"No, I am proud of Isaac and happy for him."

"I never said you weren't. I only said you might feel a little depressed that you didn't have any gifts—or *thought* you didn't at least."

"Does Isaac have this power too?"

"Actually, every human mind has the ability to create their world ahead of them."

"Did Isaac's room do this as well?"

"We can go take a look! First, tell me, what do you think your brother's room looks like? What are all the things he likes the most and imagines himself having often?"

Stella thought a moment than said, "Dragons for sure. His favorite constellation is Draco, and he reads a lot about dragons. When he was little, he sat on top of the couch and pretended he was flying on top of a dragon."

Maximus and Stella walked up her stairs, brought them back up, then continued up the spiral staircase to Isaac's room.

Maximus stopped at Isaac's entrance and stomped his foot. After a moment, the stairs began to drop.

"Hey guys, come in!"

"Hi Isaac," she said smiling as she came down the stairs. Isaac and her were very close because usually, they were all each other had for friends and his presence made her happy.

Just as she had guessed, there were dragon decorations everywhere. Stella walked around his room. There was a telescope like the one he had at home, a brown leather couch, a desk with lots of drawings of dragons scattered around it, and his bed was a four-poster, with dark cherry wood and a tan, suede duvet cover. His whole room seemed like they were camping in the outdoors of a fantasy-land. All around was dark wood, leather furniture, plants and dragon motifs. Stella loved it, and loved her brother's adventurous personality.

They visited for a little while then Stella said she was off to bed and Maximus said he still needed to go get firewood.

Maximus, in his all-knowing way, said as they left Isaac's room, "Stella, listen to me for a moment. You have many gifts and talents. The difference between you and your brother is he found them on his own and you will have to search for them, and believe they are inside of you."

Stella didn't say anything.

Maximus moved in front of her again and stooped down a little so he was looking into her eyes. Stella looked away from his painfully familiar eyes. She had finally figured out why at times, they were so painful for her to look at. They looked like her father's.

Bluntly she asked and by so doing changed the subject, "How did you know my parents?"

He stood straight again and answered, "They were very good friends of mine—I lived on the Zodiacs with your father—and I moved to Earth to help protect your parents and their child and children to come.

"Then why have I never met you before?"

"Your parents and I both vowed to not contact each other except in the most dire of circumstances. It was hard to separate like that, but it was necessary."

"Why was it necessary?"

"Stella, we could probably talk all night, but why don't you sleep, and we can talk tomorrow."

"Do you enjoy leaving me in suspense?"

Maximus smiled and looked at her again. "No, but I have

things to do before I retire as well, and I can tell you are tired. We can talk more tomorrow."

"Is this one of those times when trying to convince an adult is a waste of energy?"

Maximus smiled and placed a hand on top of her head. "Yes. I will see you in the morning Miss Stella." He ruffled her hair like she was a little puppy and she ducked out from underneath his hand and childishly smacked at him.

He laughed and said, "Good night, Stella," and he went down the stairs.

"Good night." She felt like she had a big brother that cared about protecting her. She watched him leave the lighthouse then returned to her room.

CHAPTER 12

". . . anyone that ever accomplished anything did not know how they were going to do it. They only knew they were going to do it."

Maximus

After he thought the kids might be sleeping, Maximus tried to climb the stairs quietly without being heard.

He went to the top-most room of the lighthouse and moved over to the telescope. Its gold surface had stripes of white from the moonlight reflecting on it. He placed his hands on the eye-piece end and rotated it around from facing the sky, to facing the shimmering liquid wall. Once adjusted to his liking, he moved around to the front of it, and looked into the magnifying glass. "Father, I am ready to speak to you."

Maximus then moved out of the way and turned to face the wall. A projection soon appeared there. "You look ready to go somewhere," he said.

"I am."

"You have done well with the children the last couple days."

"Thank you."

"I have bad news Maximus. Gershon has vowed if Stella does not show herself in five days' time, he will start killing Zodians by the thousands. Gershon wants those who have remained resistant to lose any thread of hope they have of the royal family returning. He wants to know where Stella is so he can kill her—in public."

"Has he discovered anything about Isaac?"

"No, he still remains ignorant that Eli and Isolde had a son."

"And this island?"

"The protection we have built around this island is unbroken. Its existence to any Earthling or Zodians remains unknown."

"I have an idea and I'm going to use the Telescope to travel tonight," said Maximus.

"To where?"

"To Pegasus. Stella's upcoming struggles are enormous and she is very far away from where she needs to be . . . mentally and emotionally. She has a fascination for Winged Horses. I thought I could convince one to come back with me to be her companion and give her inspiration."

"Sounds very wise. As powerful as her mind is . . . it must be so that she has a Winged Horse ready to be her companion."

Maximus nodded. "I will warn them of the possible upcoming battle with Gershon."

The projected man nodded solemnly then the projection disappeared. Maximus carefully and slowly pointed the telescope back to the sky. Standing in front of the eye piece, he closed his eyes and within a few seconds his entire self was zillions of tiny specs of light. Then, with the speed of a bullet leaving a gun, the mass of lights were pulled through the Telescope and blasted out the other side, disappearing into space.

Just a moment later, a flash of light appeared on the Constellation Pegasus and then materialized back into a man as fast as the blink of an eye—Maximus had landed on Pegasus. He had chosen to come to Markab, the brightest Star in the Constellation which usually meant it had the highest population and was home to the rulers or governors of the Constellation.

Maximus soon spotted a Winged Horse standing up on a rise across the field from where he stood and it looked bold and intimidating. The Horse had spotted him also and it whinnied and trotted a few pacing steps from side to side, and Maximus heard another Horse whinny in answer to him.

The Horse galloped down the hill toward him, followed

by roughly ten more Winged Horses, who took flight with their enormous wings when they descended the hill. They reached Maximus quickly and landed around him, forming a circle. These Horses were different from regular horses. Not only were they winged, but they could speak and could survive here on their own without human intervention. They were their own culture — their own "people".

The Horse that had spotted Maximus was a steel grey color that shone in the starlight. In Zeego, he loudly said, "Human! Who are you? You are not Orel or Eli who have been the only humans to ever travel here."

"My name is Maximus. Orel himself taught me to travel as he, and has given me permission to travel to you today. I am here on a specific errand, and one which is of supreme importance and urgency."

Another Horse spoke in a soft voice from behind Maximus, and when Maximus turned, he saw a Horse so white in color that she gleamed blue from the starlight. She looked more elderly, and the other Horses ceased their fidgeting and were quiet while she spoke.

"Hello Maximus."

"Hello Milady," said Maximus, knowing that this Horse deserved great respect. Her calm and lady-like presence was like a spell to Maximus. She looked like velvet to touch. Maximus could tell she was older than the others, but she still maintained enough strength to hold herself regally.

"I am Zordosa. My son has failed to introduce himself in his hurry to interrogate you. He is Sarge."

Maximus nodded in Sarge's direction.

Zordosa continued, "I am very familiar with Orel — and Eli of course, who visited here often. If you say your errand is important and urgent, then we shall take you straightway to our leader, Arrow."

"Thank you," said Maximus reverently.

Sarge was first in the air and the other horses were

following him. Maximus became concerned about how he was supposed to follow them as they flew. Before he could get too worried however, Zordosa called out, "Sarge!"

Maximus saw Sarge circle back and he landed in front of them with a loud thump.

"Son," said Zordosa, "Maximus will need to be transported to his audience with Arrow."

Sarge stiffened and looked back and forth from Maximus and his mother. Raising his neck up and tucking his nose inward, he cleverly said, "Who would you like me to get for this task, mother?"

Instead of being intimidated by Sarge now, Maximus was becoming amused at Sarge's unfounded dislike of him.

"Actually, I would like you to take him, Sarge," said Zordosa calmly.

As Sarge backed up a step, Maximus looked at Zordosa and said, "It's quite alright milady, I can travel by foot and follow you."

Sarge quickly said, "Yes, that's a smart idea. Then I can fly ahead and tell Arrow of his arrival."

Zordosa stepped closer to Sarge. "I cannot carry our guest myself Sarge, please let him ride on your back. After all, Arrow himself would offer that courtesy to Maximus."

Sarge turned sideways and hid his head from Maximus' view behind Zordosa's head and neck. Maximus could still hear him when he whispered to Zordosa, "Yes, but you and Arrow have both carried humans on your back before—I have not. How will I manage to fly with him there?"

"Son," Zordosa whispered back to him, "both Arrow and I had to do it for the first time once as well. You are young and strong and will be fine. Both Orel and Eli were natural and easy to balance. Now—we are wasting time, so go kneel next to him so he can get on your back."

Sarge sighed heavily, then without a word he walked over to Maximus, deliberately stomping each foot hard into the ground. Maximus looked past him to Zordosa who tossed her head in an upwards circle, clearly 'rolling her eyes' if she had been human. Sarge kneeled in front of him and Maximus said, "Wow, thank you!" in an enthusiastic tone, whether to try and make Sarge feel better, or to goad his temper, Maximus didn't even know himself.

Maximus wasn't sure whether to put his legs in front of the wings or behind them. Again, coming to the rescue, Zordosa said, "Put your legs behind his wings."

Maximus did so, and Zordosa cantered off a few steps, then spread her wings, stroked the air with them and gracefully rose into the air. Her mane and tail were now white shimmering curtains flowing behind her.

Sarge began to canter, and Maximus had to concentrate on keeping his balance. The sensation was strange to him. He felt insecure with nothing to put his feet in or to keep himself from slipping. He lost his balance as Sarge's wings spread. Sarge had to tuck his wings back in and swerve to keep both of them upright.

"Human!" Sarge exclaimed, "I won't be able to fly if you can't stay on by yourself."

"I'm sorry," said Maximus, breathlessly, "Unfortunately, I was never the Horseman—my brother was. Try it again."

This time, Maximus was fine until Sarge surged upwards. He slipped and grabbed Sarge around the neck with both arms to stay on. This made it difficult for Sarge and Sarge was grumbling under his breath, but he managed to get higher into the air and soon they were flying smoothly.

In just a few moments, they descended and landed by a thick group of trees that were shaped like giant mushrooms, but had translucent turquoise colored leaves hanging all around them like curtains.

Maximus dismounted.

"Through here," said Sarge walking away from Maximus. Maximus and Sarge entered through the trees by parting the long, curtain-like leaves and stepped onto dry, mossy ground. Maximus expected it to be very dark under the trees and that they would have to part many leaves to get through each tree, but was pleasantly surprised to find it still well-lit by the Stars with a turquoise-greenish glow cast by the translucent leaves, which under the cover of the trees, grew together like vines from tree to tree like a rooftop.

Maximus followed behind Sarge, whose hooves made no sound on the soft ground. He could hear voices talking and laughing in appealing whinnying and nickering sounds.

They reached the source of the voices and Sarge motioned to Maximus to pass him with a swish of his head. The silence was abrupt as Maximus walked past Sarge.

Without Sarge's hindquarters blocking his view, Maximus saw who could only be Arrow, standing on a high bulge in the mossy ground.

Arrow was truly magnificent. It was hard for Maximus to define the beauty of the horses in words, because their true beauty lay in the feeling and emotion of awe, reverence and confidence the Horses create in you.

Arrow was a deep chestnut color and his coat glistened like a copper penny. His wings matched his mane and tail, which was shimmering flaxen—golden blonde, white, red and deep brown hairs all blended together.

"Sarge," Arrow said in a voice matching his regality, "could you introduce our guest please?"

Sarge came to stand next to Maximus and said, "May I present, Maximus from . . . ." and then his eyes got wide in panic. Maximus realized he had never actually said where he was from, and to save Sarge, quickly he whispered to him, "Earth!"

"Earth!" Sarge added quickly. "He is friend of King Orel and Prince Eli. He is here on an important and urgent errand."

"Welcome friend of Orel and Eli," said Arrow in a cordial

and welcoming voice, "What is your errand?"

Maximus still hadn't decided exactly where he was going to start his story to convince one of these Horses to return with him for Stella — and on a larger scale, to get them on the side of the Zodiacs rightful rulers, should their alliance ever be needed.

He could feel the eyes of all the Winged Horses around him, and knew he must just plunge in somewhere, so began, "I am a Zodian and I followed Eli, his wife, and their daughter, Stella when they went to live on Earth, as their protector."

Zordosa made some motions and Maximus looked at her.

"I'm sorry," she said, "Eli had brought Isolde here shortly after their marriage, and that is the last we'd seen of him. I didn't know he'd gone to Earth and that they had a daughter."

Arrow said, "Eli and my sister, Zorri, were very close — he rode only her on their visits. She has always wondered why he has not returned since that day."

"Eli could not travel as a Shooting Star any longer, even though I know how much he wanted to," said Maximus, "They went to Earth to go into hiding after Stella was born."

Zordosa asked, "Why did they need to hide?"

Maximus continued, "Around the time Stella was born to Eli and Isolde, there was an uprising in the Zodiacs. Gershon, who was once King Orel's most trusted advisor, had decided he was better suited to be the ruler of the Zodiacs. He convinced all twelve stewards of Orel to follow his plan which was to control the people of the Zodiacs with a strict set of rules to, I quote, 'keep them out of trouble.' As more were joining Gershon with his promise of change and better worlds, the less influence King Orel had on his people.

"All the Zodians knew the alliance formed between the Zodiacs and the Summer Triangle by the marriage of Eli and Isolde would help the Zodiacs to be more fortified, and have more influence in the Universe than they already had. The daughter of this Union was born with great powers and great promise of becoming the most beloved and powerful princess in the Universe. With her powers, she could bring much happiness and abundance to all.

"By this time, Gershon, who at first thought he was just doing the people of the Zodiacs a favor, had now become so power hungry that he did not want any threats on his road of gaining complete control of the Zodiacs. He vowed to have Eli and his family killed, so neither Eli, nor his daughter could replace Orel and challenge him."

Maximus paused and looked at Zordosa as sadness consumed him. The hurt of Eli's death was still very close to him, and he still had not grieved properly, for Stella and Isaac needed him now. He wished he could disappear right then to save Zordosa from having to feel pain as well at the news of Eli's death. Such beauty should never suffer.

Zordosa came over, and stood only a foot's distance in front of him, imploring him with her large, concerned eyes. "What has happened to Eli and his family?" she asked.

Looking only at her, Maximus said, "Stella is now seventeen. They also had a son, now fifteen, which neither the Zodians nor Gershon and his Minion know about. Sadly— and we don't know how—Gershon discovered where Eli and Isolde were hiding with their daughter and he sent his most evil servant to kill them."

There were gasps and audible wing shuffling as the shock of this rippled through the Horses like a wave.

Tense as a statue, Zordosa slowly asked, "And . . . they . . . were . . . successful?"

"Not entirely successful," he said almost mumbling, "Eli and Isolde managed to save their children and they sent them to me."

"But Eli . . ." she said and instantly looked weak. Arrow and Sarge quickly cantered over to her as Maximus reached out and touched her neck.

"I'm so sorry milady," said Maximus.

She did not answer him but just stared at nothing and breathed heavily.

Arrow and Sarge both stood close to her and touched her with their noses. Arrow kept his head low as he looked at Maximus. "We are so sorry," he said, "At least their children lived."

"Yes," said Maximus still looking at Zordosa, "Stella is the reason I am here. She dreams of Winged Horses, though she doesn't even know you are real. A passion I can now understand was passed down to her from her father.

Zordosa's trance was broken and she looked into Maximus' eyes once more and said, "What is it you need from us? Is Stella still in danger, and the boy?"

"At this very moment? No. They are safe in my hiding place."

"Are you sure they are safe there, when they were not protected with their parents?"

"In order for Stella and Isaac to have somewhat of a normal life, Eli and Isolde could not use every protection, for then there would be no other human contact, and that is no way to raise children, though they did isolate themselves somewhat by living high in the mountains. I have lived without earthly-human contact, and now Isaac and Stella will have to as well. At my home, Orel and I have made the protection strong, and it helps that Gershon was lead to believe I am dead as well.

"They are in danger in the near future however. They are learning who they are. The time is coming that I will let them know they must choose if they will take up their destiny and save the people of the Zodiacs from Gershon . . . or not.

"Stella suffers in confidence as I am opening up knowledge of this world or universe they belong to. She does not believe she possesses any powers or is special in any way.

Gershon is calling for her to show herself within one week's time, or he will begin to kill Zodians. I fear she will not be ready."

Taking a deep breath and hoping for the best, Maximus said, "I want to ask one of you to return with me to help prepare Stella. A love for Winged Horses is deep-rooted in her soul, and she needs all the happiness and confidence she can get right now."

Zordosa stood taller, but before she could say anything, Maximus wanted to add one more thing, "Also," he said, "there might come a time when Eli and Isolde's children need a vast number of you to join on their side for a physical confrontation with Gershon's army."

Zordosa looked to Arrow and Sarge then said, "I will go to Stella."

"Mother, no," said Sarge. "The days of carrying humans has passed for you."

"I can manage, my son . . . she's Eli's daughter," she said imploringly, shifting her gaze back to Arrow.

Arrow said, "Your son is right, Zorri. Though your heart and strong willpower can withstand it, your body might not be able to physically handle the danger Stella might be put through."

"Arrow, I—" she began.

"Let me ask you, sister . . ." he interrupted, "Would it satisfy you if I were the one to carry your Eli's daughter, and protect her as you would?"

Maximus saw that this question took her aback, as it did him. He did not expect the leader of the Winged Horses to be the one returning with him.

"But why you? You are our leader here," Zorri said.

"Mostly because I don't want you to go and be in danger," answered Arrow.

"Who would take your place here?" she asked.

"You, of course," said Arrow. "And your son."

Sarge jerked his neck erect and looked surprised yet.

"Arrow . . ." said Zordosa, "I don't think we could do that. Why not send a different Horse from Markab?"

"I have always wanted the privilege of carrying a human who could form a bond with me, like the bond you formed with Eli. And she is Eli's daughter—part of the Zodian's royal family. Plus, if danger will come to our Constellation, I should be the first to know. I feel, with you and Sarge to watch over Pegasus that I could better serve at the forefront of the problem that could be facing us soon."

Zordosa dropped her eyes from Arrow and looked sorrowful. Arrow touched her with his nose. She said almost too quiet for Maximus to hear, "Yes, you are right. You are the best Horse to go with Maximus."

"I promise," Arrow said, "that I will do all in my power to protect Stella, and my family here, and all the Winged Horses I have the responsibility to protect."

Returning to his dignified stance and raising his voice again for all to hear, Arrow said as he looked straight at his nephew, "Now is the time Sergeant, to be the gentleman that Eli saw in you when he named you. Will you assist your mother in handling affairs of this constellation, and prepare all the Horses for a battle that might be in their future? You must be her physical strength."

"Yes, of course. I will do my best," said Sarge. Maximus thought Sarge looked scared and honored, nervous and excited, but solemn all at the same time.

Maximus said to Zordosa, "I want to leave you with something."

He reached into his pocket and pulled out a smooth white stone in the shape of a star that fit in the center of his palm. "This is a Star Charm. If you or any Horse squeezes it somehow, it will call me. You can use it if there is ever any danger or you need to call Arrow or myself for anything."

He braided it into her silky white mane. Arrow and

Zordosa both gave thanks to Maximus.

Arrow walked back to the high ground of the gathering place, then spoke loudly so they could all hear him, "It is decided that I will be returning with Maximus to Earth, to help prepare Stella, the daughter of Eli, to face the dangers ahead of her. Our most beloved Zordosa and her son Sergeant will assume the role of your leaders. Show them the same respect you have always shown me. I trust your two new leaders to guide us through the times of peace like we have had and might continue to have, or through times of peril, which could be at our doorstep at any time.

"I will continue my duties and responsibilities to protect our Constellation and to keep the peace. At Stella's side, I will be at the forefront and will do all in my power to keep the danger far away from here."

Zordosa and Sarge went to stand by Arrow, and slowly, the group of Winged Horses all bent a knee and bowed themselves to the ground.

Arrow said, "Thank you for your acceptance of this plan. My departure with Maximus is immediate."

Maximus watched as Arrow said good-bye to Zordosa and Sarge and then walked toward him. They parted the leaves and walked out into the night air alone. Maximus climbed onto Arrow's back and pressed his own Star Charm as they both transformed into light and were rocketed through space and pulled back through the Telescope in the lighthouse Maximus called home.

CHAPTER 13

"Be aware that as you feel good, you are powerfully attracting more good things to you."

Stella

The stomping on the stairs didn't startle Stella too much. Since she had arrived at the lighthouse, she had been hovering in the in-between of sleep and awake. She slowly got out of bed, taking her blanket with her and made her way over to the gold button. Soon Maximus was standing in front of her at the bottom of the stairs.

"No shoes again today?" she asked with a sassy-pants smile.

Maximus looked at his feet, wiggled his toes and said, "The sand is cool and soft this morning. Will you join me for a walk right now? I need to speak with you."

"Am I in trouble?"

He smiled, "No, no . . . I actually need to show you something on the beach . . . a gift for you."

"A gift?" she asked.

Again Maximus smiled and nodded. Stella noticed he looked very tired this morning.

"I'll be right there, just let me change." she said.

"Wonderful," he said, turning back up the stairs to leave. "See you outside in a moment."

Stella hurriedly dressed, leaving her shoes off and rushed to meet Maximus outside.

"This way," he said and she joined him and together they set out on the beach.

Maximus said, "I know you have been through much this week Miss Stella."

Stella liked when he called her that, like she was an adult worthy of respect but at the same time a child worthy of his protection.

He continued, "I hate to burden you with more, but there is still much you must know."

She took in a breath and held it, glancing sideways at him. He returned her glance and then placed an arm around her shoulders, pulling her in tight next to his side as they continued to walk.

"I know the things I've been telling you are extraordinary and hard to believe. I also know you've been down on yourself."

She was embarrassed that Maximus perceived so much about her.

"I want to see you happy," he said as he turned them up the beach and started to walk toward the trees, "I needed to find something to help you be happy, for the weeks ahead are not going to get easier."

She had no idea what he could be referring to, but her stomach clenched all the same.

"Which is why I am glad I came into your room and saw the mural on your wall last night," he said.

Completely confused now, she looked up at him.

"You have seen a few things this week you haven't ever before seen. Last night, I went on a journey with you in mind, and I am about to show you something you've also never before seen, which I brought back for you. He is here for *you*. To help you."

At the word 'he', Stella's bewilderment grew exponentially. Before she could do so much as squeak a response, Maximus turned her and gently pushed her through the trees.

She was suddenly rooted to the spot, for there stood her dream. Looking back at her was a winged horse. She felt drawn forward to him and looked over at Maximus for permission as she started walking toward the horse. She received an encouraging nod and smile from him. She turned again to the horse, and as she did, he started walking to her as well.

Her heart was racing, and was also filling up with warmth and spilled onto her cheek in the form of a tear. This tear didn't bother her like sad, cold tears did. She was purely ecstatic. Her life's dream — the fantasy she always let run freely in her mind — this horse . . . she felt more fulfilled and happy than she could remember feeling in a long time.

They reached each other and Stella outstretched her hand, and the horse met it with his forehead. She stared unblinking at his red, glistening coat and his multi-colored golden mane and wings and she ran her fingers through his forelock. He softly closed his eyes.

His back was about level with the top of her head. His neck was muscular and formed a perfect arch like a swan. His ears were set upon the arching neck and noble head, pointing up and slightly forward like the horn of a unicorn. His body was thick in stature, but beautifully refined by his powerful muscles and thin, soft skin.

She ran her hand over his eye, down the curve of his neck, over the muscles on his shoulders and tentatively to the captivating feathers of his wings. They felt just like a bird's, but were larger and longer than on any bird she could remember seeing. They compressed under her strokes, and then again looked untouched as her hand moved past them.

The horse never moved while she moved around him, except to turn his head slightly and keep her in his sight. She heard Maximus walk up behind her and she spun around and wrapped her arms around his waist and hugged him. Maximus sighed deeply and patted her on the back, then said, "You will never know how much pain has been lifted off my heart to see the pain lifted off yours."

She stepped back from him so she could see his face. Somewhat unable to speak still, she stammered, "Thank . . . Maximus . . . he's . . . I can't . . . I don't . . ."

He hugged her, drawing her into him again, "You're

welcome. I've received all the thanks I need just by seeing some sparkle return to your eyes. Your resemblance to your parents at this moment is startling."

This made a few more warm tears spill onto her cheeks. She felt closer and more connected to her parents at this moment for reasons she could not explain. "He's magical," she said and she turned around to face the horse again. He was still standing quiet and noble, gazing at her intently, "Does he have a name?" she asked.

"Let's let him introduce himself," replied Maximus.

Stella's head whipped to Maximus again, and then just as quickly back to the winged horse, because she heard him speak! "My name is Arrow, my lady," he said, in the language her parents had taught her.

Her mouth again was wide open, but no sound escaped her.

Maximus laughed his deep, man's laugh, and walked over to stand next to Arrow. "Yes, he talks too," he said. "When a creature is intelligent like this, we capitalize their species. He is a Winged Horse, with a capital 'w' and 'h'. Let him tell you his story — you'll be simply amazed. Arrow, where are you from?"

"From Markab, on Pegasus," he said considerately and quietly toward Stella, probably trying to soften the effects of a talking Horse.

"That's the Constellation Pegasus," Maximus added when Stella looked at him, "Just like you are from Vega on the constellation Lyra, Arrow is from Markab on the constellation Pegasus."

"How did you get here?" she asked.

Maximus answered for Arrow, "In the same way as I have mentioned to you before — as a Star, which is the same way in which you saw your dad streaking across the sky, the same way your mother sent you here. We, meaning you, Isaac and I have the ability to change our molecular density to transform ourselves into stars, focus our minds, and arrive where we intend."

Stella knew Maximus was not trying to be insensitive, but she still didn't like mention of the night her parents died. Deciding not to react, she asked, still struggling to form coherent sentences, "I've . . . never . . . are you sure?"

"Yes, I am sure Stella. This is how I went to Pegasus just last night and returned with Arrow before you awoke."

Though it was beyond anything Stella had ever before even fathomed being possible, she knew it had to be true. Nowhere on Earth did there exist a horse with wings.

With the unexplained new connection she now felt to her parents, she now understood much, like why as a family they studied the stars daily. Just one thing still troubled her, every time this subject came up, "Why was all this kept a secret from Isaac and me?" Some of the hurt and confusion that so quickly fled when she saw Arrow was creeping back.

Arrow stepped to her and put his head down at the level of her torso. Again, it felt like some sort of magic to Stella — he emanated comfort like he had a direct line to her heart from which to feed his supply of confidence.

Maximus quietly said, "Why don't you take some time to get to know Arrow, and I will go bring your brother down to meet him and then talk with you both more about that."

"Sounds good," Stella said. She was again entirely engrossed in Arrow's majesty.

Maximus turned and left. When he was gone, Arrow knelt down and spread his left wing forward. Then he said to her, "Let me carry you for a while."

Mesmerized, Stella walked up to his back behind his wing and put her leg over. He stood up and she was sitting on his back. As he started walking forward, the excitement grew all the more within her. She noted to herself how he put much thought and care into each step he took. She didn't know what she should say to him, so she contented herself by looking at his neck as it subtly bobbed up and down as he walked. His mane was like golden waves. His wings enveloped her legs like they had been made solely to shield her.

She dangled her legs casually, not feeling the need to grasp anything with her hands to stay on. She felt as if she'd been riding a Winged Horse her entire life.

It was Arrow who broke the silence between them, "Have you ridden on a Horse's back before? You feel very relaxed and balanced."

"No," she said simply, "you are the first Horse I've ridden."

"Hmmm..." he responded, "Maybe natural Horsemanship runs in your blood from your father."

"What do you mean? My father . . . did you know him?"

"Yes. He came to Pegasus several times—and he formed a very special bond with my sister, Zordosa."

"You mean, my father has been to your Star?" Stella felt a mix of thrill and again confusion as to why her parents did not share all these wonderful things about their lives.

"Oh yes, very often. His visits were not for any royal or political purpose. He liked to come just to be with the Horses. The bond he and my sister shared was a beautiful masterpiece."

Stella thought in silence. Arrow's hooves rhythmically ticked away the time as Stella was consumed in her own thoughts. Stella thought of her father riding a Winged Horse—as his favorite hobby. He probably was secretly proud of her almost obsessive interest in Horses. And maybe, she thought, he hated not sharing his secret of his friendship with Winged Horses with her.

Deep in thought, it took Stella a moment to realize that they were no longer on the soft ground of the treed area. Only when she found herself squinting in the sunlight and noticed the different feeling of Arrow's stride as he walked through the sand, did she know they were on the beach. She sighed just as she felt Arrow's ribcage expand widely under her and then heard him exhale with a gentle rattling noise from his nostrils.

She giggled and said, "Jinx!"

Arrow turned his head slightly so one of his eyes was more visible to her then said, "What does 'jinx' mean?"

"It means we both did or said something at the same exact time, and since I was the one that said 'jinx', you can't speak until I un-jinx you."

"But I am not finding it difficult to speak at all," he said cocking his nose to the side in obvious confusion.

Stella laughed aloud again, "It's just a game."

"Oh, I see. Well, I shall be silent then until you un-jinx me for sighing at the same time as you."

Stella stroked his neck. Even though it was a childish game, and he was a Horse after all, it still felt good to be so light-hearted and 'childish'.

Stella looked down the beach and wondered what it would be like to go faster. As if responding to her thoughts, Arrow gently moved into a slow trot. At this increased speed, she felt more comfortable holding his mane with her hands, but kept her body relaxed. Relaxed as she was, she felt that her body melded into Arrow's back as she absorbed all the motion.

Apparently satisfied she would not bounce off, Arrow increased his speed, and Stella's smile spread further across her face. Before his trot got too fast and bumpy, he transitioned into a smooth-as-glass canter. As he did this, they had reached the edge of the water.

Stella loved the rocking motion of the canter and felt so secure that she let go of his mane and extended her arms out like wings. To complete the feeling she was flying, she closed her eyes. Her hair was flowing and whipping behind her head like the flame on a fire. She felt weightless and deep in her imagination, she could even hear the flapping of wings.

Or was it her imagination? Stella opened her eyes. Arrow's hooves were no longer padding the beach. Instead, Stella found they were a few feet above the water — Arrow's wings spread out wide and gently flapping the salty air.

She quickly grasped large handfuls of Arrow's mane and clenched her legs and feet together against Arrow's sides. She no longer felt safe sitting up straight so she hunched over to be closer to Arrow and not lose her balance. None of these measures helped at all. She found it even more frightening and difficult to stay on, for she started slipping to the side despite the extra-firm grip she had on her Horse.

Arrow spoke a little louder than normal to be heard above the noise of the ocean and sea air as they flew through it, "Stella! You must relax as you were before!"

"I can't! I'll fall!"

"No, you won't! You'll fall if you do not relax. Close your eyes again and pretend like we are on the beach cantering."

"I don't want to."

"If you don't, we'll never be able to fly together. Don't you want to be able to fly?"

Stella hunched over a little farther and clenched a little tighter. "I just . . . I think I'll fall!"

"You won't. Just trust me!"

The thing she felt most comfortable doing first was to un-hunch her back and sit up straight. Doing this gave her an instant feeling of freedom and control over the situation.

"That's right!" said Arrow.

She could not stop the smile which began its reappearance at the corners of her mouth. She was slowly letting her legs relax and reveled in each sensation — the wind making her hair flow out behind her, the feel of Arrow's muscles moving under her legs as his wings moved up and down, the edge of his mane tickling her chin as it flowed back toward her.

She looked up in between his ears and saw the expanse of the beach in front of them, spreading on and curving around to disappear around the other side of the island. The speed at which they were passing over the waters exhilarating.

She felt Arrow lean to the side and turn so her view from between his ears changed from sand and ocean to purely ocean. She gripped Arrow's mane tighter, but willed herself to stay upright with relaxed legs and she let her body lean with the turn. Arrow completed the turn and then she saw the beach with the lighthouse.

"Much better!" she heard Arrow say over the rush of the wind.

She felt as if they truly were melding together and becoming a single being. He lowered his head and changed the angle of his wings, and they descended to the beach. He landed in a canter then slowed to a walk as he folded his wings around her legs.

"Hey!" she said suddenly remembering something. She slapped him playfully on the neck, "I never un-jinxed you!" They both laughed. Stella was delighted by the sound of his laugh—a wonderful mixture of laughter and neighing.

How she wished she would never have to leave Arrow's side. Now that they had landed, she instantly wanted to do it again and be up in the air . . . flying. Flying! She couldn't believe she had just flown . . . on a Horse's back . . . over the *ocean*.

CHAPTER 14

"There is a truth deep down inside of you that has been waiting for you to discover it, and that Truth is this: you deserve all good things life has to offer."

Maximus

When Maximus and Isaac stepped out of the lighthouse, they saw what at first looked like an unusually large bird flying in the distance. Maximus soon realized it was Arrow, with Stella on his back. Surprised, to say the least, that they had taken to the air in only a matter of minutes, he set out to meet them. Isaac, following behind him, began his questions.

"Maximus . . . am I crazy, or is that my sister riding a HORSE . . . with WINGS?"

Maximus smiled and answered, "Yes, Isaac, that is what you see."

"Where did a Winged Horse come from?"

Maximus told Isaac what he had told Stella about how he had travelled to Markab the previous night to bring a Horse back for Stella as a gift to help her. As Maximus completed his explanation to Isaac, Arrow and Stella landed softly in the sand. Again, the smile on Stella's face had the immediate effect of an identical smile on his own face. Oh, how strong her gift was — and she didn't even know she was using it.

The powerfully majestic and beautiful team of girl and Horse cantered over to Maximus and Isaac. Stella got off Arrow's back and lead Isaac forward to touch Arrow. She got him stroking his neck and cheek and stepped back a few steps to watch.

Maximus stepped forward to her and whispered, "I haven't told Isaac that Arrow can talk. Maybe you can repay him for the stinky-garbage-flower trick."

Stella's clear-green eyes looked at him, twinkling with happiness, and now a little mischief. "Arrow," she said in

Zeego, "what do you think of my brother?"

Arrow answered, "I think he is very kind. Like you, Milady."

Isaac stepped back quickly, tripped on his own two feet and fell in the sand. He whipped his head around to look at his sister in an "are you kidding me?" type expression.

She laughed cheerily along with Maximus, "Yes, Isaac — Arrow can talk!" she said.

They all enjoyed a moment of laughter and mutual affection. Stella shared her experience of flying, Isaac became more comfortable with Arrow and Maximus settled himself in the sand, watching the scene before him with much gratitude for the safety and happiness of his two charges — even if deep down he knew it might only be brief.

Gradually, Stella and Isaac came to sit by him, and the Horse stood behind Stella, hooves and knees only inches from her body. Maximus could tell Arrow intended to make good of his promise to protect her and had already formed a deep affection for her.

As the chatter quieted down, Maximus knew that soon, Stella would remember that he was going to answer some more questions.

It was nearing lunch-time, and the sun was getting higher and hotter. Luckily, on a small island in the middle of the ocean, there was always at least a small breeze to keep the heat bearable, and even pleasant.

Just as Maximus had guessed, as the children got quieter and settled down, Stella looked at Maximus. He saw incredibly how much more calm and happy she seemed. *Finally*, he thought, *I have done something right.* And in the same stream of thought came: *and now I'll probably ruin it by telling her she must face Gershon in only a few days or Zodians would start dying.*

"Well," said Stella to him, "Isaac is here now. Should we talk some more?"

"Yes," said Maximus, but all that he could come up with was a long pause. After a few moments, he looked over to Isaac and Stella. They looked concerned and confused for him. Maximus forced a smile, "Sorry. Just clued-out there for a minute."

"Are you alright?" asked Stella.

"Yeah . . . yeah, I'm fine. Stell . . . why don't you get me rolling here and ask a question or something?"

"Uhm . . . yeah. Well, what I keep wondering is why we didn't get told any of this stuff about where we're from. Like, my dad . . . he never told me he went to Pegasus all the time, or even that there was such thing as Winged Horses."

Maximus saw a little shadow of the hurt return to her face.

"This is what I know," he began, "Remember I told you how your parents moved here when you were a toddler? And the reason for that being there was someone threatening to kill you?"

"How could I forget?" asked Stella.

"I'm going to tell you who that person is. I'm having a hard time with this because when I tell you about him, your life will change. You won't be able to go on with life as normal."

"It isn't normal anyway," interjected Isaac, "We're not normal."

"Yes, that is true. Your parents kept everything a secret to give you as close to a normal childhood as you could have. Whether it was the right decision or not is not my place, or yours, to decide. That's what they thought was best to keep you safe and happy."

He paused to look deep into Stella and Isaac's eyes. He wanted to emphasize this point. He didn't, or couldn't have them upset by their parents' choices.

"Do you agree that they had the right to decide what is best?"

They both nodded.

Maximus continued, "It was our understanding together, before going into hiding, that if you were sent here, it was time. The time to tell you everything and prepare you to do what must be done . . . should you accept. The fact that you get to choose? You can thank your parents for that. If you'd have grown up in the Zodiacs — you would have been forced into the roles I am about to tell you of — and your lives would have been miserable and full of fear — always having to guard your lives. Be grateful to your parents for giving you a childhood. Be grateful they let you grow in peace, safety and love."

It was silent for a moment. Then, Stella looked at him somberly and said, "What roles? What do we get to choose?"

"You get to choose if you want to become the rulers of the Zodiacs you were born to be — or not."

Maximus could see Stella and Isaac had no idea how to respond — and it was too big a concept anyway, so he moved on. "Because of the attack on your parents and yourselves, we now know that the people you have been hidden from found you. How? We don't know for sure."

"Can't they find us now then?" asked Isaac.

Maximus sighed, "Protection on this island and lighthouse is stronger than your home. As far as we know, it's impenetrable."

Stella, with voice slightly raised asked, "Why couldn't we have had the same protections?"

"One major reason. Again, it comes down to your parents wanting you to have a happy childhood. This lighthouse is completely secluded, to keep the protection at its utmost, I have had no other human contact — Earthling or Zodian — for these now fifteen years. You would have had to do the same — which means no friends, and no wandering outside a certain radius. That would be no life for a child . . . or for your parents.

Stella said, "That's basically how we lived our life anyway—but, alright—they found out where we were and they saw us."

"They saw your parents, and they saw Shooting Stars leaving the scene. They still don't know who the second star was. But they know you escaped the attack. The man that was sent to kill you, his name is Dreold. He is the most feared of Gershon's Minion."

"So, are they still looking for us?" she asked. Arrow bent his head down over her. "For you, Stella, yes. But they're not necessarily 'looking'."

"What are they doing?"

"Yesterday, I found out that Gershon demanded you show yourself in five days, now four. In other words, come out of hiding, or he will start killing innocent Zodians by the thousands until you emerge. Why he is giving you time instead of just saying 'right now' is strange, but he does have a way of convincing people he is kind and merciful. He traps all in his lies."

"But . . . what? Won't he kill me if he knows where I am?" She abruptly stood up, staying close to Arrow. She looked agitated. Arrow remained standing still and strong by her side.

"We need to make a plan to prevent that from happening." He paused. "Of course, you don't have to show yourself at all, but could stay here forever."

"And let people die because of me?" she said a little frantically, "I couldn't do that!"

"I know. I knew you would feel that way. There is much I can teach both of you to guard yourselves. Isaac, they won't remain ignorant of you forever—but we need to try. A male heir of Eli and Isolde would send Gershon into a frenzy right now. But, the time might come when news of your existence will be greatly needed by the Zodians."

Stella stepped forward toward Maximus, Arrow

mirroring her. "If they want ME dead, and I am their female heir, won't they send all their forces for Isaac?"

"Yes, that is what we are left to assume."

"We can't let anything happen to him. They must not find out."

"Stella, I'll be fine," said Isaac.

"Isaac," she argued back, "we can't fight them."

Maximus did not want to feed Stella's insecurities any longer, so he said in a firm voice, "Stella — when you arrived here, I told you about your parents and their powers and I said that you and Isaac were born with those same powers. I can teach you to become Shooting Stars among other things . . . and we can do it within the next few days."

Isaac jumped to his feet. "Really?" he asked.

"Yes, I have no doubt of it."

Stella said, "So we learn to zoom around the sky and move things. These people are evil and can harm us. We still won't be enough."

Completely changing direction to respond to Stella in a round-about way, Maximus bluntly said, "Your grandfather — Eli's father — is still alive."

They both stared at him, stunned silent. Then Stella stuttered, "Th . . . then why . . . why doesn't *he* remove Gershon from power? Where has he been in all of this?"

"Gershon rose to power deep within Orel's kingdom, which is the Zodiacs, by turning people toward him with his fake promises and lies. Gershon has so many Zodians under his influence that Orel, and those who still remain his followers are severely outnumbered, and their influence is mostly non-existent."

"Well if he can't win . . . we surely can't," Stella said.

"Let me remind you again of what you have in your favor which Orel has lost. First, you have your freedom. Gershon will not know where you base yourselves as he does Orel."

"How will he not know once we show ourselves?" Isaac

asked. "Won't they trace us back here?"

"I will explain more of that later—but, in a few words, Orel gave us something here that used to be his. It keeps us hidden from Gershon. Secondly, you have extra powers because your mother was Princess of Vega. Your births created a union of the Constellations, and that union can benefit all the good influence in the Universe—and give evil a little harder time at succeeding. And, Eli, your father, is the son of Orel."

They both stared.

"You mean, this Orel person, *he* is our grandfather?" Isaac asked.

"Yes."

Stella and Isaac had no response to this so he continued, "So, those who have remained out of Gershon's influence and loyal to Orel will surely be bolstered by news of you . . . and Isaac when the time is right. They will come out of hiding and join you. It is also possible that the hope you will instill in the people of the Zodiacs can turn the majority of them back to you, leaving Gershon in the minority. But, that will be a long process which will take much painful effort to be a success. If we can find those who are already on your side, we can begin to build an army of sorts. Gershon will not go down without a severe fight."

Stella leaned against Arrow's shoulder and dropped her head against his neck. "This is all very overwhelming," she said.

Isaac asked, "What does Gershon do that is so bad?"

There was much political jargon and talk Maximus could use, but he wanted to answer him simply enough so a child could understand. He said, "He thought it would be better if all the people in the Zodiacs were MADE to obey the rules. Not only has he made it so the rules are enforced using violence and most often death as a punishment, he has given *more* rules. In HIS mind, these rules will create even more 'peace and harmony'—for he believes he knows what is best for each person, and that his knowledge of what is best can rule the Zodiacs the best they ever have been ruled before.

"The worst part of it all is he is so good at lying and deceiving, that he has most of the Zodians convinced that he is right, that his way is the best way. And, he demands recognition and praise from everyone, and wants Orel to admit that he was right—that he is doing better than he did.

Many of these people—our people—like thinking they are being taken care of, but truly are miserable as they live in fear of making any mistakes, and as they surrender their lives and all decision-making powers."

Maximus could keep going, but decided he had ranted for quite long enough and made at least the majority of the most important points.

"But, that's no way to live!" said Isaac.

"I'm glad you feel that way. Humans need to be able to make choices, decisions, and mistakes most of all. It's the only way we evolve. Right? We Zodians would never have achieved the brain power to do the things we can, being controlled as Gershon is now controlling." Maximus felt political heat and venom returning to him as he spoke of these things.

"But why will these people who like him and his ways even want us?" asked Stella.

"Because of your innate power to restore hope that has been lost, you will remind them of what can be possible again."

Isaac, sounding very mature said, "Then I want to do this. At least our parents taught us about the stars. Maybe this is what they eventually wanted for us. We're like them. We don't even really belong here on Earth."

Maximus answered, "They DID want you old enough to choose for yourself. But yes, they also want the best for the Zodiacs. The choices they had to make—I wouldn't want to be in that position . . ."

All was silent again as Maximus gave them time to contemplate. He watched Stella stand and run her fingers through Arrow's mane. In a quiet voice, she asked, "Do we have more family on Vega?"

"I am unsure of your blood-relations—but as a daughter of their princess, I think it would be the best place to present you. The people of the Triangle should be able to put up enough protection to keep Gershon from harming you."

"It is all still very confusing," she said.

"I know. I'm sorry."

"I still don't understand where Orel is, how we're safe here at the lighthouse, how Gershon will see me when I'm on Vega, and . . . other things I can't even remember now."

Isaac walked a couple steps to stand next to Stella and Arrow. "So, can I just clarify?" he asked. "To the Zodians . . . are we . . . royal? I mean, you said we had to choose if we wanted the throne and you're telling us about our family who are all rulers and princesses and the like."

"Yes, Isaac," Maximus answered," Orel, Eli, Isolde and you are the royal family—you have the most evolved minds of all who live in the Zodiacs."

Maximus watched them look at each other in astonishment. After a moment, Isaac looked at him and said, "Now that we know who we are and what we can do . . . it'll be hard to just sit here and do nothing. Especially if Zodians will be dying every day."

Maximus nodded. He knew Isaac would feel that way. "And you, Stella?" he asked.

"There is no other choice," she said, "We can't let people live in misery and die in misery if there is something we can do about it. I'm just . . . scared. I don't know if we or rather I can live up to the expectations that everyone has of me."

Before Maximus could answer, the one who could do a better job at reassuring Stella spoke to her, "You can," said

Arrow. He lifted his wings and moved them gently up and down. She smiled. Obviously that was enough of an answer for her.

"Let's go get lunch," Maximus said, ready to be done the very intense conversation and all the emotions it brought.

Maximus was relieved there were no melt-downs and that they both made noble decisions. As they walked back to the lighthouse, he thought of a picture on his desk of his beautiful Cecily. He held on to his hope that she was still alive and well. She was the only thing he regretted leaving behind in the Zodiacs—and now it was time to return.

CHAPTER 15

"Let us remember, as far as we can, that every unpleasant thought is a bad thing literally put into the body."

Gershon

Gershon paced in front his cave. His anger made him a danger to be around. He was furious with Dreold for letting Eli's and Isolde's daughter escape. It had taken fifteen years to track them down! And they were on Earth! This was shocking to Gershon. Earth was so far behind in evolution, that he never would have thought anyone from the Zodiacs would ever want to go there. He threw a glass candle and breathed heavily as he watched the hot wax splatter and drip down the stone wall.

He only wanted one thing at the moment—to be rid of Orel and his family forever. He stopped pacing abruptly in front of his high-backed stone chair which was padded with skins of foxes from Velpecula. Then he spun around harshly and sat. His anger cast a foul and vile energy that hung over him.

He fought against thoughts of Orel—the thorn in his side—even though Gershon had once loved Orel as a brother. Through those long years in which he had served Orel as his advisor, he had been taught to use more of his brain capacity than he ever thought possible. He learned to become a Shooting Star and travel between the Zodiacs.

All Gershon could think of now however, was how Orel was treating him—like an outcast—banished from his presence. Orel refused to acknowledge Gershon for anything he was doing for the Zodians.

Gershon first suggested the implementation of Twelve Stewards, one for each Zodiac, so Orel did not have to be bogged down with the everyday minor affairs of the ever more populating and evolving Constellations.

Orel embraced the plan, and invented the Telescopes, one for himself and twelve more. The Telescopes were for communication and transportation. Progress was slow in teaching the Stewards to transform and travel as Shooting Stars, and the Telescopes made it possible for them to start their jobs as Stewards right away.

The invention of the Telescopes was a monumental achievement for Orel, and Gershon was yet again amazed by the incredible things he could create.

Still however, Orel was constantly burdened by the Zodians and was saddened by many of the things they did. It had pained Gershon to see Orel that way.

Gershon had seen a way around this. The people of the Zodiacs did not need the freedom to make poor choices and forget about Orel, who had made their bounteous lives possible. Gershon saw that the freedom and bounty made the Zodians proud, and that pride had ultimately led them into trouble.

What if they weren't given so much freedom? They needed to be obedient to Orel before they got the freedom and knowledge to expand their abilities. Plus, Gershon could tell them what was best for them and show them how to live better lives. If they didn't believe him, he'd have to prove it. They'd come to thank him.

In addition, with Gershon's plan, his subjects would be constantly reminded of who they owed their thanks to. In his mind, it was an unthinkable action to forget about Orel, and now himself.

Gershon thought that if Orel had accepted the plan of the Twelve Stewards, he would love and accept his new plan to remove some freedoms from the Zodians and use stronger rule enforcement as well. Orel refused and Gershon felt hurt by the chastisement he received.

Not able to let go of his hurt, he set about to do it without

Orel's permission. He would prove Orel wrong—and show Orel that he was right. His plan couldn't be discovered by Orel until it would be too late for him to reverse anything.

He started with the Stewards. He slowly gave them small amounts of additional knowledge and power—until power and recognition became all they craved and felt they deserved.

Then, as Orel was getting close to discovering what Gershon was doing, Gershon told the Stewards Orel planned to take all their power away—then switched them to his side by promising them the power and they wanted by doing things his way.

But Gershon knew the Stewards, now called the Minion, would have to be ruled in much the same way as the Zodians, just not as obvious, so that he maintained ultimate control.

It had taken long years to track the royal family down. Orel had two sons, one already dead, and then Eli. When things began to crumble for Orel and build for Gershon, Eli went and married the princess of Vega of the very powerful Constellation, Lyra. Zodians were bolstered by this union and when they had a child that promised such ability as they have never before seen, the Zodians started to fight against Gershon.

Gershon set out to put a stop to it immediately, but somehow his plans were discovered and all of the royal family disappeared—including Orel. Gershon was wracked with nerves every day about where they were and what they could be doing.

When he found them, he had hoped to dispatch Eli's family in complete secrecy from the Zodians. He did not want to lose any favor by letting it be known that he had set out to find and murder them. But now that their daughter was still out there, thanks to the failure of the disappointing Dreold, he must act quickly.

But the realization came to him that if the Zodians knew the royal family was dead, all those who were resisting him in wait for their return would succumb. It was his plan then to have Stella appear herself and he would lure him to her, let the Zodians see her, and then do the deed himself for all to see.

He inwardly congratulated himself for this plan and reveled in his cunning genius.

CHAPTER 16

"There is no dream that may not come true, if you but learn to use the Creative Force working through you . . . The key to power lies in using what you have . . . freely, fully . . . and thus opening wide your channels for more Creative Force to flow through you."

Isaac

In Isaac's not-so-distant past, he had actually grown weary of Stella's constant 'protectiveness'. But now, he found himself a little lonely—maybe even slightly jealous if he wanted to admit that to himself. But, she had been sad and depressed for some time, and it was wonderful to see her happy again now that she had Arrow.

After lunch, she told him she was going outside to check on Arrow, and then ended up being gone for a while. Wondering where she had gone—Isaac went outside the lighthouse to see her as only a dot in the sky—Arrow's wings spread in flight.

With mixed feelings of being happy for her, lonely, and somewhat jealous, he went back to the lighthouse with the intent of returning to his room. As he walked across the large communal living space towards the stairs, he heard Maximus call him from the kitchen which was wrapped halfway around the circumference of the lighthouse against the outside wall. Another wall was built to section it off from the living room.

Obediently, Isaac changed his course and headed for the kitchen. Maximus was finishing the after-lunch clean up.

"I noticed you're feeling a little left out since Arrow arrived," Maximus said when he entered.

Isaac inwardly scolded himself for letting his emotions be so obvious.

"No, not at all!" he answered, "I am very happy for Stella! She finally has something that keeps her smiling. Besides, I'm finally getting some peace and quiet without her hovering over me like a queen bee protecting her hive."

Maximus didn't laugh, nor did he look convinced. It was hard to hide anything from him. He tossed the towel on the counter and walked over to the table. Sitting down, he said, "I'm glad you're happy for Stella; I am too. Come and sit."

Isaac joined him at the table. "When do we start training?" he asked.

"Right now."

Isaac sat up straighter. "Should I get Stella?"

"In a minute. Let me ask you something first."

"Okay."

"What do you think about searching for a companion for yourself?"

Isaac felt the same gratefulness he had when Maximus had guessed that he had discovered some of his powers.

"I think that sounds amazing!" he blurted. But then instantly, he was flooded with guilt. "Actually," he said, "no, I'm fine. Let's just do the training so we can make sure we get Stella to Vega on time." The guilt came from the realization that Stella might think he was taking away the one thing she had that he didn't.

Maximus was quietly studying Isaac which made him want to squirm. Then he said, "Alright. That's fine. We will train, and if you should come to change your mind, let me know."

Isaac nodded. He felt disappointed, but worked hard not to let it show.

Maximus said, "Let's just say however, that we were to team you up with a creature of your choice . . . what would you want?"

"Never thought about it really . . . I didn't know all of this before. What kind of creatures are there?"

"Well, it's quite simple really . . . just as your sister got a Winged Horse from Pegasus, which is a Constellation shaped as a Winged Horse . . . so have all the Constellations taken on the form of the animals which inhabit them."

That seemed like a strange thought to Isaac. He knew many of the Constellations well from their family nights looking at the stars. He asked, "Canis Major and Minor? Is there a bunch of dogs and wolves running around those Stars?"

"Not the sort of dogs you think," said Maximus.

"What sort of dogs then?"

"The animals on the Constellations might *look* somewhat the same as they do on Earth, but in intelligence, they are much different. And that's why we capitalize their species in our grammar. The Dogs on these Stars can, like Arrow, talk and communicate. They are organized like little communities. On Canis Major and Minor, their accommodations aren't too different from wolves or coyotes though. Like I said, they look the same as wild dogs here, so no thumbs or walking around on their hind legs or anything."

"I find it hard to believe there are Stars full of Giraffes wandering around on the Camelopardalis," said Isaac.

"It might be hard to, but you can believe it! Sometimes there are other creatures living among the dominant creatures of the Constellation as well, and occasionally, humans are led to live among them. But humans are not dominant on the Constellations which are in the shape of creatures outside of the Zodiacs. However, the *Zodiacs* that are shaped like a creature, like Taurus the Bull or Aries the Ram are populated *mostly* with humans, but have a huge population of the creature whose shape the Constellation has formed."

"Wow. So, will we get to see these places if we learn to become Shooting Stars?"

"I don't see why not. In fact, it may become necessary. It will take a lot of training, so you best be willing to work diligently."

"'Course I'm willing!"

Just then, Isaac heard Stella return. He could see her through the open door of the kitchen. She was humming to herself and had a bounce in her step. Isaac had seen this before—on movies or something. If he didn't know it was the Horse she was enamored with, he'd think she was in love with a boy.

"Hello?" she called.

"We're in the kitchen," Maximus answered.

She joined them and sat down at the table. Upbeat, she asked, "What were you guys talking about?"

"Oh, you mean while you were out *checking on Arrow*," Maximus asked in a teasing tone. He threw a wadded-up napkin at her like he was one of the kids.

Her fair, freckled cheeks blushed pink. "Sorry," she said through a not-well-hidden smirk. "I couldn't resist. I could fly all day."

"I bet!" said Maximus, "Eli was always sneaking away to Pegasus. But," Maximus continued, "you will need to spend a little less time flying for now, and more time with me, as you have a LOT to learn in the next few days."

"I know," Stella said, face turning serious again. "I will."

"Good," said Maximus. "Well, training is what we were going to discuss, then I started telling Isaac about the creature Constellations. I asked him if he could have a companion like you have Arrow, what he'd pick."

"Oh!" she said. "That's a great idea! Isaac should have a companion too."

"She thinks you should have one too, Isaac," Maximus said punching his arm.

"Well," Isaac said, trying to remain nonchalant, "what are my choices?"

Maximus quickly explained to Stella that the creature Constellations took on the form of its inhabitants. She was very excited about this, because she also knew many of the Constellations from her parents' teachings. Typical of Stella, she asked about Unicorns. "There are Stars full of Unicorns in Monoceros?" Her eyes twinkled with anticipation.

"Yes," said Maximus, obviously enjoying their fascination. "According to your father, the Unicorns of Monoceros are almost any color and shade you can think of. They have many magical properties, and if I remember correctly — they are also very 'snooty'. They can talk, but only choose to speak to certain people — and most definitely not men. They never spoke to Orel or Eli," then added more to himself, "I wonder if Eli ever took Isolde there? She probably was pure enough for them."

"Wow," said Stella.

He continued, "There is Ursa Major and Ursa Minor, the Bears . . . a very interesting and also highly developed Constellation. There is Aquila, the Eagle. Not highly populated, and the Eagles like to keep to themselves, but will 'mingle' with other species when the occasion calls for it. There is Lepus, the Hare; Leo, the Lion — of course in the Zodiacs; Vulpecula, the Fox; Serpens, the Serpent — kind of spooky to go to Stars full of snakes, but Orel has done it; there are also Stars full of Lynxes, very rare. And one of my favorite Constellations is Phoenix — such magnificent and gifted birds live there."

"What about water animals? Such as, dolphins? Are there Dolphins on Delphinus?" asked Stella.

"The constellations in the form of water animals, like Delphinus, Hydrus the Water Snake and like Pisces in the Zodiacs which is in the form of fishes, are mostly made of water, but like Earth, they have land masses as well and other creatures living on the land. But yes! Delphinus' waters are heavily populated with Dolphins! I know it's hard to believe, but this is the way our Universe is made. There is also Draco of course . . . where the Dragons live."

Isaac couldn't hide his smile when Maximus looked directly at him. "Can you tell me more about them?" he asked hopefully.

"Oh yes. There are Dragons galore—some with amazing powers and some with powers that are locked inside of them, yet to be revealed. Dragons are great architects. Their buildings are enormous and elaborate. However, Draco is one of the most dangerous Constellations to travel to. They seem to always have battles there amongst themselves. There are really different groups on the separate Stars, each wanting complete rule over the entire Constellation.

"The Dragons on Gamma Draconis—which is the brightest Star in the Constellation—are mostly welcoming of humans, and are interested in the Universe at large. The evil Dragons might also be interested in what goes on in other Constellations, but only because they see the possibility of more room to hatch eggs and populate. The idea of having power all over the Universe is most appealing to them."

He paused, a bit of a troubled look coming over his face, "I've actually always feared the possibility of Gershon getting these Dragons on his side. The Battle of the Zodiacs can grow to be a Universal War. Arrow has realized this as well. Mostly, the creature Constellations will be in our favor. If they choose to join us, it will be to keep their homes free and unencumbered by this war. We might have an easier time than Gershon winning their 'vote', so to speak. Gershon will of course lie to them and promise them things they will not get in the end—but luckily for us, creatures (better than humans) can discern good from evil very well. And most creatures are 'good'. The ones who will like Gershon however, will be dangerous and troublesome. Like Serpens, or some of the evil Wolves on Lupus. Even some Bears—for there are around twenty six Stars full of Bears—lean toward the more vicious side.

"My point is . . . we already have Pegasus on our side. Isaac needs a companion—something strong and even frightening to others. We need to keep him safe—keep him alive. If we can talk to the Dragons before Gershon does . . . well, we have a lot of reasons to go to Gamma Draconis."

"Are you . . ." Isaac stuttered, still whirling from the turn this conversation had taken, "Are you saying . . . that we are going to see Dragons?"

"I can't think of anything more appropriate," said Maximus. "You love Dragons, and if they choose to support us, and one decides to return with us — you'll be better protected with the Dragon than with any other creature I can think of."

"Bring a Dragon . . . here?" Stella asked in a small voice.

"If you can turn into Shooting Stars within the next few days, we can do it before going to Vega. Then, we could leave Isaac here protected by the Dragon . . . just in case our secrecy here fails, or any other unforeseeable misfortune would happen."

"How big are the Dragons?" asked Stella.

"Pretty big!" he said smirking, "It could use your little pony as a teddy bear."

Her eyes widened more. Isaac knew what she was worried about. It wasn't that she wanted something bigger than Arrow, or that she felt undercut again — it was that she was worried about her Horse sharing the island with a large, fire-breathing Dragon.

Stella looked at Isaac and he was relieved to see a smile flickering at the edges of her mouth. "I guess no more riding the back of the couch pretending it's a dragon Isaac!"

Isaac laughed a mostly nervous laugh. He could be dreaming. Were they really talking about Dragons and the attempt to bring one here to this island specifically for him?

"It's what you want, right Isaac?" asked Maximus.

Isaac nodded quickly.

"Great!" said Maximus, standing up. "I need a little time to prepare — then you two can join me at the top of the lighthouse. There is something there I have to show you —

and it is where we'll do all our training. I'll call down to you when I'm ready."

He left the kitchen. Isaac looked at Stella, and for a moment, he let himself be the little brother that he really was and hugged his sister. It was part a celebratory hug, part as a thank you hug—but mostly it was a hug to get comfort and love. He missed their parents very much . . . and he knew she did too. Stella would always understand him better than anyone else could. They were brother and sister.

CHAPTER 17

"Most people define themselves by this finite body, but you're not a finite body.
Even under a microscope you're an energy field."

Maximus

Maximus was sitting on a stool in front of the Telescope in the highest room of the lighthouse. He knew he had told the children it would be just a few minutes. However, his exhaustion consumed him. What he needed most was a nap . . . a long, long nap joined with a full night's sleep.

Willing himself to make it through the rest of the afternoon and evening, he got off his stool and pointed the Telescope at the wall. All Maximus did to see who he wanted to see was speak to the telescope as if he were speaking to the intended. Maximus only ever spoke to one person, which was Orel.

Soon, Orel's projection appeared there. Maximus felt relieved in his presence.

"Stella has taken to Arrow as we hoped," Maximus said, "I was able to tell her of Gershon, and his demands, without her melting down and trying to run away. I consider that a success."

"Well done," Orel said with an encouraging smile, "Now, are Stella and Isaac ready to begin their training?"

Maximus sighed. He felt nervous to be the one to teach them. He looked at Orel imploringly and said, "Yes. I told them I would call them up shortly, after I had a few minutes to prepare."

"And, what do you need to prepare?"

"Honestly . . . a good night's sleep sounds the most appealing to me. Other than that . . . I just wanted to . . . to talk to you, I guess."

"I know you feel overwhelmed Maximus, and you do deserve the rest. Remember, this is what you came here for, to be here for the children in a crisis. Stay awake with them a little longer today. Wait with them while they work. Then you can sleep soundly and happily tonight knowing you did your best and gave them your all."

He looked at the projection of Orel as he felt his tiredness being replaced by motivation and said, "I have not yet taught anyone to transform, is it difficult?"

"It will be easier with these two than it would be with anyone else, for they have their parents evolved minds passed on to them already. You have the Telescope as well, which they will use until they do not need it anymore."

"Where should I start?"

"Convince them they are infinite matter and what that means."

Maximus said, "I have a feeling Isaac will transform more quickly than Stella, because he already discovered powers of creation. I have a suspicion he can do more, but hasn't shown me yet."

"Yes, Isaac has discovered some of his gifts on his own, though you know as well as I do that Stella is just as gifted and skilled—she is just one of those that has to be shown the way. Do you feel ready to call the children up now?"

"As ready as I can be. I know I should have been preparing for this. I guess, deep down, I never wanted to believe anything could ever happen to Eli and Isolde."

"I know," Orel said with sympathy in his voice.

Maximus nodded at the ground.

Orel said, "Should I go now so you can bring my grandchildren up here?"

"When will they meet you?"

"When they ask—and when they're ready, or when they are in dire need of me." Orel smiled at Maximus then faded away.

CHAPTER 18

*"There is no time for the Universe
and there is no size for the Universe."*

Stella

Stella was waiting anxiously for Maximus to call them up. The concept that she could become a Shooting Star was still slightly out of her reach, but her confidence was a little stronger now that she had Arrow.

"Isaac! Stella!" she heard Maximus call, "Stella! Why don't you go ask Arrow to come inside and join us upstairs?"

She was elated and zipped past Isaac and out the door. She didn't have to go far, Arrow was standing only a short distance away from the door. He brightened when he saw her.

"Maximus said you could come inside! He wants you to join us for our training!"

"Well," said Arrow stepping forward, "let's not keep him waiting."

Stella spun around excitedly and Arrow followed her into the lighthouse, ducking his head and tucking his wings to make sure he cleared the door-frame.

When she and Arrow reached the bottom of the stairs, Arrow stopped short.

"What's wrong?"

"Those look a little complicated for me, and I'm nervous that they are too weak to hold my weight."

Stella stomped on a stair. Indeed the sound was not as solid as she would have liked it to sound. "I would have to agree," she paused and they looked each other in the eye. Stella smirked as understanding passed between them. Why walk when you can fly? "I should probably just take the stairs this time. I don't want to weigh you down."

He spread his wings and said, "I'll race you."

Arrow began beating the air with his wings and through herculean effort, rose vertically into the air. Stella watched in amazement for a moment and marveled at his strength.

Then she remembered they were racing and started taking the stairs two at a time. She reached the top landing huffing and puffing. Arrow was standing square and bulging his chest out trying not to look out of breath. "You don't fool me," she said panting, "I know you're out of breath too."

He visibly deflated in a playful manner, and Stella was smiling as she knocked on the door.

"Come in," she heard Maximus say.

Stella entered with Arrow in tow, his nose close enough to her neck she could feel his warm breath. After entering the threshold, they stood just inside the doorway and looked around. There was an unusual mixture of things Stella had never seen before—like the silvery liquid which ran down a section of the wall like a waterfall. She was positively transfixed by an enormous golden telescope. It was at least ten times the size of hers at home. The lens was bigger around than her head. Prompted by Maximus and by a nudge from Arrow's nose in her back, she walked forward to it and stood next to Isaac, who seemed equally as transfixed.

She looked at Maximus who was standing with his hands locked behind his back, rocking from his heels to his toes with an expectant smile. She made the comment she knew he was expecting, "This is the most amazing telescope I have ever seen."

Isaac added, "I've never seen another one like it."

"You are both correct," said Maximus, "this Telescope is the most amazing there ever has been and there is not another one exactly like it. It can do more than just help you see the Stars." He unlocked his hands and reached out to stroke it as if it were his prized pet.

"What else can it do?" asked Isaac.

"Much. But for our present purposes it is going to be your portal to travel to other Stars. Until you can do it without the Telescope that is . . . and many have never achieved travel as a Shooting Star without it. But you two should be able to use it easily. Your minds are further developed due to your parentage. But for now, you'll learn to use the Telescope."

Stella's nerves were in a place that she couldn't put a name to, but it was somewhere between dread and excitement. Maximus started pacing back and forth. "Your first lesson is to understand a couple important facts. You must grasp these concepts and believe them to be true if you are ever to transform yourselves and become Shooting Stars." After saying this, he made eye contact as he passed in front of them.

Stella knew he was looking for signs that they understood, and she nodded to him along with Isaac to show she comprehended. Maximus stopped to face them and said, "Here it is then," he paused and with his hand motioning each word, he hammered out the next few words, "everything is made up of the exact same thing." He looked into their eyes again before going on, "Everything! Is made up of the exact same thing. Your hand is made up of the exact same thing that the ocean outside is made of. Your hair is made up of the exact same thing as the bowl you ate your breakfast in. Stars are made of the exact same thing as the sand on our beach."

He resumed his pacing, and a look of wonderment came over him, "You see, *everything* is energy: the Universe, this Earth, and each human and creature. Our organs and skin which are made up of cells which are made up of molecules, which are made up of atoms."

"And atoms are made up of light and energy!" Isaac almost shouted, startling Stella and Arrow so that they jumped a little.

Maximus looked at him and smiled, "Exactly," he said. "See! You knew that, but did you ever contemplate the meaning?"

"No, I guess I haven't before."

Stella wanted to clarify, "So, the one thing everything is made up of is energy?"

Maximus answered, "Yes, that's exactly right. You are an energy field."

Stella looked around the room at objects and for the first time was able to look past their physical matter, whether it be wood or steel, plastic or organic, and she knew that truly, they were all the same thing—energy—just arranged and appearing in different ways.

She caught Isaac's eye. They smiled at each other then they looked back at Maximus who was again rocking back and forth from heel to toe in a bouncy way. Arrow was the one who spoke next, "Can I learn to transform as well?"

Maximus contemplated, "I believe you could," he paused, "eventually. Stella and Isaac have a great advantage being born from such evolved minds. But, anything is possible Arrow! If you can remove your limitations and expand your mind, you could no doubt develop some powers. Then your children could benefit, and if they expand theirs even more . . . you see how the process goes."

Stella's anxiety bubbled to boil-over in a split second, "Arrow will be able to come with me though won't he?"

Maximus asked, "Do you want him to?"

"Absolutely!"

"Then yes! Every possibility already exists. Remember, you and Arrow are made up of the same substance—energy. All you must do is be united in purpose and mind, and truly become 'one'."

"That's easy," she answered.

Maximus looked at Isaac, "It will be possible for you to transform your Dragon along with you as well, even as large as it will be. Size does not matter to the Universe."

Stella asked, "So, how do transformation and the

Telescope work together?"

"Right," Maximus said. He walked over to the Telescope and placed his hand on it. "Once you learn to transform your bodies and companions into pure light and energy, the Telescope will pull you in. It will be pointed toward the sky, then it will 'shoot' you there. You will appear to anyone looking at the night sky as a shooting star. I'm not sure how Orel invented this or what science is behind it . . . but it works! The 'how' doesn't matter. All you need to know is it can take your transformed matter and send it travelling through the Universe."

Smartly, Isaac asked, "At what speed? Even at the speed of light, travelling from Star to Star could take years."

Maximus answered, "Yes, you will be travelling at a speed that scientists on earth have been unable to measure."

"Which is?" Stella prompted.

"The speed of thought."

Isaac looked impressed.

"The speed of thought?" Arrow asked.

Isaac answered, "The speed of thought is faster than anything that has been measured, in fact, scientists are still unable to measure the speed of thought like they can the speed of light and the speed of sound."

Stella felt queasy at the thought of being shot out the Telescope like a cannon ball travelling faster than the speed of light or sound. Then she remembered she'd already travelled as a Shooting Star, the night their mother had sent them. It was bitter-sweet. It was comforting to know she'd already done it, and she remembered feeling warmth and seeing the glowing lights. The bitter part of the memory was that that was the last time she'd seen her mother. Remembering still hurt, so she turned her thoughts away quickly before the tears came.

She also remembered another thing that hurt about that memory. She looked up at Maximus, hoping her face hadn't turned red with the prospect of crying, "Maximus, why were Isaac and I unconscious on the beach after the first time we travelled as Shooting Stars?"

"I think the transformation was a lot for your bodies to handle the first time—and you didn't know what was happening to you."

"So, you don't think that will happen again?" she asked.

"I think you might be a little disorientated and probably exhausted the first few times—but no, I do not think you will lose consciousness again. Mostly because you will be aware of what is happening to you, and you'll have had practice at it."

Still, she felt nervous, and try as she might not to, she still doubted she could do it on her own. But, to avoid another lecture from Maximus on how brilliant and capable she was, she kept her doubts to herself.

CHAPTER 19

"Most of us have never allowed ourselves to want what we truly want, because we can't see how it is going to manifest."

Isaac

Isaac was enraptured with all of this possibility. Playing it out in his mind, he saw one big problem. "Wait," he asked, "How do we get back once we are away from the Telescope?"

"Ah . . . that. Yes. Well, if times were better, you'd just be able to use other Telescopes."

"The other Telescopes?" Isaac and Stella asked in unison.

"I thought you said there weren't any others like this Telescope," Isaac said.

"No, I said there is not another Telescope EXACTLY like this one. Orel created one Telescope for himself and one for each of the twelve Zodiacs. They were to give his Stewards as a way to travel and to communicate with him and each other. This one was Orel's. It's not like the other twelve because it has the ability to create a sort of invisible force for miles around it, and everyone and everything inside that radius is undetectable if they follow certain rules.

"How did you get it? Why doesn't Orel have it?" Isaac asked.

"He has other ways to protect himself. He gave this to me when I followed your parents here to help them." Maximus' face went from an exuberant expression to withdrawn and even mournful in seconds.

"What's wrong?" asked Isaac.

"Oh . . . I . . ." he looked like he didn't want to answer.

"Maximus?" he prompted.

In a quiet voice he said, "I just wish Eli wouldn't have refused taking the Telescope from Orel."

Again, both Isaac and Stella spoke in unison, "Why did he

refuse it?"

"Many reasons. One is the same reason I told you before. He wanted his kids to have as close to a normal life as possible. I have forgone human contact, because the Telescope makes this place completely secret. It was necessary I stay hidden in its protection for a long time. If I left it, I'd risk being found. Eli made me take it—when he didn't want it—to keep me safe."

Stella asked, "How did our family stay hidden so long without it?"

"Your parents had to stop using their gifts. If they used them a surge of tremendous energy would travel through the Universe, and Gershon and his Minion would be able to follow its . . ." he paused, ". . . ripples—and be able to pinpoint its location."

At that moment, both Isaac's heart and stomach seemed to drop to the floor and he felt like he was going to vomit. He must have swayed a little because Stella had moved to him and grabbed his arm. "Isaac, what's wrong?" She sounded far away.

"Isaac, say something!"

He didn't want to speak for fear of opening a flood of emotion. Plus, what he had just discovered would disgust them. He was disgusted at himself. Stella shook him a little.

He said with eyes wide but seeing nothing, "I know how they found us. I know how. It was me—I did it. It's my fault. They found us when I was using my powers in the woods. It's my fault!" And then he started crying. He thought Stella would realize that their parents were dead because of him and let go of him like he had a disease. Instead she wrapped her arms tightly around him.

Maximus knelt in front of him and said, "Isaac, listen to me. It was not your fault."

"Yes it was!" he almost shouted, "If I wouldn't have done that, they wouldn't have found us. I probably made ripples that let them find us!"

Stella had begun to cry. It was almost imperceptible, but Isaac knew the signs. Soon, she'd probably revolt from him.

"Isaac," Maximus said, "How could you have possibly known about everything you've learned in the past few days?"

Isaac resumed staring at nothing, sniffling and wiping his steady stream of tears with his sleeves. He knew Maximus didn't expect him to answer. After a moment Maximus said, "The only way you can be at fault is if you have all the information and deliberately tried to do damage."

Isaac was refusing to be comforted. In his mind—it was his fault. Maximus kept pressing, "Isaac, you never meant anybody harm by testing your gifts. Gershon and his Minion are the ones who mean harm. It is their fault and theirs alone. You discovered your amazing powers and your dad and mom would be proud of that. They are probably looking over you now, pleading with you as I am not to blame yourself. Such gifts and powers cannot be concealed for long, and I know they feel proud about what you can do and that you discovered it on your own.

"Plainly put Isaac, if you insist on blaming yourself for something that is not your fault, you'll never feel good enough to achieve transformation and return to the Zodiacs in your father's place."

Isaac focused his eyes and looked at Maximus. He still felt awful. Then Stella sniffed and wiped her eyes, then pulled him to his feet. Maximus stood too. "Come on Isaac," she said, "you can't blame yourself. What happened is not your fault."

Still, he did not look her in the eye—shame was like an anchor keeping his chin down and shoulders slumped. Stella grabbed his chin and made him look at her. "Isaac, you're my brother and I love you. Please, let's just keep working so we can make them proud."

Isaac thought of his parents. Could they possibly be proud of him? Or did they blame him? Despite himself, he took a deep breath. At the moment he still found it hard to talk, but he allowed himself to hug Stella tightly. He would do his job and protect the family he still had with all his might. He would say he's sorry to his parents and Stella by fiercely defending her and by doing the job that now fell to him in his father's absence.

CHAPTER 20

Is happiness in the destination or the journey?

Maximus

Maximus was holding his breath with a tight chest as Stella and Isaac were hugging. He hoped that Isaac would not dwell on the idea that it was his fault. Maximus scolded himself for not seeing this before. Possibly it was true? Was Isaac using his gifts the reason Gershon found them?

Isaac and Stella stopped hugging and Stella faced Maximus. She said, "Anyway, I think the original question was 'how do we get back without the Telescope?'"

Jumping into action, Maximus said, "Right! Let me show you." He went to a window sill where sat a little porcelain box with seashells pressed into it. He opened the lid and pulled out a small handful of charms. Each charm was the size of a thumb-print. They were in the shape of a five-pointed star and were etched from white, almost translucent rocks.

"You will have these," he said and held out his hand for them to see. The white stars had begun to glow a little in his hand. "They glow when they are in the hand of someone who has the mental capacity to transform."

Stella reached a hand forward but she drew it back.

Isaac asked, "Can I take one?"

Maximus gave him one and said, "As you go through the Telescope with this, it will imprint itself to you — memorizing your unique genome. Then, when you are away, it will only work for you. When you want to return hold your hand around it, then transform into light and energy, think of the Telescope and the lighthouse, and the Telescope will pull you back."

"At the speed of thought . . ." Stella said, sounding a little disbelieving.

"Yes," Maximus said, trying to remain patient with her doubts. "If you've been there in the mind, you'll go there in the body. Your thoughts are the most powerful thing you possess. The biggest reason most people don't achieve the level of mind power that your family has is everyone tries to understand 'how'. And if they don't see *how* something is possible, then they believe it is *not* possible. You must not let yourself be one of those people who limit themselves, Stella."

Her eyes shifted to the floor and she nodded. "So," he continued, "just believe Stella. These things are possible. I can tell you that because I believed – and then experienced. You do not need to understand the 'how' for these incredible things to happen."

She nodded. Arrow nudged her forward toward Maximus and said, "Take one of the Star Charms. Don't be afraid that it won't glow in your hand."

Maximus set the charm down on the stool. He wanted it to stop glowing so that the teenage-girl in Stella wouldn't blame its glowing on the fact that Maximus had been holding it.

She reached out toward the stool and lightly took it in her fingers, folded it into her palm and closed her fist around it.

Maximus watched with anticipation as Stella looked up at Arrow, took a deep breath and opened her palm. Maximus saw the glow of the charm reflecting in Stella's eyes – and then the glow lit up the smile which was spreading across her face.

She looked at her brother and he smiled and held his own glowing charm up in the fingers of one hand and pointed to it with the other.

They were ready.

CHAPTER 21

"To expand our identities, we find that affirmations
are tools we cannot do without. When joined with good
intentions and consistent actions, affirmations overcome
and eventually convert old thinking patterns."

Stella

Stella's star charm already felt like another extension of her own body and she never wanted to be without it.

"Let's move away from the Telescope for now," Maximus said, "You're not going to travel today—just transform as much of yourselves as you can."

They all moved a few windows away from the Telescope. "Now," continued Maximus, "it's as simple as just setting your minds to the task and trying."

Stella's heart was pounding fast and she wondered if Isaac's was too.

Maximus went on, "I will give you some things to think about and repeat to yourself. You can make your own personalized affirmations and they will help you focus your powers. When you affirm something, you declare it to be true. You say it positively. An affirmation can be a phrase you say to yourself to put yourself in a positive state of mind and build belief in yourself. It can be as simple as 'I know I can do this . . .' and any variation of that. Ready to try?"

They nodded.

"This is what I do," Maximus said. He glanced at the Telescope and took a few more steps away from it. "I close my eyes and start imagining myself turning into light. I repeat in my mind simply 'I am light and energy. I am made up of the same substance as Stars. I am light and energy.' I picture my body glowing—breaking up the physical matter and revealing what it truly is."

He stopped speaking and closed his eyes. Right before Stella's eyes his body had begun to look tingly with specs of light. Soon, the form of Maximus was made up of millions and billions of pin-pricks of light. He was now an energy field, alive with dynamic light.

It was, by far, the most miraculous thing Stella had ever witnessed. She looked at Isaac and gasped. "Isaac! You're doing it too!" she said.

Pin-pricks of light were beginning to show on his cheeks and on his hands and arms. Stella saw him look down at his hands and they instantly turned back to flesh and bone again. Maximus had returned to form as well.

Isaac was looking back and forth between them and said, "I didn't do that on purpose! All I was doing was saying in my head the things Maximus was saying and trying to memorize them. When he transformed, I just imagined how wonderful that must feel."

Maximus smiled at him. Stella wondered why she hadn't thought to do the same thing. Isaac made everything look so easy.

"Well done, Isaac," said Maximus beaming. Then he looked at Stella, "Are you ready to try?"

"I can try," she said.

"Close your eyes or look at anything that will help you focus only on yourself," he said.

She decided to close her eyes.

"Go ahead and try it again, Isaac," she heard Maximus say, "Now, clear your mind. Start thinking about the Stars and about infinite matter. Everything is light and energy. You are made up of the same stuff as Stars. Imagine the warmth, the possibility. Your body is trillions of atoms. Just keep thinking of these things. I'll be quiet now and let you try."

Stella was imagining her body growing warm with dots of glowing light replacing her physical form. *I am light and energy. The same stuff as stars.*

"Yes Isaac!" Maximus said, interrupting her thoughts.

Instead of looking at her brother who was surely glowing again, Stella told herself she could do it too, and she kept repeating those things to herself. She found herself relaxing, breathing deeper and feeling at peace—and happy. She was warm.

"Excellent Stella!"

She opened her eyes and looked at the skin on her arms and hands. To her complete joy she saw she was shimmering like her skin was encrusted with millions of microscopic jewels that glowed from within. She looked at Maximus who was smiling at her.

She looked to where Isaac was standing before she had closed her eyes. Only, he wasn't there. She looked around the room and saw a glowing mass of light moving over the ground.

"Isaac!" she screamed just as he passed in front of the Telescope which was pointed to the sky. In a horrifying moment, Stella saw him get sucked in through the eyepiece of the Telescope like he was dust to a vacuum.

Even though it was useless, Maximus and Stella ran over to the Telescope and looked outside. There was nothing to see.

"WHERE DID HE GO?" she yelled.

CHAPTER 22

"Whatever is going on in your mind is what you are attracting."

Isaac

Isaac knew exactly what Maximus meant when he said you felt full of infinite possibility. He felt far away from troubles and pain. He felt like *anything* he wanted, he could achieve.

He had transformed back into light as soon as Stella had closed her eyes. After Maximus saw this, he had turned around to watch Stella work. Isaac felt free to experiment a little bit. He wanted to move. He felt different, but he was still himself, right? Could his brain still tell his feet to move? He tried it. Just like that, he was moving, but didn't necessarily feel the 'thunk, thunk' of walking. Instead, he felt like he was sort of gliding and hovering over the ground.

Weightless, that's what Maximus had said it felt like. Isaac agreed. He was weightless but also completely aware of every bit of himself.

This is amazing, he thought. *I wonder how quickly we can go to Draco? I want to see the Dragons. .*

Isaac heard Stella yell his name at the very instant he felt himself being pulled swiftly in one direction. He was swirling, twirling and flying. Then he landed on some hard ground, instantly returning to his flesh and bone self.

He felt the ground rumbling beneath his feet. He heard roaring and flapping and he looked up and saw two Dragons—and they were fighting each other.

CHAPTER 23

"Everyone has a fair turn to be as great as he pleases."

Stella

"Where did he go?" Stella repeated frantically, "What happened to him?"

"The Telescope sent him somewhere," Maximus said sounding equally as frantic, "I'm so surprised . . . He would've had to be thinking of someplace as he passed in front of the eye of the Telescope."

"Draco!" she said. "He's in Draco!"

Maximus' eyes widened. "Of course. We must get to him quickly. Not all Dragons are necessarily cordial. Did he take his Star Charm with him?"

Stella looked around, hoping she would not find it—but her stomach sank because it was sitting on the windowsill next to where they had been standing.

"No, it's there," she said and went over to it. She picked it up and looked back at Maximus, "What does that mean? Can he come back?"

He didn't answer her, just went to the eye of the Telescope. "I'll bring him home," he said and then transformed and was gone through the eye of the Telescope.

Stella worried. "Arrow, Draco has so many Stars, how will Maximus find him before anything happens to him?"

Arrow stepped closer to her and she threw her arms around his neck and sobbed. "I can't lose him too. He's my brother. Not my parents and my brother!"

After a meaningful pause, Arrow said, "Isaac is strong and the smartest of us all. He'll be safe."

She knew that he was, and probably would be safe, but she still let the tears flow freely into Arrow's thick mane. Any step toward something sad or stressful and it made all of the sadness over her parents open up again and flow out full force.

As she cried, she resolved to deal with the agony of waiting for them to return as best she could. She would get a heads up on practicing transforming Arrow with her, so she would be ready to go anywhere needed when they returned.

When would that be?

CHAPTER 24

"When you visualize then you materialize."

Isaac

There were claws the length of Isaac's own hand pounding and scratching into the ground. There was roaring filling his ears and it smelled like molten rock and singed skin.

The Dragons trampled closer to him and suddenly, he was swept up under an enormous arm. He felt his clothes getting snagged on humongous scales as he was lifted into the air.

He screamed from the sudden upward thrust. Below him, he saw a black Dragon rising up into the air behind them. Behind the black Dragon was a circle of a dozen or more Dragons looking up at them from the ground.

The black Dragon was gaining on them, and the Dragon carrying Isaac sped up. Isaac worried both Dragons liked the sudden appearance of a rare meal and were now going to fight over him.

Isaac felt the Dragon grip tighter and then almost lost his stomach as they went into a barrel-roll toward the ground and then banked hard to the right. He flew low to the ground at a speed Isaac had never physically felt before. The Dragon then pushed his wings down so hard, the jolt upward made Isaac fall forward through the Dragon's arm. He almost fell out, but the Dragon gripped him tighter and did not drop him.

The Dragon growled and hissed and made other sounds as if trying to form words, but Isaac could not understand him. Then, loudly over the swooshing of his wings, the Dragon used words that Isaac understood, even though they weren't English words. The Dragon was speaking Zeego.

"I'm taking you to the King and Queen of Draco," the Dragon said. "They will know what to do with you. You are human, yes?"

"Yes, I'm human," Isaac shouted back in Zeego.

"No need to be frightened, the king and queen are sympathetic to other creatures."

Isaac looked forward and saw an enormous castle-like structure made of thousands of colored stones melded together.

The Dragon landed on his back feet first, and then the arm not holding Isaac touched down next. Very gently for a huge creature, the Dragon stretched out his arm and set Isaac down on his feet.

When Isaac saw the Dragon full-on, he was astonished. He always imagined Dragons in average reptile-color greens and browns, but this one was anything but average. He looked like the sun. His scales were shimmering in oranges and yellows with what looked like the tiniest flecks of gold.

Isaac stood frozen, his mouth agape. Surely, this was the most beautiful thing he had ever seen. He looked for the right words in Zeego, feeling very grateful his parents had practiced the language so much with him. "You're magnificent," Isaac said slowly. "Do you have a name?"

"I am called Helios," the Dragon answered with a dignified voice.

"HEEL-ee-ohs?" Isaac said, wanting to clarify the pronunciation.

"Yes, Helios, it means 'sun'. And you are called?"

"My name is Isaac."

Just then, another Dragon landed very close to them and on instinct, Isaac darted to the other side of Helios and looked around him to see the black Dragon that had been chasing them.

The black Dragon spoke to Helios in Zeego, obviously wanting Isaac to understand him, "I knew you were bringing that ugly little man-child to your beloved King. He doesn't belong here you know. Only Dragons and the things Dragons hunt on Draco. Is that what he is Helios? Your meal? Or are you too tender and sweet to exterminate him?"

"He's going inside, Onyxus," Helios said.

Irritation flashed across the black Dragon's face. Onyxus.

Helios roared, and in response, two more Dragons came out of the entrance of the castle, saw the black Dragon, roared, and then a few more Dragons came out. Isaac looked at Onyxus to see what he would do. He stayed staring straight back at all of them. His upper lip curled in a disgusted sneer.

A dark green Dragon approached Isaac and spoke to him in a language Isaac could not understand. Helios answered so Isaac could understand him, "Isaac. He appeared suddenly right in the middle of a little . . . disagreement Onyxus and I were having. I scooped him up and brought him straight here. All I have learned is his name."

Taking the lead from Helios, the green Dragon addressed Isaac directly in Zeego, "Where are you from? How did you get here?" He seemed a little hostile.

All the Dragons stared, waiting for an answer.

"I came here from Earth."

"Earth? In the Solar System? You come from a long way. How long did it take you to get here?"

"I think only a few seconds . . . I just learned how to transform into a Shooting Star and I think I went in front of the Telescope and I was thinking about how much I wanted to meet Dragons on Draco. Then I felt a pull, and I was swirling, and then I landed in the middle of a Dragon fight."

The Dragons looked at him as if he were insane. Isaac nervously rambled on, "Then Helios here—he picked me up and brought me here, and—"

He fell silent as the Dragons were looking at each other and speaking very low and imperceptibly.

The green Dragon said, "Helios, did you know your young detainee here is the second human visitor today?"

This news shocked Isaac. Who had been there just before him?

"No, I did not know that," Helios answered.

"Also came here as a Shooting Star. His proposal was quite disturbing. He wanted to keep us on stand-by to use for a possible future battle."

Isaac's heart was pounding. It just couldn't have been Maximus. He was with him all day! He knew it must be somebody from the other side. At this thought, Isaac became cold. He hoped whoever it was had left already so they did not see him.

"Called himself Dreold," the green Dragon continued. "He said he was from the Zodiac Constellation, Gemini. Apparently he was left steward over Gemini by Orel — who we know of course. But Dreold said Orel was fallen from power, and Gershon, once Orel's advisor, rules the Zodiacs now. Dreold offered us travel to other Stars — and more power in the Universe to go with it — in exchange for our allegiance to Gershon in a battle among the Zodiacs."

Helios said, "I do not want to be part of a massacre or anything of the sort. What did you tell him?"

"Want to know your problem Helios?" Onyxus interjected. "You can't see the greater purpose. Dreold gave us a stone . . . which Titus here is keeping ransom for *King* Adamas. That stone will transport us to a different Star — away from Draco — and from there we can go anywhere. The Universe, Helios . . . right there within our grasp. Who cares what we have to do to get there."

"I care," Helios growled, "and I'm sure King Adamas does as well."

"Yes, yes . . . *noble* King Adamas. Thinks we're too good to be used as leverage in a human battle and says we have all we need right here in Draco. I actually agree that we shouldn't be used by humans. But, *really*, we'd be using *them* to spread our populations to countless worlds, and — "

Helios interrupted, "Onyxus, surely King Adamas has logical reasons for turning Dreold down. I think I know why as well. If *you*, of all Dragons are attracted to Dreold's proposal, his..." he paused looking for the right word, "*disposition* must be of a darker nature."

The other Dragons chuckled at this. Onyxus snarled with his lip curling.

"Perhaps," Helios continued, "We should take this human inside and see what Adamas will do about his being here."

Onyxus' lip twitched again. "After you," he said sinisterly.

Helios looked at Isaac and said, "Follow me," and started walked towards the entrance.

Isaac obeyed. Isaac was taken up in complete amazement as he passed through the entrance of the Dragon's castle. The sizes and colors of the stones the Dragons built with were magnificent. The ceiling was exceptionally high, and up the sides of the walls were openings into what Isaac guessed were the Dragon's caves.

Isaac's eyes followed the path up to the front of the great hall. On each side of the path Dragons were staring at him. At the front of the room stood two Dragons: One was a large, midnight-blue colored Dragon, and the other was smaller and dazzling sky-blue. Directly behind the two Dragons was a translucent yellow stone of incredible size—larger than any of them. With the light shining through it, it was a miniature sun in its own right.

All the Dragons sparkled and glistened in the multi-colored lights of the shining stones which freckled their expansive hall in a multitude of colors. Once closer to the front of the room, Isaac could see the smaller Dragon's scales were not only sky blue, but they shone like the gleam of tropical water. She looked royal and was unmistakably the Queen of Draco. Everything about her was more refined than the larger Dragon who had to be the King.

Coming to a stop, Isaac glanced shyly at the majestic, dark blue King and then looked to Helios for some direction.

"There haven't been humans here in almost two decades, and now I get two in the same day," said Adamas. His powerful voice vibrated through Isaac.

"I didn't get to meet your last visitor, King, but this is Isaac—from Earth," said Helios, "He travelled here as a Shooting Star and appeared in the middle of a disagreement between Onyxus and myself."

"Very good for bringing him here straight away, Helios. Onyxus, you're here again? I thought you would keep your distance after our last disagreement when Dreold left."

Onyxus answered from the back of the room, "As it happens, oh great King, I ran into your son Helios and was able to let off a little steam with him. Of course I had to come here and see how *this* visit went."

His son, Isaac thought. *Helios is a prince then!*

Adamas said to Onyxus, "Keep your distance and stay back there." Then he turned to Isaac, "Human, I see that you are but a child. Do you come on behalf of Dreold? I already made our answer clear. In fact . . ." he turned and walked to a pedestal that held a long black crystal inside an extremely thick glass sphere. He took it gingerly in his teeth, brought it to Isaac and placed it in his hands. He continued, "You can take that back to him. We will not need it."

"Your majesty," Isaac said respectfully, "I do not know Dreold and I came here on my own."

Adamas paused and looked long and hard into Isaac's eyes. Isaac was terrified, but he looked back into his eyes for what felt like so long that his eyes began to water and burn.

"Very well," boomed his voice again, "I am King Adamas and this is my Queen, Alethia. You may now speak your purpose here."

Isaac felt terrified to speak, but he cleared his throat and said, "I am at the other end of the same war which your other visitor spoke to you about."

Alethia spoke in a sweet but bold voice, "A small boy,

such as yourself, in a war?"

"Yes . . . well, I've been through a rather difficult time recently. I have just learned who I truly am only a few days ago."

"And who might that be?" she asked.

"I am the son of Eli," he said.

"Eli—Orel's son?" asked Adamas.

"Yes," said Isaac. "Gershon and his Minion actually don't know about me, but he knows about my sister. They found our family and they killed my parents. They wanted to kill Stella too, and they would have found out about me, but my mom sent us away to Maximus."

"Maximus?" thundered Adamas. Then more quietly said, "It can't be the Maximus that was Orel's eldest son, because Maximus died, just before Eli disappeared from the Zodiacs."

Isaac was stunned speechless. At that moment, a lot of puzzle pieces came together. That's why he followed Eli to protect him and that's why he knew how to be a Shooting Star, needed to be undetectable, and why he cared so much about them. He was their . . . Uncle. But, why keep that a secret?

"We're terribly sorry about your parents," Alethia said.

Isaac nodded.

"Maximus came here as a small boy," said Alethia. "I remember him."

Adamas asked, "What were you hoping to accomplish by coming here?"

"A companion," he answered directly, before he fretted over how it would sound. "I feel like I'm facing dangers too big for me. Stella has to go to Vega, and she will let herself be seen by Gershon from there. A Winged Horse on Pegasus agreed to be Stella's companion, and all of Pegasus knows about the impending war."

The Dragons were silent and looked deep in thought.

"How many are on Gershon's side?"

"More than are not on his side I believe. Maximus thinks once the Zodiacs are completely owned by Gershon, he will set his sights to other Constellations."

"Meaning, he'd bring the war here." Adamas sighed, and on his exhale, smoke came out of his nostrils. He said, "Seems like our paths will cross with humans no matter if we try to avoid it or not."

"My King," said Alethia, "Orel, Maximus and Eli are full of integrity just like this one. They are not all like Dreold and Gershon—but it sounds like all the good ones might become extinct and we'll be forced to deal with only the evil."

Adamas answered, "You're saying we should help and send a protector with this boy?"

She nodded.

Adamas looked at Isaac, then at Helios. "Helios, come with the Queen and me. We need to discuss this in private. Titus, you as well. Excuse us for a moment, son of Eli?"

"Yes, of course," Isaac answered.

The four Dragons exited into a room off the side of the great hall and slid a large stone door closed behind them.

Isaac was left with tired arms holding the glass casing that held the black crystal . . . and with the other Dragons. He felt too nervous to turn around and count them.

To his right he heard some rumbling growls and then the mocking voice of Onyxus. He looked and Onyxus had his arms up in the air like he was surrendering. "Down beasts, I just want to ask the boy a question or two. There is no crime in that. Here," he said and picked up his own tail, "if it makes you feel better, you can hold on to the tip of my tail so you can . . . *correct* me if I get out of line. Good little Dragon. Now, let's go talk to him."

They approached Isaac and he clutched the stone hard next to his chest, knowing the appeal it held for Onyxus.

"Hello, Izzzzzzzaac."

He was so close that Isaac could smell the rotting of his

breath. Then, Onyxus opened his mouth to ask his question—but in one motion, he grabbed Isaac with his enormous arm and clenched him to his chest—pinning the crystal in between them. He whipped his head around to burn the Dragon holding his tail and shot up into the air.

It was pandemonium. Onyxus was flying toward the exit but Isaac saw it being blocked by Dragons. Onyxus changed course abruptly and flew straight up to the ceiling. As he flew in a vertical line up the castle, he grabbed Isaac by the ankle with his free arm and yanked him out. The sudden force of being flung upside down in flight made Isaac drop the glass cylinder, and as it was falling, Onyxus reached out and snatched it.

Isaac had never before felt such panic. He saw Helios zooming toward them and hoped against hope that he would get to them in time—he was close. Then Isaac saw Onyxus put the glass cylinder in his mouth. He chomped down on it so hard that Isaac was splattered in blood from the Dragon's mouth, and the next instant they were to wherever that crystal was set to transport them.

CHAPTER 25

"It's better to wear out than to rust out."

Maximus

"Where is a blasted Dragon when you need one?" Maximus grumbled to himself as he was panting from running around Gamma Draconis—the most heavily populated Star in Draco. From what he could remember from being there as a small boy, there were Dragons everywhere you looked, but now he saw none—or Isaac.

He stopped running so he could try to remember details about when he had been there as a boy. He remembered being quite scared, but then there was one smaller Dragon, scales the color of the sky and as shiny as polished silver. She was nice to him. She was the Queen . . . he thought harder . . . *in the Castle of Colored Stones.*

He hadn't done short-distance travel in a long time, but was sure that's where they all were, so he transformed and thought of the castle. A second later, he landed right in the middle of the great hall in the castle and found himself in utter chaos. Hundreds of Dragons were agitated and he had to keep jumping out of the way as to not get stepped on or knocked over.

Finally, through the chaos, he saw the shimmering sky-blue scales of the Dragon he hoped to see. She was pacing frantically in the front of the room.

"Silence!" boomed a thunderous voice.

All at once, the Dragons stopped and turned to face the front of the room. Maximus could see the Queen now as she looked around. Her face was stricken with worry. Then she spotted him.

"A third human!" she yelled. "Adamas!"

"Your majesty," Maximus shouted, "you know me! I came here as a boy many decades ago with my father, Orel."

"Maximus?"

"Yes."

"Isaac is your nephew then?" asked Adamas.

"Isaac!" he said and ran to the front of the room as Dragons parted for him. "You've seen him? You said there was a third human, who was the other?"

He looked back and forth from the King and Queen's faces. He saw a strange thing happen—a tear came out of Alethia's eye and evaporated into steam almost instantly.

"Oh no, what happened?" asked Maximus.

Adamas' thunderous voice answered Maximus, "Dreold was the first. He wanted us to join him and we said no, but he left us a crystal to transport us to him if we changed our minds. I thought Isaac was coming on behalf of Dreold so I gave him the crystal to take back with him.

"Then Isaac explained who he was and what he came for so Alethia, Helios, Titus and I went out of the hall to discuss it. We heard a commotion and came back fast. We saw that Onyxus had seized the boy. Helios flew to go rescue Isaac. He had just grabbed Onyxus ankle when he broke the glass cylinder that held the stone and they vanished out of the air— all three of them."

Maximus yelled, "No!"

Alethia asked, "Maximus, what do we do? Do you know where they went?"

"I . . . I don't know where they are. I need to get home to the Telescope to try and find out where."

"Maximus, wait," said Alethia, "Helios is our son—the Prince of Draco. And, I feel responsible for Isaac getting taken. We were foolish to leave the room with Onyxus so near. We knew he wanted the crystal. Please, can I go with you? I want to help find the boy and get them out of there safe."

"Alethia," said Adamas, "I should go. It's too dangerous—you need to stay here."

"Adamas, I don't have the power to keep things in order here like you can. Let me rescue our son and the boy and you stay here."

Adamas nodded his head and they both looked at Maximus.

"We must go now," Maximus said. He was trying not to think of the possibility that Gershon might kill Isaac the moment he learned who he was. Onyxus would probably tell Gershon right away who the boy was—as if his image wasn't proof enough that he was Eli's son.

Adamas and Alethia touched noses and said good-bye. Tough and intimidating Adamas looked tender toward his Queen.

Maximus stepped to Alethia and put his hands on her and closed his eyes. A moment later the air where they stood was blindingly bright, with trillions of specs of light. And then they were gone.

CHAPTER 26

". . . your purpose is what you say it is. Your mission is the mission you give yourself. Your life will be what you create it as, and no one will stand in judgment of it, now or ever."

Isaac

Isaac woke up shivering and holding his painful head. Right before he passed out he knew that the crystal was taking them nowhere good.

He got up off the cold, slate floor, still holding a hand on his forehead. He could hear chains being clanked and pained roaring. He turned toward the sound and saw Helios chained to the floor so tight he couldn't even lift his head.

"Let me see the boy!" Helios shouted.

"Shut up, Helios," said Onyxus, "Dreold went to get us an audience with his master. Prepare to never see that boy again—they're going to love the gift I brought for them."

"How could you Onyxus?"

"I'll say it one more time Helios . . . SHUT UP. If you hadn't started trying to attack everyone you saw, you could have been with me, instead of against me and then you wouldn't be in chains."

Helios started, "You are—" then was interrupted by a loud rush of voices.

Isaac saw a large group of dirty looking men coming into the cave-like room.

"Bind the boy!" he heard one of them shout. "Gershon will be here any moment."

Isaac had nowhere to run. Two foul-smelling, sweaty men forced him around harshly and placed shackles on his wrists and ankles. Then they jerked him forward toward a throne and anchored him to the floor in front of it.

Dozens of men gathered around Helios wielding long spears that had electricity spiking between its two-pronged end.

Helios looked like he was getting ready to yank free of the chains if he could, but Isaac didn't want him taking chances with those electric spears.

"Helios!" he yelled.

Then the pain in his head quadrupled as one of the men who had bound Isaac smacked him in the back of the head. "Don't open your maggot-mouth again—unless you are told to!" a guard shouted.

Helios was quiet. Isaac knew he had understood his meaning—don't fight. Yet.

Onyxus went to the front of the room with a man that sent fear through Isaac. Was it Gershon? But he didn't sit in the throne. The man smirked at him and Isaac was chilled to the bone with trepidation.

Everything about the atmosphere was dark and evil. It was cool, dark, and damp. Twisting lines of green light reflected from a large and eerie pool of water.

Isaac was shaking, both from horror and cold. A hush fell over the gathered people and another man entered swiftly and came to sit on the high backed throne made of a shiny, dark metal.

The men that obviously worshipped this man were fanning out around the throne in a semi-circle. They looked like terrified children in front of the strict school principal. They bowed and forced Isaac to as well.

Gershon. Isaac was horribly transfixed by the sight of him. Sheltered as he was by his parents on their little mountain, Isaac had never imagined such vileness was possible.

Gershon's hair was dark gray and thin. He had the kind of mouth that was always naturally open in a sinister way — showing his long, thin teeth crammed closely together. His skin was sickly yellow as were his eyes which were piercing Isaac with furrowed brows.

Gershon appraised Isaac for a long time with cold eyes, then to Isaac's terror, Gershon leaped out of his throne and came swooping down on Isaac. He grabbed both sides of Isaac's face with his ice-cold hands and jerked it back, forcing Isaac to look him in the face.

Gershon had his lips pulled tight over his teeth and they pressed into a hard line as he looked over Isaac's face.

"Eli had a son!" he yelled, half sounding like a question. "This boy looks just like the coward. Are you Eli's son, boy?"

Isaac couldn't talk. Fright filled him to the brim and clogged his throat.

"Sire, if I might," Isaac heard Onyxus say — for the first time not sounding sarcastic or cynical, "This is indeed the son of Eli. I have brought him for you."

Gershon started breathing very rapidly, still gripping Isaac's face but looking at Onyxus.

When Gershon didn't respond, Onyxus went on, "And this other Dragon grabbed hold of my ankle when I touched the genius crystal you left for us. He is not sympathetic to your plans. I will exterminate him for you if you wish."

Gershon's fire-like eyes flitted toward Helios, then he fixed them on Isaac again. He asked slowly, his chest tight with rage, "How. Did. You. Get. To. Draco?"

Isaac's pain was escalating as Gershon's grip was tightening.

"HOW BOY?" He shook him.

Helios roared and Isaac heard the spears singeing his scales.

Isaac shouted over the commotion, "Shooting Star! Telescope!"

Gershon squeezed Isaac even tighter. "Answer quickly boy. Which Telescope? Who taught you?" Then, completely manic, he spit on Isaac's face and shouted, "Your parents are dead!"

Isaac's head was swimming and he felt he might black-out again.

"I don't know if you know about me, boy," Gershon's voice shook with fury, "but I do not have much patience. Open that pipsqueak mouth of yours and ANSWER ME!"

Isaac knew he couldn't answer any of those questions. He already felt responsible for his parents' death. He couldn't let Maximus or Stella die because of him as well. He was not going to talk to Gershon. He ignored the spit on his face, tried to straighten up, and looked purposefully back at Gershon, forcing himself to breathe steadily and not look away.

Gershon straightened his back like a cobra preparing to strike.

They stared at each other for a few moments.

Then Gershon growled, "Is that how we're going to play?" He moved his face only inches from Isaac's. "You know I can and *will* kill you right here and now if you don't do exactly what I tell you, right?"

"Yes," Isaac said boldly, still not looking away.

Gershon let go of his head and smacked him hard across the cheek. Fuming, he said, "No. You know what? We're going to do things MY way. You will stay alive, and I will make you suffer until you do what you're told.

He spun around and went back to his throne. He sat, then raised his arm in the air and said, "Take him to a cell! And give him a few volts. That should start to turn him around."

Dreold motioned to the guards to wait and then rushed up to Gershon's side to whisper something into his ear, but Gershon waved him away angrily.

Gershon looked back at Isaac and an evil grin spread across his face. "Oh yes. I don't think you two have met yet." He cackled. "Isaac, meet the man who killed your parents."

Now Isaac knew why this man made him feel so cold and he felt sick looking at him.

Helios began struggling again and didn't stop when the electric spears were shocking him.

"Helios, stop!" Isaac shouted.

Gershon had moved over to Helios and put his hands in front of him. In a split second, Helios could not move any longer, and his roars of pain turned shrill and loud. Isaac wished he could cover his ears. What was he doing to him? Gershon said through gritted teeth, "I could kill you right now Dragon—but I want creatures like you on my side. We'll change your mind."

Then, Gershon looked like an idea he very much liked entered his sinister mind. His rage was gone, but his new expression was even more terrifying. He looked crazed—thirsty for something, and eerily happy. He dropped his hands and released Helios then turned back to the guards. "Take them away. NOW! Dreold, we need to talk!"

CHAPTER 27

"... lean not unto thine own understanding."

Stella

Stella was pacing nervously on the beach in front of Arrow and . . . a Dragon. She had about fell over backwards when she saw Maximus appear with it on the beach — but there was no Isaac.

When Stella rushed out to the beach Maximus introduced them and said Alethia would fill her in. He said he had to talk to Orel and darted off to the lighthouse before Stella could get a word in.

Alethia told her everything that had happened on Draco. Her brother was missing and could possibly be facing Gershon. Stella could barely breathe but she couldn't hold still.

Finally, Maximus returned and he looked distraught.

"Maximus! What did he say?" Stella asked.

"He said he probably knows where they are . . . but he won't tell me, because he doesn't want us to go."

Instantly Stella was mad — *fuming* mad. She dropped her grip off his arm. "Who is he to say what we can and can't do? If he knows where they are, he's going to tell us!"

"Stella," Maximus said looking at her now, "He said he knows the way Gershon thinks now, and he's confident Gershon will decide to keep Isaac alive. He'll be more valuable to him that way."

"Well, how can he be sure?" she asked testily, "He's the one that is in hiding because of Gershon. How should *he* know?"

"Stella, you need to have respect. He said we cannot go because we will be killed. He said he trusts Isaac to find his way out of there on his own."

Alethia cried out, "But what about Helios?"

Maximus forced a smile, "I'm sure a Dragon-lover like Isaac won't go anywhere without the Dragon that tried to rescue him."

"Maximus!" Stella shouted at him. "We just HAVE to go."

"Stella, we cannot go. You need to stay alive. That's all there is to it."

"Isaac needs to stay alive too!"

"He will. Trust Orel."

"I don't even know Orel. How can I trust him?"

"Because I do. Do you want to get to know him?"

Stella thought about this person who had only ever been talked about in conversation. "Right now?" she asked.

"If you'd like."

"No . . . no. Not right now." She felt too angry at this stranger who was supposed to be so powerful. Maybe she should meet him and tell him what's on her mind! No . . . he wouldn't change his decision. If he wouldn't tell Maximus who he knew so well, he wouldn't tell her.

Maximus said, "I trust him Stella. You can too. Isaac will make it home. *With* Helios," he added looking at Alethia.

Stella felt helpless. She felt wronged and angry. She was terrified about what could happen to Isaac. Without a word to any of them, she walked around Maximus and went inside to hide in her room. They all let her go undisturbed.

CHAPTER 28

"Decide what it is you want. Decide what you're willing to give up. Set your priorities. Be about it."

Isaac

The volts of electricity Isaac received had left him on the floor, feeling sick and useless. The cells were cave like holes in the stone walls that had bars on the front. The insides of the cave had a netting of wire around the walls and on the floor. There was nowhere to escape the electric shocks.

He tried to roll to his side, but just moaned because it hurt too bad to move.

"Just lie still for a while—you'll feel better soon," said a female voice. A young female voice—*a teenager*, thought Isaac.

"Whhhh..." Isaac tried to say but talking hurt too. He tried again. "Who . . . are you?"

"My name is Rikenzia. You don't have to talk right now. Just rest."

But Isaac wanted to talk to her.

"Where? You?" He left it at that hoping she knew what he meant.

"I'm in the cave right across from you. Just rest."

"Why . . . are you here?"

"You listen to instructions really well don't you? Alright, I'll talk—you rest. I'm here because I was hiding with my group, but one day, I was distracted and got careless and was caught."

"Wha . . . What group?" Isaac asked.

"Shhhh..." she said, and then went on more quietly, "One of the few groups that still have enough brains to know Gershon is a lunatic. We're searching for Orel . . . and his lost family."

She paused and Isaac could hear clinking from her cave, like she was throwing gravel at the metal bars. Then she whispered, "When you're feeling better, you can tell me who you are." *Clink. Clink. Clink.*

Isaac knew instantly he was going to tell her exactly who he was. She'd been searching for him, and his family, hadn't she? Isaac pushed through the pain and rolled onto his side then pushed himself into a sitting position. He looked out from the cave, through the dim and very narrow passageway. Then he saw her. Even in the dim light he could see she was beautiful. Probably around fourteen or fifteen years old. Long, dark hair, big eyes and a personality that could not be hidden.

"Wow, you recovered fast," she said quietly.

Isaac saw her eyes were a light brown and still had sparkle in them . . . like being caught in a cell that was electrically charged wasn't affecting her at all.

"How are you?" she asked, tilting her head to the side a little.

"G . . . good," he stammered, also trying to keep his voice quiet. Then composing himself he asked, "Where are you from Rikenzia?"

"Capricornus. Where are you from?"

Isaac very carefully stood up—he didn't want to fall over in front of her. Who knows what embarrassing things she had already seen. "I was born on Earth," he answered.

"Earth? Like circle-the-sun-that-passes-through-the-Zodiacs Earth?" She had said it somewhat loudly and put her hand over her mouth to quiet herself.

He looked up and down the aisle and didn't see anyone. "That's the one," he said and flashed a smile he hoped was charming.

"How did you get here?" she asked.

"It's a very long story."

She looked at him expecting him to continue, but he

didn't want to rehash that right now. He moved on, "My name is Isaac, by the way."

"Hi, Isaac. You look very familiar to me but I can't pin it down. Plus, I don't know anybody from Earth, so I can't possibly know you."

"Rikenzia," he said still in hushed tones, "I'm going to tell you who I am, but don't freak out and call attention over here."

She looked at him curiously.

"Eli had a son," he said and watched as understanding dawn on her face.

In a whisper-shout she said, "That's why you look familiar! You look just like the pictures I have seen of him!"

Isaac nodded.

She started pacing the front of her cell and kept looking at Isaac. Suddenly, she stopped and asked, "Where is the rest of your family?"

"My . . . my parents died just a few days ago. Gershon's Minion found us."

Isaac's physical and emotional pain were running too close to tell them apart.

"Oh, Isaac. I'm so sorry." She hung her head looking devastated, then looked back at him and said, "But Stella is still alive, and so are you! Oh, Isaac, what joy you'll bring!"

He tried to smile at her.

"Do you know where Orel is?" she asked.

"No, I still haven't met him. I just learned about who I was a couple days ago."

"Wow. And how did you end up here?"

"I learned how to transform into a Shooting Star and I accidentally went in front of the Telescope while thinking about Dragons on Draco. Then an evil Dragon grabbed me and bit this crystal that Dreold left there and it transported us here — and another Dragon, Helios, who was trying to save me is here too."

Rikenzia's mouth hung open. "How did you learn so fast?" she asked, by-passing the rest of the Dragon story. "Who taught you? Which Telescope? Don't they all belong to the Minion?"

Isaac liked that she could fire off questions as quickly as he could. But, they were almost the same ones Gershon had asked and he didn't want to answer her for fear they'd torture her for answers if they found out she knew. He instinctively knew his secrets would be safe with her, but he didn't want to put her at risk—and he didn't want to intrude on Maximus' secret. He had faked his death for his own reasons, which reasons Isaac wanted to find out.

"I can only answer one of those questions. And if these guards come, I want you to pretend we never talked or even looked at each other."

She didn't say anything.

"Promise," Isaac said.

She looked at him thoughtfully then said, "I promise."

"I'm not sure how I learned so fast. It was just easy for me. My teacher said I had an advantage being related to Orel and Eli."

"But, those knuckle-headed so-called *Stewards* learned how, right? And they're not related."

"I guess so," he said, not sure what her point was.

"Can you travel without the Telescopes?" she asked.

"I've never tried," he answered. Then he got excited because he remembered the Star Charm. He had forgotten about it in all the non-stop commotion. He searched all his pockets. Nothing. Then he remembered he left it on the stool. Why had he done that?

"Missing something?" she asked.

He didn't answer.

"Isaac?" she asked gently.

He looked at her.

"Can you teach me how to be a Shooting Star? We *have* to

get out of here. As quickly as possible. The Zodians need to know you're alive. We need to *keep* you alive."

She looked so hopeful and sweet. Isaac tried not to think of the improbability of them escaping without a Telescope — or Star Charm, but he couldn't dash her hopes so he said he'd teach her.

She looked ecstatic. He didn't want to get her hopes *too* high, so he said, "Realistically Rikenzia, I don't know if it's possible without a Telescope."

She whisper-shouted again, "Isaac! Never let me hear you talk like that again! You learned how to transform in only a couple days. You are the son of Eli! You're born to lead the Zodiacs. You descend from Orel who *created* the Telescopes. Surely you, of all people, know that *anything* is possible."

Isaac blinked at her boldness. She was right though, and a smile crept up his face.

"Actually," he whispered, "I transformed the first time I tried."

She smiled back at him. "So we're getting out of here?"

"We're going to try."

"Isaac . . ."

He threw his hands up in surrender, still smiling. "Sorry! Sorry! *Yes*, we're getting out of here."

"That's better," she said.

"But we have to take a Dragon with us."

Her eyes got wide and she looked so incredulous that Isaac had to stifle a laugh. He liked this girl.

CHAPTER 29

"Most of the time, when we don't see the things
that we've requested, we get frustrated. We get disappointed.
And we begin to become doubtful . . . Take that doubt
and shift it . . . replace it with a feeling of unwavering faith."

Maximus

Maximus, Alethia and Arrow stood in silence for a while after Stella left. Maximus could tell that Alethia was grieving. She had her head hung low and her wings were drooping.

He said to her, "I can take you back to Draco. You can be with Adamas until Isaac returns with Helios."

She shook her head.

"There is not much you can do here," Maximus said, "Let me take you back."

She moved her head imperceptibly. Maximus couldn't tell if it was a nod or a shake, but he took it as a nod. He moved over to touch her and closed his eyes. He started transforming but where his hand was touching the Dragon was growing hot and it tingled with sharp, painful prickling. He came back to form.

She was refusing to go and he could not transform her.

He looked at Arrow who was gazing up at Stella's window.

Arrow looked at him and asked, "Do you think she will still be willing to go to Vega?"

Maximus wondered how differently Gershon would act to her coming out now that he had Isaac.

"Well," he answered, "she must. I worry about the people on Vega though. Will the Minion be able to get there and torture them to try and find out where Stella is?"

Arrow asked, "That is where Isolde, her mother was from,

right?"

"Yes," answered Maximus.

"And Isolde was their princess, correct?"

"Yes, she was."

"Now, Stella is their princess. They will rejoice in her return. No doubt they will protect her—fight for her I mean."

Maximus knew that was true. "Yes, Vega is still the right place to go. A Star away from the Zodiacs—not under Gershon's control."

"I can go too," Alethia interjected.

Maximus was surprised. "Why would you want to go there, your majesty?"

Alethia said, "I need to DO something and be useful! If the sister of Isaac needs help, I want to help. I can help protect her people until Isaac and Helios return.

Maximus was slightly concerned about how Stella's people would react to a Dragon, but hope started to seep through him. "Thank you Alethia. That would be wonderful."

She brightened and put her neck erect again and tucked her wings in close to her body. "When do we go?" she asked.

"Tomorrow. We need to go tomorrow."

CHAPTER 30

"Experience is not what happens to you; it is what you do with what happens to you."

Isaac

Isaac had started teaching Rikenzia right away. They had to keep pausing to look as helpless and distraught as possible when guards would pass by in front of the cells. When they could talk, he repeated a lot of the same things Maximus had taught him. Rikenzia was a sponge and not once asked Isaac to repeat himself. Isaac paused to ask her, "Is it making sense? Do you have any questions?"

"It makes perfect sense. Can I try to do it now?"

But Isaac didn't get a chance to answer her. He received a shock all through his body. A second later, the same two men who had bound him before were pulling him out of his cell. Isaac felt sick, in pain, and mostly did not like being torn away from Rikenzia. He looked and saw she was on the floor too. *That's it*, Isaac thought, *we're leaving.*

The foul-smelling men dragged Isaac to the cave-like room with the green lights reflecting off the water. They took him up to the throne where they could hook him to the chains, but they didn't put the chains on him.

Isaac stood unshackled in front of the terrible form of Gershon. Gershon still had the evil-genius expression that made Isaac very nervous. Over to the right of Gershon, Isaac could see Dreold and Onyxus watching him, but Helios must have been moved.

"Isaac, my boy!" said Gershon. His voice had changed tones. Instead of filled with rage and loathing, he was faking cheerfulness. Cautious, Isaac said nothing.

Gershon went on, "There is no need for you to stay in that cell any longer—or for shackles." He got off his throne and came to stand in front of Isaac then threw his arms out to the side and said, "I am going to announce your existence to the Zodians!"

Gershon stared at Isaac waiting for a response. Isaac offered none.

"See, Isaac, I know you can talk. Unfortunately, the silent treatment won't work anymore. I need you to talk to me." Gershon's voice was still faking cheerfulness, but suppressing his anger sounded like it was getting more difficult.

Isaac finally said, "Let me see the orange Dragon."

Gershon's face turned red. He said through gritted teeth, "The first thing you choose to say to me is a command?" He turned around and went back to his throne, as if he needed it to remind him he was the one in charge.

Once sitting on his throne, he said, "You have more cheek than your cowardly father, I'll give you that much."

Now it was Isaac's turn to be angry. Gershon laughed. "That's better," he said. "You actually do show some personality, and can even get a little angry. That's just fine by me little boy."

"Now," Gershon continued, "What bugs me, Isaac, is having to hunt down the opposition one by one. I'm tired of it. The time is at hand where all the Zodians must obey, or be permanently punished."

"My genius mind has enlightened me to the fact that if they knew about you . . . and that you were working with me . . . well, you see my point. All at once! I could have them all at once. Even more effective would be to have your sister standing by our side too." He laughed again.

Isaac felt sick. He wanted out so bad he thought about attempting to leave right then. But, he couldn't get Helios or Rikenzia out of his mind. He needed to get in contact with Helios. To tell him to be ready to go—to think of leaving.

Very bravely, Isaac did not acknowledge anything Gershon had just said and repeated, "Let me see the orange

Dragon."

Gershon stood abruptly and to Isaac's confusion, swooped out of the room on the opposite side Isaac had entered. Isaac looked at Dreold and Onyxus. They smirked at him maliciously like they knew exactly the kind of torture that was headed Isaac's way.

Isaac could hear roaring on the other side of the stone wall. It was Helios. He sounded hurt. Isaac's adrenaline started racing and he almost started running toward him, but Gershon came swarming back into the room and again towered over Isaac. He thrust his fist into Isaac's chest and held it there. A little winded, Isaac looked down. Two scales, shimmering in orange and yellow with flecks of gold was gripped in Gershon's boney fingers.

"There is part of your precious Dragon, who NOW has a broken wing! You can snuggle with those scales in your CELL!" His shouting was ear splitting, and Isaac felt sick — Helios now had a broken wing and ripped out scales.

"First though," Gershon said, venom still thick in his voice, "you're coming with me. Then, after a night in your cell, I have a feeling you'll change your mind and tell me the answers I want. OR, I can rip your Dragon to pieces scale by scale if my electric shock therapy is not working on you."

He clenched Isaac's arm in his fist and took him forcefully out the same opening he went through to get to Helios. They wove through a long and skinny tunnel and then emerged outside of the cave. There was a ledge not too far in front of them. Gershon forced him out to it and Isaac wanted to run the other direction. As he looked over, he could see that the pit looked bottomless — just blackness extending on and on. He felt queasy and scared.

Then he heard something over to his left and looked to see Helios chained down tightly to the ground, guards circling him with spears that were sparking with electricity.

Gershon jerked him away and started leading him the

opposite direction of Helios along the ledge. Isaac looked up at the sky around them. Under different circumstances, it would have been a breathtaking view. There were other Stars, so close and large, that Isaac could see the colors of their surfaces against a midnight blue, almost purple sky. Gershon jerked him around and then he was facing . . . a Telescope. Shaped exactly like the one Maximus had, but this one was made of dark colored metal.

Gershon turned it around to face the outside wall of the cave instead of facing the sky. He placed his hand on it and stood there for what Isaac felt was a long time. Gershon didn't remove his hand from the Telescope until a faint, bluish light was reaching the wall. He took his hand off the Telescope and yanked Isaac around to look at him and put his face right in his.

"You've seen nothing of what I am truly capable of Isaac. Do you believe that? You'll do exactly what I say or that Dragon dies tonight."

Sick to his stomach, Isaac nodded.

"You're starting to come around . . . partner. Now, I want you to stand next to me in that light, and look happy. You don't even have to talk." He dragged Isaac to the edge of the bluish light and demanded. "Look happy."

To save Helios, Isaac obeyed. The light was bright and he felt it on his skin like it was toasting him. Gershon entered in behind him and immediately, the light turned a pale green.

"Citizen Zodians," Gershon said, addressing the Telescope like a camera. "I have an exciting announcement to make." He looked at Isaac and then back at the Telescope. "Do you recognize him yet?"

Gershon poked a fingernail into Isaac's back and Isaac remembered to smile and look happy. He wished he could undo everything that was happening right now—vowing to himself he would.

"Yes, that's right! Eli had a son. I have found him for

you. Eli was trying to keep him away from you. I give you —
your prince! We rule together now! When you are with me,
you are with him."

Isaac was seething inside with hatred and disgust over the
public personality Gershon was showing. He hoped that
despite his outward look of forced happiness, the Zodians
would be able to see past it and know he was NOT in
agreement with him. He thought about shouting out what he
really thought about Gershon, and how he killed his parents,
but he wanted to escape first — with as many as he could take
with him. He would make it right when he wasn't being held
prisoner.

Gershon was saying, "We will be coming around to all the
Stars of the Zodiac Constellations so that you might meet
him."

Isaac looked at Gershon's yellow face with astonishment.
Gershon dug his finger farther into Isaac's ribs and Isaac
looked back at the camera.

"Carry about your tasks. Follow your Stewards. The Son
of Eli is here!"

With that, Gershon stepped out from the projected light
and it turned blue. When he touched the Telescope again, the
light disappeared.

Looking back at Isaac, he said mockingly, "Oh yes, yes
dear little child. You will walk by my side, or you will see just
what happens when you disobey. The atrocities will be your
fault." All seriousness had returned to his voice. "Now — if
you obey," he paused for a moment, "then all Zodians will be
saved from themselves. All I want is obedience. You will
save them from harm's way, Isaac."

Isaac had enough. He blurted, "YOU'RE the one putting
them in harm's way!"

Gershon lashed out at him with the back of his hand and
caught Isaac hard on the cheek. One of Gershon's rings
caught the edge of his lip and cut it open.

"Oops," Gershon said and let out the most bone-chilling, evil laugh Isaac had ever heard. "I guess I can't beat you up and take you around to the Zodiacs all bloody can I?"

"In that case," Isaac answered, not reacting to the pain, "take all the swings at me you want." Isaac was surprised by his own bravery.

Gershon laughed again. "You are so entertaining! However—give me an order one more time, and I *will* beat you bloody, and then you'll stay locked in a padded room until you heal, and then we will STILL do my plan. You're my trophy, Isaac! In fact," he paused as a creepy smile crawled higher up his face, "tomorrow, when your sister comes out of hiding, I will . . . *persuade* her to join us as well."

He laughed shrilly. "Sometimes my own genius shocks me. You are KIDS. I don't need to *kill* you." Then he looked serious and menacing again and spoke almost to himself, "No. Not kill you. You will be better used by my side."

As quickly as the seriousness had come, Gershon returned to looking insane and crazed. He spun around in circles with his arms stretched out wide. Isaac's fear doubled. Gershon was demented. Isaac's stomach did an uncomfortable twist as Gershon suddenly stopped and bored into Isaac with his stare.

"Now," Gershon said, "You can stay here with me, and I can get you food and drink and a comfortable chair—IF you tell me about what you've been doing since your parents so tragically . . . passed. Or, you can return to the cell. You already know how comfortable it can be in there."

Isaac had of course already made his decision and said, "I'll go to the cell."

Red surged up Gershon's neck and made his yellow face turn a sickly brown. His fist looked charged to backhand Isaac again. Isaac braced himself for it as Gershon raised his hand in the air, but to his surprise, Gershon did not hit him. He snapped his fingers and commanded, "Take him back!"

Gershon's guards started dragging him away. Gershon

shouted, "Don't worry Isaac, I'll take good care of your Dragon for you!"

Isaac was being roughly pushed back toward the cave entrance. They passed Helios and the last thing Isaac heard before being shoved back into the tunnel was Gershon's bone-chilling cackle.

CHAPTER 31

"The conditions of conquest are always easy. We have but to toil awhile, endure awhile, believe always, and never turn back."

Isaac

Immediately when Isaac was thrust into his cell, he was welcomed by pain zapping through his body. When it was over, he wanted to cry. His body involuntarily twitched several times before he could lay there still.

He looked across to find Rikenzia.

"What did they do to you?" she asked. "You're all bloody on your lip and you look horrified."

Still fighting back his emotion, Isaac didn't want to reply just yet. He felt Gershon's torture was weakening him. He wondered why Rikenzia seemed so strong and unperturbed by being locked up and shocked all the time.

She must have known he didn't want to answer, because she said, "I can tell you something that might cheer you up. I practiced what you told me the whole time you were gone. I think I'm getting it. I just think about images of you, Eli and Orel doing it. Well, I've never personally seen any of you doing it, but I've heard stories and descriptions of what it looks like."

She paused for a moment and then gasped. "What is that in your hand?"

He had almost forgotten. Helios' scales. He fought the exhaustion and pain, stood up, daringly put his hands through the bars and handed her one of the scales.

"Gershon ripped them off my Dragon when I said I wanted to see him."

Rikenzia looked appalled, and then she looked back down to the scale she was holding in her hands. They stood in silence for a few moments. Isaac could feel something from the scale. It felt warm and Isaac felt a faint connection to

Helios, almost like he could hear him breathing. Isaac placed the scale in his pocket to protect it and told Rikenzia to do the same.

"Rikenzia?" he asked quietly.

"Yes?"

"Do you know anybody else who is locked up here?"

"I don't know, I can't really see anybody else. A lot of people have gone missing though."

Isaac contemplated what to do next. He knew his plan: escape. How to do it and take Rikenzia and Helios with him he didn't know. Then, what about everybody else locked up here? The thought exhausted him and he sunk back to the ground, slumped over his legs and hugged his knees. Exhaustion soon overcame his pain, and eventually, his thoughts faded, and he was able to fall asleep.

CHAPTER 32

"What you resist persists."

Stella

Stella was lying on her bed, trying not to think of her anger at Orel and she wished she could stop worrying if Isaac was warm enough, if he was in pain, or if he was scared. The more she resisted these thoughts, the harder they pressed into her mind.

Wait, she thought, was tomorrow the day they were going to Vega? Everyday seemed to last a lifetime to her on the island. It must be tomorrow. Why Vega? How would she 'show herself' to Gershon when they didn't even know where he was?

She jumped to her feet and left her room filled with blazing determination to get answers from Maximus. She stomped through the sand to him then said, "I don't get how, or even why we are going to Vega. How is this all going to work?"

Maddeningly calm, Maximus told her, "The Telescopes are created to be able to transmit images to each other."

Stella looked at him with wide, expectant eyes and pulled her shoulders up toward her ears in a shrug. "But all the Telescopes are on the Zodiacs—and here."

"Ah . . ." he said, "I didn't tell you—Orel made one more as a wedding gift for your mother."

"My mother? There . . . there is a Telescope on Vega?"

"Yes, a very special one."

"And, we'll use that how?"

"It will project your image to Gershon's Telescope and he'll be able to see you.

Stella swallowed down her fear at the thought of a man that wanted her dead seeing her.

"And Alethia," Maximus continued, "is going to come. She is going to stay on Vega to help protect your people. At least until she is needed elsewhere."

Stella nodded a thank you to Alethia, but she was now too overcome with nerves to want to know why the people on Vega would need protection.

Stella walked over to Arrow and wrapped her arms around his neck, burying her face in his mane. Even though she knew her troubles were lurking right around the corner, she could escape momentarily in the feel and smell of the horse.

Feeling like she could talk now, she let go of Arrow and asked Maximus, "What do I do or say?"

"I'm not sure Stella. We'll just have to see what he says. We'll all be there with you and we will help you. We just have to decide our core principals — what we can base all our decisions and actions off of."

Stella said, "Like the fact that our number one priority is to keep Isaac alive."

"And you."

"And Isaac."

"Yes. Both of you."

"So, we do whatever Gershon wants to keep Isaac alive," Stella said.

Arrow stepped forward, head raised high and said, "Not if it means hurting you, Stella."

Stella looked at him and felt a twinge of regret. Even though she felt very close to Arrow and didn't want to hurt him, Isaac was her brother. If there was a choice of who to keep happy, she'd pick Isaac over anybody or anything else in the Universe. In response, she just stroked the feathers on his wings.

Stella looked at Maximus again and he looked full of sorrow. He said to her, "You haven't seen very much in your protected life, and that is where I fear we have all made mistakes. You should have been able to know what was going on, and for us to talk to you about it. But childhood is so precious — and you should not be burdened by such things."

Stella felt a sudden determination to prove she could do this — to save Isaac. "Isaac and I have a lot of responsibility because of who we are. And now we're old enough to understand the true meaning of that. I understand why we have been raised the way we have, and I'm ready to embrace it now."

Maximus looked at her and she was surprised to see tears in his eyes. He said, "You definitely are ready to take responsibility for who you are. I just saw you mature into a true Princess right before my eyes."

CHAPTER 33

" . . . it has been scientifically proven that an
affirmative thought is hundreds of times more
powerful than a negative thought."

Isaac

Isaac woke up sometime in the middle of the night. He was unable to move at first from the tension and soreness in his body. He listened for a minute, and could hardly hear anything, except for a distant snoring—the guard by the door most likely. Everyone else must be asleep, or silently awake like he was.

He projected his voice as quietly as he could. "Rikenzia, are you asleep?"

From a dark area in her cell where Isaac couldn't see her she said, "No, I'm not asleep."

She sounded sadder than Isaac had heard her before. In fact, even in their dire circumstances, he hadn't often heard her be anything but determined and upbeat.

He wanted to move closer to her. He got up from the cold, damp floor, fighting the pain and walked to the front of the cell. Now he could see her in the dim light. "What's wrong?" he asked her. In his mind he answered his own question, *'What ISN'T wrong?'*

He heard her sigh. "I just have a hard time at night—I miss my family."

Isaac didn't want to think about family right then. He changed the subject. "Can I ask you a question?" he asked.

"Of course," she answered.

"What was it like . . . where you live?"

He waited in silence for her to answer.

Eventually, she said, "I'm one of the few kids like me, Isaac."

"What do you mean?"

"I mean, not brainwashed. My parents taught me what was *really* going on and as much as they could about how it was when Orel ruled and what we used to get taught in schools about using our gifts. Other kids—they believe Gershon is great. A man to be loved. And they hardly even know they have special abilities."

The thought of loving Gershon made Isaac slightly repulsed. "Where are your parents?" he asked.

She shifted her legs and crossed them. She stared down at the ground as she said, "I don't know. I . . ." and her voice caught.

Isaac saw that she couldn't go on talking about them, and he regretted bringing it up as that was a subject he had been trying to avoid himself. He decided to ask a different question. All of the cells were quiet and he could hear the guard still snoring, so he felt it safe to rest his elbows in the squares of steel that kept him locked in. He put his face up close to the bars, almost touching them with his chin and tried to see Rikenzia better. Before, her presence seemed as strong and fiery as a lion. But now, she seemed tiny, frail and looked the same way Isaac felt. He wondered if during the day, he looked as brave and full of life as Rikenzia did.

"How did you get captured?" he asked.

"I was pretty good at pretending to be a Gershina, which is a child of Gershon. The kids attend his schools every day and are his hope for the future he wants, which is to say completely ignorant puppets. Anyway, I knew all of their little phrases and things from watching them in the market from our hiding place. So, I was picked to go into the markets to get food."

She paused and stretched her legs out in front of her and leaned back on her hands. She still was not looking at Isaac however. She was lost in her story. "But, my dad," she sighed and Isaac could hear her pain, "was caught somehow and put into prison on Capricorn. We don't know how they found him. It had happened just the day before I got caught. I was pretty upset, but we were all so hungry. So, I bought food and the worker said the typical, 'Gershon is Great', and instead of forcing myself to say it like I usually do, I just turned and left. Stupid. I was so stupid. They were already looking harder for others in the area because they found my dad. The worker reached forward and grabbed my arm and he saw tears in my eyes . . . quite different from the little emotionless robot child I was supposed to be.

They used the stick on me, but I only cried silently. I would not tell them where my mother was. Then they brought me here. Gershon wants to know where the 'rebels' are hiding. He tries to get me to talk."

She paused for a long time and Isaac waited silently, riveted by her story.

She looked over at him and with tears in her eyes said, "I hope they haven't found my mother, too."

Isaac wanted to comfort her and he *really* wanted to turn her back into the strong 'day time' Rikenzia. He wished he could banish the bars separating them and go over to her.

He abruptly stood up straight and dropped his arms down by his sides. Rikenzia got up and came to the front of her cell, "What is it? Are you alright?" she asked quietly.

"I just . . . well . . . everything is made up of light and energy, right? That is what we transform into to become Shooting Stars. I never thought of transforming things that don't have life before though."

"But you have before," Rikenzia interjected, "Your clothes come with you don't they? Or do you show up naked everywhere?"

Isaac looked at her face and was happy to see the playful spark returning to it. He said, "I guess you're right! I just never thought of it before or made a conscious effort to make sure I stayed clothed."

"Probably because you are brilliant and everything you touch is affected by you."

He looked at her square and whispered, "Even the bars?"

Her eyes widened. He asked himself why this simple idea for escape didn't come any sooner. "Should I try?" he asked in such a quiet whisper he wondered if she heard him.

Rikenzia tried to peer up and down the narrow passageway. The guard's snoring still went on like a never-ending lawn mower.

Isaac had another thought—which was the one he tried to avoid thinking about—the thought about how his parents had been found. "Kenzie," he whispered, "I think Gershon can detect powers being used. He might know the instant I try."

"Remember I can transform now, too. I've been practicing and Gershon hasn't noticed anything that I know of."

"Oh yeah!" he said trying to keep his voice quiet still.

Rikenzia said, "I can transform, but I'm pretty sure I can't shoot across the Universe as a Star yet."

"I'm not sure I can either."

"I know you can. You're Eli's son."

Isaac felt the pressure on him for being Eli's son. "I hope I can," he said.

"Isaac . . ." she said.

He was amused by her bossiness. "You win. I CAN."

"That's better."

"But, I'm nervous about trying to take you . . . and Helios."

Rikenzia started walking slowly back and forth, careful not to make any noise with her feet. She was like a pacing tiger—soundless, and just as fearless.

"The question is," she said finally, "what can go wrong?"

He answered, "I could fail at doing it and then we'd be stuck here and who knows what Gershon will do to us."

"Yeah . . . that would be bad. Uhm, never mind. Let's not think of what can go wrong, because we just need to do it," she said and stopped pacing and looked at him expectantly.

"Like, right now?"

"Yes, right now. You were the one who said you wanted to get out quick."

"I do. Stella is supposed to appear tomorrow and she might do something stupid to save me. I can't let her do that."

"Then let's go!"

Isaac's head was now busy with the noise of all his questions and worries.

"Isaac!" Rikenzia said in the loudest way she could without waking the guard up.

He looked and her.

"You've gone white," she said, "Listen. I know we can do this. We have to. Think of your sister. Think of Helios. Think of Maximus," she paused then added, "Think of me."

Isaac took a deep breath, looked her in the eye, and nodded with purpose.

She started pacing back and forth again, and Isaac could practically see the wheels in her head turning.

"First," she said, "we, and by *we* I mean *you*, have to get these bars to melt away or do whatever you do. Do you think you can do both of ours at the same time?"

They both stepped forward to peer around and see the guard. Isaac guessed no one had ever tried to break out before, because the guard was obviously not concerned at all. His mouth was gaping open, and Isaac was certain his sleep was deep enough he might not notice—if they were very quiet.

Isaac felt in a hurry now . . . he wanted out of the cell before the guard woke up. "Yes," he said, "I'll try and do both at the same time."

"Where are we going after we get out?" she asked. "The only place I know how to get to is Gershon's *throne*."

"That's actually where I want to go."

She looked at him as if he were insane for a split second,

and then comprehension dawned, "Right," she said, "Helios."

Isaac nodded. They looked each other in the eye for several long moments and Isaac knew that he would do anything to keep her safe.

It was time to go.

CHAPTER 34

"You can start with nothing and out of nothing and out of no way a way will be made."

Isaac

Isaac reached through the bars and tried not to think about the guard waking up and shocking all the prisoners. Once he was touching Rikenzia's bars with as many fingers as could reach, he gripped the bars of his own cell and with one last glance at Rikenzia, he closed his eyes.

His nerves were rushing around inside of him like noisy children on a sugar high. He mentally told himself, 'Stop. Think.' He felt his breath, he felt the bars. *We are the same. Light and energy.* He envisioned himself standing next to Rikenzia without any barriers separating them. He felt the feelings of freedom, and of exhilaration and peace.

Then his hands were no longer holding bars. They melted and vanished into warm specs of light. Isaac heard Rikenzia gasp and opened his eyes to see her covering her mouth with her hands.

With metal no longer between them, they stepped toward each other through the glowing specs of light into the narrow passageway. Rikenzia stepped to him and wrapped her arms around him, pinning his arms to his sides.

"Thank you, thank you!" she whispered, "You are amazing."

It was sort of awkward standing there with his arms pinned around his sides, not being able to hug back, but he felt himself smiling at the fact that *she* hugged *him*.

They were both smiling.

Rikenzia whispered, "Are you ready to go?"

"More than ever. Let's get out of here. First step—the guard."

She nodded.

Isaac took a step forward and accidentally kicked a loose rock into the wall. They both froze. The guard snorted a little and rolled his head, but then started snoring deeply again.

Rikenzia gave Isaac a small finger-poke. Isaac looked at her and she whispered so quietly it was almost inaudible, "Do you not know anything about stealth? Watch me, and go toe to heel." She put a finger on his shoulder. "Watch me."

Rikenzia started forward, toe, heel, toe, heel. She watched the floor and then to Isaac's surprise started moving pretty fast without making any sound. Isaac followed suit. He didn't see anyone else awake or moving in their cells as he moved by them.

The guard's chair was directly in front of the door. Isaac and Rikenzia tip toed up to him. As they approached, Isaac scrunched up his face from the awful odor that was emanating from the dirty, drooling man that was supposedly a guard.

Isaac glanced at Rikenzia before continuing on with the inevitable and terrifying task of opening the heavy metal door behind the guard and squeezing past him without getting caught. He had expected Rikenzia to look frightened, but was taken aback to see she looked like she was stifling a laugh. When she noticed Isaac was looking at her, she rolled her eyes and mouthed, 'He's pathetic', and she waved her hand over her nose in a 'stinky' gesture.

Isaac smiled regardless of the panic in his stomach.

Rikenzia stepped past him, put her hand behind the guards head and on the doorknob. She started to turn it slowly and to Isaac's horror, the doorknob didn't move at all. Rikenzia snapped her head around and looked at Isaac with wide eyes. Isaac read her lips even though he didn't need her to tell him, "It's locked from the outside."

No wonder such a pathetic guard had been placed inside the door.

"What do we do?" Isaac mouthed back.

Rikenzia took his hand and pulled it to the door handle,

"Dissolve it—like you did the bars," she whispered into his ear.

He looked at her and Rikenzia squeezed his hand.

Isaac was more nervous here, standing right next to a guard who could wake at any moment than he had been back in the cell. Isaac closed his eyes, but he still could not concentrate on transforming. It was taking too long—nothing was happening. He tried to take his hand off the doorknob, but Rikenzia, whose hand was still on top of his, squeezed and pushed down on his hand again so that Isaac could not move. He looked at her and this time, Isaac saw a new desperation and fear.

"You must," she mouthed, "Please."

He could do it for her. Pushing all fear aside as best he could, he focused on what needed to be done. The lock was just a part of himself. He was light and energy, just like the girl touching him. He thought of her, so pure and beautiful, and he thought of how confident she made him feel.

Warmth spread through him. He heard Rikenzia gasp. He opened his eyes, or what would have been his eyes if he were in his body. Isaac, and now Rikenzia were a mass of microscopic specs of light and energy. And still, they were entirely themselves—able to see and act just as if they were their flesh and blood bodies.

Isaac had not meant to transform their bodies, but his determination to save Rikenzia was great enough to accomplish more than he expected to.

Then, he heard another gasp—one quite different than Rikenzia's. He saw that the guard was awake, staring open mouthed at the light which had been their bodies a few seconds ago. He felt Rikenzia's energy—it was urgent and scared. It moved into the side of him as if pushing him forward. Their fear moved through each molecule of each other and as it did, Isaac felt their bodies returning to their flesh and bone mass.

Isaac's panic energized him to act fast. The ready-to-sprint guard was looking quickly between their in-between-light-and-mass bodies and where the door was supposed to be.

Isaac and Rikenzia both launched themselves through the curtain of light that had been the door. Unfortunately, before they hit ground they had transformed all the way back to their bodies. Isaac felt his shoulder jam into the hard floor.

As they scrambled to their feet, they saw the guard scuttling around on the other side of the lights, obviously too scared to touch it. He started yelling for reinforcements at the same time as Isaac saw him reaching for the switch that would electrify all the cells and cause the prisoners intolerable pain.

Isaac dashed back toward the doorway and reached in to grab the guard's wrist. As he did, he felt the guard pull down on the switch and Isaac's stomach wrenched as he heard the cries and screams of the people still trapped in the cells.

Acting fast, he stepped back through the doorway, still grasping the guard's wrist. He put his other hand on the guard's arm and he forced it up and turned the switch off. Isaac could hear whimpering. Isaac glanced at the doorway and to his alarm he saw it started materializing again and then the guard began to pull down on the switch again.

Isaac jerked the guard's arm upward to get him to let go of the switch without pulling it down again. The guard did not budge however, and Isaac saw his knuckles were white from gripping the handle of the switch. Isaac could only think of one thing to do, and as willpower replaced revulsion over touching the disgusting guard, Isaac reached his head forward and bit his arm, digging his teeth into the knuckles and tendons. The guard yelled in pain and let go of the switch.

The door was solid in big patches now and Isaac could hear Rikenzia pleading on the other side. The guard kneed Isaac in the groin and Isaac crumpled to the floor in pain. The guard tried to step over Isaac to the door, and desperately against the pain, Isaac reached up with his legs and kicked the guard's stomach with both feet.

As the guard was falling back, Isaac stood up quickly and leapt through the partially materialized door. He felt shards of it scrape him and then he landed painfully on the same shoulder as he had just a few moments before.

Rikenzia instantly helped him to his feet. Through the parts of the door that were still only light, they could see the guard, also again on his feet and sprinting toward the door.

Isaac wanted to run, but he needed to make sure the guard stayed in there and could not come out. He moved to stand in front of the door—it was almost completely solid again with holes in places that were still only light. In the few milliseconds it took for the guard to get to the door, the only part of the door that remained only light was around where the handle had been.

Isaac and Rikenzia both threw their weight against the door as the guard started pushing against it from the other side. He started yelling and screaming and as Isaac and Rikenzia used all their strength to keep the door from opening—pushing and sliding with their feet against the slippery slate, Isaac willed the handle to materialize again.

Isaac and Rikenzia both shouted in surprise as the guard's hand and arm shot through the light where the handle needed to be, and reached for them. The door finished materializing completely and they spared a few moments to stare wide-eyed at the arm now protruding from the door and flailing around. Under different circumstances, it would probably look comical—but Isaac could only think of how long it would be until someone walked this way and saw it. They could hear the guard's hysterics through the door, but the sound wasn't carrying far.

Then, they dashed as fast as they could without slipping. Soon, everyone—even Dreold and Gershon—would know of their escape.

So great was their speed down the seemingly endless narrow passageway that they practically flew over the ground. They both knew the way. Isaac focused on Helios.

They stopped at the door which lead to Gershon's throne. Quite unbelievably, no one had seen them make it this far. They stood there panting for a few seconds before either of them had any extra breath to speak.

"Are you ready?" Rikenzia asked breathlessly.

"I don't know what to be ready for," he answered.

She looked grave and nodded. "I know. But we've gotten this far. What's the plan?"

"Get to Helios, transform, go back to the island," said Isaac.

Rikenzia took a deep breath and said, "I will stay as close to you as I possibly can—I don't want to get left behind."

"I could never leave you behind."

Then they heard what they had feared. Shouting and running. "Escape! Escape! Isaac and another prisoner have escaped!"

"Let's go!" Rikenzia whispered frantically. She reached her hand out to the door to push it open. Locked. Before they could so much as look at each other however, they heard the locks being undone from the other side of the door. They darted away from it in the opposite direction of the shouting. There weren't any nooks to hide in, and as they heard the door open, they froze in place. Isaac hoped that the darkness was complete enough to hide them where they stood.

Out from the door emerged Dreold. The sight of him drove all remaining doubt and fear from Isaac's mind. He was reinvigorated to his cause. He remembered his parents— he remembered Stella.

Dreold dashed toward the shouting and noise then Isaac and Rikenzia snuck back toward the door and stepped inside of it. The moment they entered, a Dragon roared. Onyxus was standing next to the throne. He was puffing his chest out and sneering at them. His black scales almost glowed from the green lights sparkling on them. He looked toxic — poisonous — and his expression was dangerous.

Through his curling lip, he said to Isaac, "Well, well, well. What do we have here?"

"Where is Gershon?" Isaac asked, and did his best to sound unshaken.

"Oh, never you mind, little boy," he said, putting his paw back on the ground. "And don't you fret, because I shall not alert him — I can handle a few little brats on my own — and he will reward me for it."

Isaac felt a flare of mixed anger and daring rising in him. He shouted at Onyxus, "We're leaving! With Helios. Do not stand in our way!"

Onyxus mockingly said, "Oh no, I'm so scared." He stepped one step toward them and said, "You're not going anywhere."

Isaac felt Rikenzia step up behind him and put her lips up to his ear. "We can't fight him Isaac."

"Oh look," Onyxus said, "You broke a little jail pigeon out with you. Hey pidge — don't be frightened — I don't eat disloyal little filthy things like you."

Isaac balled his fists up, not sure what he wanted to do with them, but they were aching to inflict pain on Onyxus, who was now laughing at them with huffs and puffs of smoke coming from his nostrils.

Rikenzia put her hand on Isaac's shoulder.

"Well now," Onyxus said, now sounding more serious, and dangerous, "We need to restrain you until Dreold returns."

Without warning, Onyxus burst toward them. Rikenzia screamed as they both started sprinting toward the exit that lead to Helios.

"Helios!" Rikenzia yelled, "Isaac! Call him!"

Onyxus roared and Isaac felt the Dragon's paw and claws

grip around his upper arm and halt his progress.

"Helios!" Isaac yelled.

They heard Helios roar in reply, but they were both now struggling against Onyxus, who had both of them by the arm. The struggle was futile, but they continued on. They heard Helios through the wall—roaring in frustration—obviously not being able to break his bindings. Then Isaac felt something. The scale was growing hotter in his pocket and all at once, he knew what to do.

"Helios! Helios! Listen to me!" shouted Isaac.

"Don't speak to him!" Onyxus said, and started to squeeze Isaac's arm so tight, the pain was making Isaac gasp.

Isaac concentrated all his strength to shout at Helios, "Think of leaving here with me!"

"Oh no you don't!" said Onyxus. He tweaked the arm he was squeezing and Isaac felt something snap.

Isaac tried to scream but the pain was too great. He heard Rikenzia crying but he was motionless. He wanted to give in to the blackness that was closing in on him but he held a picture in his mind—the lighthouse. Freedom. No pain.

"Kenz," he said, "The scale. Touch it. Think. You're the same. As it. As me. Think."

Onyxus shouted at him again to not speak. But it didn't matter, that was all he could say. It was all he could do just to think.

Faintly, he heard footsteps entering the room. But warmth had consumed him by then. Pain was no more. Rikenzia. Helios. Join them. He felt even warmer, as if there were more of himself. He felt complete, like they were all there.

He could hear men yelling and a Dragon roaring. He wanted to leave it. He wanted to be home in the lighthouse. Isaac felt like he was swiftly being carried away—his whole self—Helios and Rikenzia with him. And then just a moment later, they were somewhere different. It was quiet. Isaac knew it was safe and he let himself materialize again, and then he gave into the pain and blacked out.

CHAPTER 35

*"We all possess more power and greater
possibilities than we realize . . ."*

Stella

Stella was supposed to be sleeping but instead was staring out her window. She jerked when she saw a massive Shooting Star break through the atmosphere and land on the beach.

"It *has* to be Isaac," she said breathlessly and she ran down the stairs and out the lighthouse. She was immediately joined by Maximus, Alethia and Arrow in running to where it landed.

They stopped at the edge of a massive crater of melted and hardened sand. Stella could not yet see who was at the bottom because it took a few moments for her eyes to adjust to what the moonlight could illuminate. Then she saw glittering orange sparkles and she did not understand.

Alethia said, "It's Helios!"

Maximus said, "He did it—Isaac got both him and the Dragon out."

"Let's get down there!" Stella said.

Maximus looked at Alethia and said, "Let us go down first. I'm not sure how much room is going to be down there."

Alethia nodded and said, "Just hurry, please."

Maximus looked at Arrow and said, "We can't slide down. If Isaac is unconscious, I don't want to slide into him. Would you—"

Arrow cut Maximus off and answered his unfinished question, "Sure. Of course. Get on."

"Both of us?" asked Stella.

"I can manage," he said and knelt down and they climbed on.

Alethia urged them on—anxious mother that she was. Arrow stepped to the edge of the crater and told them to hold on. He put his hooves together and jumped off the edge as his wings spread wide. He started pushing the air to slow himself down. It wasn't too far down, so Arrow had to work hard at slowing his speed before they touched down.

Stella was keeping her eyes on the sparkling, orange Dragon, and looking around him, trying to see where Isaac was. She didn't see him until Arrow had touched down with a bit of a rough impact. Isaac was just a dark lump, lying on the ground. Stella's heart lurched.

Stella and Maximus leapt off Arrow and rushed to Isaac. He was by Helios' head. When they knelt down beside him, Stella saw that he was indeed unconscious. She could not make out much in the darkness, but Helios' scales were reflecting the moonlight, and Stella saw that Isaac looked very pale. Too pale. She started touching him and feeling for his pulse.

Relief flooded her as she felt his vein pumping under her fingers. She started examining him for damage, using mostly her hands as the lighting was poor. She didn't have to look far. "Maximus!" she yelled, "His arm!"

He had a cut on his lip that looked sore and several smaller scrapes and bruises. What was most alarming was his upper arm. It was very swollen, very bruised, and very distorted.

"Broken arm," said Maximus.

Helios was beginning to stir, and they looked around. As Stella looked at the Dragon, she could see he too was very injured. He looked worn down, tired, and burned and cut in several places.

"Helios," said Maximus in Zeego, "Easy now. There are a lot of people down here and I don't want you to hurt any of them."

Helios' eyes flew open and he raised his head. His body shuddered and he looked terrified, which terrified Stella. She didn't want him to start panicking.

"It's alright, it's alright!" she shouted. "Isaac transported you here. We're not going to hurt you."

Helios lay still again. He looked at Isaac and looked worried. "Is he alive?"

"Yes," she answered, "But he has a broken arm and he is unconscious."

"Who are you?" he asked. "Where am I?"

"I am Stella. I am Isaac's sister."

"Who is he?" Helios asked looking at Maximus.

"I am their guardian," Maximus answered him for Stella.

Helios didn't say anything for a second, and then after a moment he said, "There is something under my wing."

"What do you mean?" asked Stella.

"I think it's a person. I can feel them under my wing."

Maximus jumped into action and went to Helios' wing. He said, "Can you lift it?"

"I can't," Helios answered. "It is broken."

Maximus heaved the wing upward and moved it. Helios groaned.

Maximus picked up an unconscious person and Stella saw that she was a very pretty girl, about Isaac's age. Her long dark hair draped over Maximus arm.

Maximus said, "Your brother is amazing. He got not only himself — but a Dragon and this girl out of there, too."

"I know," Stella said, "Can we get him to a doctor?"

"We can't let him leave this island again. They will detect him."

"Well, then, can you fix his arm?" she asked, again frustrated at how everything normal in her life had changed.

"No," he said, "but I know who can."

"Let's go then," she said, jumping to her feet.

Arrow stepped over to them, ready to help. Just as Maximus started to lift the girl up toward Arrow's back, she came to, gasped and started to jerk around. Maximus almost dropped her but pulled her toward him and sank to the ground on his knees so he didn't fall down as she struggled.

"You're safe! You're safe!"

She still fought him—but Maximus did not let go. Louder, Maximus said, "Isaac brought you here. I'm Maximus—and Stella is here, his sister."

She stopped fighting immediately.

"Maximus?" she asked.

"Yes," Maximus answered.

She threw her arms around his neck. "You are Orel's son! You are not dead after all!"

Stella looked at Maximus' face as his eyes flitted over to her nervously.

The girl let go of his neck and said, "Isaac said he was from Earth. Is that where we are? Is that where you have been?"

"Uhm—"

She didn't wait for an answer but turned to look at Stella, "Stella! Isaac's sister!"

"Yes," Stella said.

Then the girl saw Isaac at Stella's feet. "Oh no," she said, and she squirmed out of Maximus' arms so she could kneel next to Isaac. "What's wrong with him?"

"His arm is broken," answered Stella, then she looked at Maximus and Arrow and said, "We must go now."

Maximus nodded then said to Helios, "Your mother is here, Helios. Be still, I will send her down."

Helios looked heartened, then said, "Please take care of Isaac. He saved me. I was supposed to save him, but he saved me."

Stella was feeling urgent and said, "Maximus!"

Maximus said, "Alright. I will hold Isaac on Arrow while he flies us out of here."

Arrow said, "Then I will come back for both of you girls."

Stella looked at Arrow with concern. She remembered the vertical lift off inside the lighthouse and how it had taken much effort. Now, to do it with a full grown man and a teenager seemed like it might be too hard for him.

Stella watched as Maximus balanced Isaac on Arrow then climbed up behind him. Maximus leaned Isaac back against himself — gripping him tightly. Maximus looked nervous, but he gave the cue to Arrow that they were ready.

"Just hold on tight with your knees and thighs," Stella told Maximus.

Just as Stella had suspected, the lift off was extremely difficult for Arrow. He grunted and slowly rose off the ground. His veins were popping and had a focused, even pained expression.

After she saw them disappear above the lip of the crater, Stella realized she had been holding her breath. She and the girl glanced at each other, hearing only their own breathing, and Helios' pained breathing behind them.

They both looked up again as Arrow came swooping down. They backed up closer to Helios to give Arrow space to land. Upon landing, Stella reached out and touched his neck. She felt sweat there, and he was breathing very heavily.

"Let's go," Arrow said through his breaths. He knelt down so they could reach his back.

Stella got on Arrow first, behind his wing, and then instructed the girl to get on behind her.

"Now hold on tight to me," Stella said, "Hey, before we go, what's your name?"

"Rikenzia."

"That's beautiful."

"Thank you."

Stella tightened her knees on Arrow's side and wrapped her hands into the long, thick strands of his mane. He took that as his cue and started pumping again. This time, without an unconscious body and amateur Horse rider on him, he gave a little jump into the air. Rikenzia stifled a startled yell — but they both remained tight against his sides.

Stella could feel every muscle in his back flexing back and forth as his wings moved up and down. She knew they weren't as heavy as Arrow's last load, but to do this lift a second time was taking its toll on him.

Stella was holding her breath again, and for a moment she thought Arrow might give in and fall back to the ground. But then, his wings started going faster, and Stella felt more lift. Arrow made it over the lip of the crater, straining and pushing, and landed not so gracefully as usual.

Stella heard Alethia going down into the crater. She stood on the edge, baby blue wings spread wide, and instead of jumping off and flying, she scooted into the crater, keeping her feet on the side to skid down—using her claws and wings to keep her slow.

Arrow snorted, sounding utterly drained.

Rikenzia and Stella dismounted. Stella said, "You did amazing, Arrow. Thank you so much."

Arrow bobbed his head once. In the brighter moonlight, she saw how much he was sweating, and she could feel the sweat and Horse hair sticking to her pants—but she didn't mind at all.

"Where is Isaac?" asked Stella.

"Maximus took him to the lighthouse," answered Arrow. "Top most room."

"Stay here and rest, Arrow."

Not waiting for an answer, Stella started darting as fast as she could in the sand toward the lighthouse. Rikenzia was close behind her.

They reached the door of the lighthouse, breathing heavily, but they didn't stop and burst right through.

"Wow," said Rikenzia as they navigated the furniture.

"Yes," Stella said with a small smile as she remembered the same feeling, "I know."

They took the stairs. Stella's legs were burning from the intense work out she was putting them through. Finally, the girls reached the top and they stood outside the door for a moment and tried to catch their breath. Stella could hear two adult male voices and she was confused. One was Maximus' voice, and the other, Stella did not recognize.

Very curious now, Stella tentatively knocked on the door.

The talking stopped and Stella heard footsteps coming toward the door. When Maximus opened it, Stella looked past him to try and see Isaac, and also who the voice was coming from. She saw Isaac laying on the floor by the Telescope. He was still unconscious.

"So, what are we doing? How are we going to fix his arm?" asked Stella.

"You need to meet someone, Stella."

"There is somebody else in here with you then?"

"Sort of," he said, "not technically."

She glared at him, tired of being confused.

"I'll just show you," he said.

They walked to the Telescope and Stella saw it was pointed toward the waterfall of shiny liquid. Then, she stopped in her tracks when she saw a man projected there by the Telescope. Stella found she was unable to move forward anymore. The man was familiar. She felt as if she knew him, but she knew that she didn't.

The man motioned for Stella to keep walking forward. She had the oddest mixture of feelings between apprehension and trust and moved forward. She stopped when she got next to Isaac, then looked away from the projection to her brother at her feet. Even in an unconscious state, Stella could see pain on Isaac's face.

Seeing her brother like this spurred her braveness forward. She looked back at the projection and said, "Maximus said he knows who can help my brother. Is that someone you?"

A deep voice which was as calming as a warm breeze gently spoke to her from the projection. "Do you know who I am?"

Stella glanced at Maximus and Rikenzia. Rikenzia was staring at the projected figure with water filled eyes. Maximus was looking at Stella and he nodded when their eyes met.

Then, Stella knew that she *did* know who the figure was, even though she had never seen him before, and only recently learned of him.

She cleared her throat and then said, "You are Orel. My— my grandfather."

"Yes," he said calmly.

"Are you going to help Isaac?"

"I could help Isaac if I were there."

"Where are you?"

"I am no place that has a name or anywhere you can fathom."

Stella felt heartbroken and—lonely. "Then, who is going to help Isaac?" she asked, fighting back sudden tears.

"You are. I will instruct you perfectly on how to do so."

Stella said through sudden tears, "I know that you could come here right now," she said, "You can do anything. Do you just not want to?"

"Stella, child," he said, still gently, "I know that you do not understand. I can only leave from where I am when the majority of the Zodians want me back."

"But, there are those who do want you back. Are you just going to ignore them, because they are only a minority?"

"For those people, I lay in wait. Those people will have leaders to help them get through until I can return."

Stella wiped her face and looked at him. She knew what he meant. Sadly, she said, "I am not a great leader—I cannot be you."

"You don't have to be," he said, "and you are capable of more than you think."

Just then, Isaac stirred. It was very fleeting, but they were all looking at him now. Maximus and Rikenzia came forward and knelt down by him. Isaac groaned in pain, and Stella's frantic urgency to act was back.

She looked up at Orel again and said, "What do we do?"

"You can heal him."

Stella's voice rose with the sudden flare up of anger at these words, "No, I can't! He's suffering—we need to help him *now*."

"Stella." Orel used a different voice. It was not angry, but it wasn't a slow breeze anymore. It corrected her anger and she was now listening to him with her full attention.

"You are my granddaughter. I can heal people's wounds. With Isolde's blood running through your veins as well, you, dear Stella, have the power to heal both physical and emotional wounds."

She did not dare contradict him. She felt complete respect for Orel now that she had stood in front of him and spoken with him. If he said she could do it, then she had to put her trust in him.

She looked at Maximus as they knelt around Isaac. She asked him in a low voice, "You can't do this?"

He smiled at her softly and said, "You need to do this. You *can* do this."

He reached across and put a hand on her shoulder.

She looked at Rikenzia.

Rikenzia said, "I saw Isaac do incredible things today, and I believe you can do incredible things too."

Stella felt buoyed up by the love and support of all the people around her. She looked back at her grandfather and said, "Tell me how to do it."

CHAPTER 36

"Our job is not to figure out the how.
The how will show up out of a commitment and belief in the
want."

Stella

Stella felt nervous and slightly embarrassed to have all these eyes watching her as she attempted to do something she had never done before, so she was grateful when Maximus, Rikenzia and Arrow all backed up several steps to give her room.

Isaac was still motionless, but his breathing had become more rapid and he was now sweating.

Orel said, "Hold your hands gently on either side of Isaac's arm."

Tenderly, Stella put one hand in between Isaac's side and the broken arm and then put the other hand on the outside of his arm, barely touching it.

"Now, Stella, you are not a scientist, nor a doctor. So you do not need to know everything that has to happen inside his arm for it to heal. The type of healing you can perform does not require that you know the *how*. It only requires belief that it *can* be healed. The only scientific knowledge you need to have is that each cell in the body can regenerate and heal itself, as if it were brand new. What you are going to do is ask the damaged cells to purge themselves and come back as new and perfect."

Stella was taking very deep breaths while listening to Orel and looking at Isaac.

"There is one more thing, Stella."

She looked back up at him and held her breath for a moment. He sounded very grave.

He continued, "The healer does have a price to pay. As the pain leaves him, it will have to go somewhere. Since it is your hands that will be doing the healing, the pain will transfer into you for a time. But, it will leave you if it finds nowhere to stay."

Stella's heart thudded even faster and she was biting her lower lip. Even at the prospect of pain, she would not and did not back down.

"I'm ready," she said.

"I know you are," Orel said with fatherly affection for her in his voice. "Focus on Isaac's arm. Focus on it being whole."

She did. She closed her eyes to better be able to put images of Isaac being whole and perfect again. She listened to Orel's voice in her head and did everything he told her.

"*Feel the energy passing between your hands. Ask the cells to regenerate. They will respond to the energy you create.*"

As Stella did everything she was told, she felt her hands grow steadily hotter.

"*Good Stella. All the energy is charging itself. The cells are regenerating. The injury is healing.*"

Stella's closed eyelids could not keep out the bright light coming through them. She opened her eyes slowly as she held the picture of the healed arm in her mind. It looked like she was holding an orb of glowing, fire-hot light where Isaac's upper arm had been.

Then, without doing anything to change what she was doing, the glowing orb turned to blue light and it cooled dramatically to the temperature of ice.

"It is done," said Orel. "Remove your hands."

She did, and instantly the pain hit her. She gasped. It was all over her body—prickling and stabbing her relentlessly. She was closing her eyes tight and rocking back and forth. It hurt. All she could focus on was the pain. Physical pain— emotional pain. Oh, how she missed her parents.

Somewhere in the distance, over the sounds of her own grief, she heard a voice telling her, "*Be cleansed of it Stella. It has no place in you!*"

She tried to listen because she wanted the pain to leave. It had no place in her.

"You are free from pain, Stella. It has nowhere to live inside of you."

Yes it does, she thought, *my heart.* As she thought this, the pain seemed to zoom to her chest. She clutched her hands to her heart and curled up on the floor in the fetal position.

Someone came and knelt over her. Maximus. He put a hand on her head and spoke softly in her ear, "I know that you miss your parents, but you must cleanse the pain out of you. Think of everything you still have — think of us."

Then she heard Isaac's voice. "Stella? What's wrong with her? What happened?"

Isaac. Happiness and affection flooded through her body and swept the pain out with it instantaneously. She sat up and locked eyes with her brother. There he was — alive and they were together again.

CHAPTER 37

*"If you're worried or in fear, then you're bringing
more of that into your life throughout the day."*

Onyxus

Dreold demanded that everybody except Onyxus leave
the throne room immediately, and he locked the door behind
them then he and Onyxus began shouting at each other.

"How could you have let them escape? You're a fire
breathing, claw-ridden BEAST with sharp teeth!"

"Do not insult my abilities pathetic human." Onyxus said
furiously. Steam was issuing from his nostrils. He was
containing the flame inside of him with much difficulty.

"Oh . . . Pathetic? What good are you going to be to me,
OR Gershon if you cannot even detain children?"

Onyxus couldn't hold it in anymore. The fire came up his
throat and with a feeling of complete vengeance—he let it go.

Dreold jumped to the wall to dodge it. "Dragon!" he
yelled.

"Human!" Onyxus yelled back. "I did not come here to be
a servant for humans."

Dreold walked up to Onyxus and with malice thick in his
voice, he said, "If you ever want other Stars, you will be
whatever we want you to be."

Onyxus glared at him—hatred burning inside.

"Now," Dreold said, walking toward where the throne
was, like it was his, "we still have time to fix this before
Gershon knows what has happened. He is out on an . . .
errand."

Dreold turned back around as he reached the throne. He
stood in front of it with the back of his knees right at the seat
like he was going to sit down, but he didn't. Looking at
Onyxus, Dreold said, "Now, what do you know Dragon? Did
they say anything before they left?"

"Nothing of importance," said Onyxus, still seething with annoyance, "just that he wanted to leave with Helios—and he did."

Dreold's shouted again, "Yes, but WHERE?"

"It's not like they chatted about their travel plans with me!"

Dreold growled in frustration and flopped down on the throne.

"Uhm," said Onyxus, "I don't think you're supposed to sit there."

"Oh, shut up. Gershon isn't anywhere near right now."

They both were silent for a moment. Then Dreold said, more to himself than to Onyxus, "I knew it. I told him Eli's son would be capable of travelling without a Telescope. He should have been kept under stricter guard, in an isolated and closely watched prison. Gershon underestimated him—said he was just a stupid kid and didn't want him to get any 'special treatment'. Well, now he's going to pay for his mistakes. But of course, we will be blamed for it. He'll never admit his mistake."

Onyxus knew he did not want to be on the receiving end of Gershon's wrath. "What do we do then?" he asked.

"We have to leave here, and we have to find them, and we have to do it now. I was counting on you having some sort of lead as to where they went—but for now, we just have to get out of here."

They started walking toward the hole in the cave that led to the Telescope outside. Onyxus was thinking hard as they walked. He tried to think of things Isaac had said on Draco to Adamas and Alethia—but he had been so focused on planning each detail of his escape, that Isaac's words were mostly tuned out.

Then he recalled hearing something about the Winged Horses on Pegasus being informed of what was going on, and that they were preparing for battle.

Dreold and Onyxus stepped out onto the ledge, and the tungsten colored Telescope glinted at them from the light of the nearby stars.

Onyxus told Dreold what he just remembered.

"We will go there then. They might know where the little brats are hiding," said Dreold.

Onyxus asked, "And how will you get this information from them?"

Dreold smiled a terrible smile. He said, "There is very little that separates myself and Gershon — and in many ways, I am better. I have enough powers to protect myself there, and to get what I want. And you are a Dragon quadruple their size."

"I have no doubts Winged Horses taste delicious — but I can only eat so many, know what I mean?"

Dreold snickered, "You're scared."

Onyxus growled.

"Here you go Dragon," Dreold said as he walked over to a group of clear crystals protruding from the wall. He put his hand on one and said some words Onyxus could not hear. Then he pulled and the crystal came free. Dreold turned back to Onyxus, smiled maniacally again, and tossed the crystal a few feet and caught it again. He walked straight past Onyxus and to the Telescope.

Onyxus watched as Dreold held the sharp end of the crystal up to the magnifying end of the Telescope. In a matter of seconds, the crystal was sucked into the Telescope like it was a knife cutting butter. When it had completely disappeared inside, the Telescope started freakishly spinning, whooshing and squeaking as it did.

Onyxus backed up a step and Dreold's eyes flickered toward him again. Dreold laughed again, then he walked away from the spinning and squeaking Telescope and over to a cavern in the wall behind the Telescope where sat dozens of thick glass cylinders. Onyxus was watching him, but then he looked back toward the Telescope when it stopped abruptly.

Dreold stepped toward the magnifying glass end again and pushed the cylinder in so the rim of it melded into the magnifying glass. "I can't touch it with my skin now," said Dreold. "It will severely burn any human's skin."

Onyxus watched and waited for whatever was going to happen next. Then, in the same way the crystal had entered, it emerged, but it looked different. The shape was the same, but the color was a shiny black. It hung eerily suspended in the middle of the cylinder, not touching any of its sides.

"There," Dreold said as he pulled the cylinder away, "you can use this in case any of those ponies give you trouble."

Onyxus jumped as he heard something through the hole to the cave—Gershon's voice—yelling and angry. He looked at Dreold who also looked suddenly panicked. Onyxus bounded forward away from the door, and Dreold launched himself toward Onyxus. He was cradling the crystal and did a somersault on the ground. Then he touched Onyxus leg as they came in contact with each other. As fast as a flash of lightning, they lit up, and were gone.

CHAPTER 38

"Perseverance and audacity generally win."

Zordosa

It was a quiet and peaceful night on Markab. Zordosa stood with Sarge on a hill and watched over a large group of Winged Horses, taking turns grazing and sleeping. There was a warm breeze. Zordosa felt at peace and confident.

In a split second of time, all of the quietness was traded for chaos. The herd of Horses looked up as a Shooting Star, glowing brightly green, broke through their atmosphere and zoomed over their heads. It kept going until it was out of site, and then there was a loud crash.

As one, all of the Horses started running in the opposite direction of the crash, which was toward the rise where Sarge and Zordosa were standing.

"Stop!" they both yelled at the oncoming stampede.

Again as one, with very little bumping into each other, the Horses skidded to a halt, leaving long gouges in the ground.

Zordosa spoke to them, calmly and assertively, "You all must hide. I have a very bad feeling about this."

Sarge said, "Go to the dome trees and do not fly there. We will go investigate."

The Winged Horses took off galloping past Zordosa and Sarge then Sarge started their gallop in the opposite direction—toward where the green Star had landed.

An instinct had taken over Zordosa and her age did not matter. She kept perfect time with her muscular and long legged son. They galloped for some distance, over open hills and then toward a thick grouping of tall trees.

Her nose caught onto a burning smell and they slowed to a walk. Zordosa had only seen fire a few times when Eli had made them to keep himself warm. Eli had taught her it could be dangerous, so the site of flames was unnerving to her.

Zordosa separated from Sarge just a little, so that they could navigate through the thick trees better and conceal their presence. Sarge, who was a dark steel grey would not have as much difficulty hiding as Zordosa would have being bright white.

It was difficult work to walk with hard hooves on a surface that had a lot of debris. Zordosa heard voices and she stopped and listened, still a safe distance away. Sarge had stopped too. The voices were arguing with each other in Zeego.

"Shouldn't I be carrying that?"

"And how do you expect to do that? Are you going to walk around on your hind legs so you can carry it in your paw?"

"Tie it around my neck."

"With what, Dragon? I don't see any stinking rope around here."

Dragon? Not good.

"You can make one with these leaves."

"Are you kidding me? You think I want to waste time building you a necklace?"

"How else do you expect me to get back to Gershon's Lair if we get separated?"

"Your fear of these stupid little ponies amuses me, Dragon."

"I'm not scared of these tasty snacks. I just want to make sure I can get out of here!"

"Fine!"

Zordosa could hear branches and leaves being tore down. She was tense, and when Sarge appeared right next to her, she jumped.

Sarge reached his mouth out for the Star Charm in Zordosa's mane. Zordosa too knew it was time to call for help. They had heard all they needed to hear. Dragon.

Gershon.

Sarge took the Star Charm tenderly in his front teeth and wrapped his lips around it. He pressed down lightly so that he did not break it, then let go. The Star Charm blinked with light a few times. It had worked. Now, they had to keep safe until Maximus arrived.

It did not take long for the Dragon and Gershon's servant to start traipsing through the woods toward the clearing. Sarge and Zordosa stayed in front of them and out of sight. The Dragon was making so much noise trying to navigate the dense trees that Zordosa did not have any fear of the sounds their own hooves were making.

One of them said, "I just want to find the stupid beasts quick and make them tell me about Stella and Isaac."

Zordosa froze in place at the edge of the clearing.

The Dragon spotted her just as she realized her mistake. "Dreold! I just saw a flash of something white through there!"

Zordosa sprinted into the clearing and spread her wings, but after only a few long strides, she was where Horses fear to be most—trapped. There were no physical barriers holding her back like ropes or nets. But, the air around her held her in a vice-like grip. She could not even turn her head or move a leg but she could see the man's face and she saw a frighteningly excited look on it as he held his arms out in front of him toward her. Sarge charged straight at the man.

Zordosa was momentarily released and she could move again. She turned around to face the man and watch Sarge, and then in an instant was constrained again.

"Stop!" the man yelled at Sarge. "Or I will hurt her!"

Sarge, who had been nearing striking distance, slid to a halt. The dirt stirred up from his back hooves sliding in the ground hit the bottom of the man's legs. Now they were standing eye to eye, Sarge was breathing heavily and looking furious. The man looked amused.

"Well, well, well. Two brave little ponies with wings."

Zordosa saw Sarge snort and paw the ground.

"I don't have a lot of time," the man said, "so let's get straight to business. I know that Pegasus has been very recently involved with Eli and Isolde's children. I need to know where they are. Now."

Sarge looked frantically at Zordosa, and she wished with all her might she could respond.

Then the man did something and Zordosa's body writhed and spun in the air, and a horrible sound she couldn't control was escaping from her.

The pain stopped and she crumpled to the ground trying to remain conscious — but darkness was threatening her. She heard the man talking again and saw he now held Sarge like he'd been holding her.

He said, "You can still talk while I hold you like this, pony. Now, do you want to feel the same pain that the pretty little white Horse just got a lethal dose of, or would you like to tell me about those children?"

Zordosa knew Sarge wouldn't talk and she wished she could protect Sarge from the pain she was feeling.

CHAPTER 39

"Experience is a hard teacher because she gives the test first, the lesson after."

Sarge

"Talk Horse!" yelled Dreold. "I know you can."

Then Sarge felt the pain. It was a burning and gripping pain that filled the insides of his body. It was unbearable and all Sarge wanted to do was escape it. Then, as suddenly as it had come, it stopped—and so too did the grip upon him. He fell hard back to the ground. He was not very coherent, but he saw more lights whooshing around. He heard more voices—and he heard trees being split apart and knocked down. The image of his mother being flat on the floor came to his mind and he shot up to his feet in an instant.

She wasn't there. He started galloping toward the spot where she had been. But quite a different sight than what he expected greeted him. It was Arrow, running toward him. Sarge slid to a halt again.

"She's been moved!" Arrow shouted above the noise of roaring and yelling. "She's safe! Now get out of here!"

Sarge did not move. He was transfixed by the sight of not only one, but three Dragons in total. The light of Pegasus' Stars shone brightly on their scales—a glistening light-blue Dragon, and a golden yellowish-orange Dragon were pinning the black Dragon on the ground. On the black Dragon's chest was a stone of some sort, in a clear case.

The golden Dragon had his massive paw pressed down on the side of the black Dragon's face, keeping it tight against the ground.

"Sarge!" said Arrow. The roaring subsided, and all that could be heard were the whooshing sounds and the cracking of trees.

Sarge did not look away from the Dragons. Then, he saw three figures of something human — small and young — one male, two female. "Are . . . are those Eli's children? There are three?"

Arrow snapped his head around and said, "No, no, no!" and started galloping back toward the children who were on their way to where the Dragons were struggling with each other. Sarge followed him.

In a moment, they were all standing around each other — Dragons, Winged Horses, and humans.

The young human boy said, pointing at the black Dragon, "That is Onyxus! He was the one that kidnapped me to Gershon's Lair."

Arrow looked at the Dragons for a moment, then turned back to the young humans and said, "We told you to stay inside the dome trees. What if Dreold sees you?"

The children did not look remorseful at Arrow's scolding. The female with hair the same color as Arrow's mane asked, "Where is Maximus?"

All of their heads, minus the black Dragon's, turned to look back at the trees. It looked like a battle zone. Trees were alight with flames and lit up objects were zooming back and forth.

"Still fighting Dreold," answered Arrow.

CHAPTER 40

*". . . nothing new or different can ever happen to us
until we decide to make new and different choices."*

Stella

Stella watched the trees, feeling nervous and sick. It hadn't been that long ago when she had witnessed a scene like this. On that night, she lost two of the three most important people in her life. Maximus had become just as important to her. Especially now she knew he was their Uncle.

She saw Isaac move beside her, and she looked over to see him running toward a small object on the ground. She and Rikenzia ran after him and stopped as he dropped to his knees in front of the object. Stella looked and saw it was a boulder.

"What are you doing, Isaac?"

He did not answer her. He placed his hands over the boulder but did not touch it. In no more than a few seconds, it had a glow around it and he picked it up off the ground — still not touching it. He rose to his feet and lifted it higher.

He looked at Stella, and she looked back at him, completely stunned. Yet again, he had discovered a power he had without anybody telling him he had it, or how to use it.

"Stella, this isn't the first time I've made objects move. I can help Maximus fight!"

"No," she said flatly.

"Look!" he said, and he pushed his hands forward and the rock zoomed out of sight.

"I know you CAN, Isaac, but you just . . . I can't . . . just, no. You have to stay safe."

Isaac looked at Rikenzia. Stella looked at her too. She shook her head at Isaac which Stella saw disappointed him. They all looked around as the sounds of Horse's hooves came galloping up behind them — Arrow, and a steel grey Horse.

Arrow said, "Let's get you three back to the dome trees."

Before any of the children could argue, a loud bang rent the air, making them all jump. As they looked around, they barely saw the streak of green light before it left the atmosphere of Markab. Dreold had left. What did that mean? What happened to Maximus?

Stella took off sprinting to the trees. She ran through the grass faster than she had ever ran before. She had to find him. "Maximus!" she yelled.

"Stella!"

She stopped, heart pounding, scanning the tree line to see if she could see where his voice had just come from. There he was, over by the Dragons.

She ran to him, only vaguely aware of the group running behind her. When she stopped in front of him, she saw cuts and bruises all over him, but he still looked whole and reassuringly alive. Stella could not help herself—she hugged him and he hugged her tightly back.

"Hello, Sarge," said Maximus over Stella's shoulder.

Stella let go of Maximus and turned around to the Horses and Dragons. The steel grey Horse called Sarge answered Maximus, "Thank you for coming when we called."

"We said we would," said Maximus.

Stella looked around to locate Isaac and when she saw what he was doing, she called out, "Stop, Isaac!"

Maximus pushed her to the side and ran to Isaac but she and Rikenzia followed right behind him. Isaac was moving directly toward the Dragons, his eyes set on the black one.

When Maximus caught him and held him back, Isaac looked a little annoyed, "I just want to look closer at what Onyxus has around his neck. It looks familiar, like the exact crystal that he bit when we got transported to Gershon's Lair. Maximus, you have to get that crystal away from him. If he gets a hold of it, it will take him back to Gershon, and then he'll know we've been here."

Stella's body responded to this news by tingling and tensing. Gershon could not bring an army here to the pure and peaceful Pegasus. She had seen all those Horses in the domed tree area, and was in heaven. She did not want them harmed.

Just then, she saw a large group of Horses walking slowly over the nearby rise toward them. A beautiful and elderly Winged Horse, white and bright, was out in front of the herd. The other Horses stayed respectfully behind her. Even Onyxus stopped struggling as the Horses approached. Sarge cantered over to them.

Stella was watching them in awe, but then her attention was caught by Maximus moving over to Onyxus to look at the crystal. Onyxus growled at him, and Alethia and Helios pushed down harder, digging their claws into him.

The Horses were upon them now, and they started to fan out around the humans and Dragons.

Maximus grabbed the band around Onyxus' neck that the crystal was attached to and pulled at it until he found the knot. Onyxus started to struggle mightily, but Alethia and Helios were able to keep him down and Maximus was able to undo the knot and pull it from his neck. Onyxus tried thrashing again and his tail came very close to Isaac, who jumped back as Stella's stomach jumped to her throat.

Onyxus spoke, sounding muffled and squashed, "No human can grasp that crystal without getting severely burned."

Nobody responded to him.

"Don't take it out of that glass cylinder, Maximus. It will transport you to Gershon's Lair," said Isaac.

Stella felt panicky that Maximus was holding the crystal so close to himself.

Helios said with voice straining, "I don't mean to intrude or anything, but what are we going to do about Onyxus?"

At that precise moment, Onyxus gave a particularly nasty

thrash, and Helios' body slid down his side and Onyxus yanked his arm free. Alethia still held on and she was being ripped around by Onyxus' continued thrashing. The Horses were all backing up, and Maximus hurriedly rushed Stella, Isaac and Rikenzia out of harm's way.

Once at a distance, they turned around to watch. Stella was watching transfixed, and unable to move of her own free will. It was terrifying watching the Dragons battle.

Maximus was standing in the middle of them, and he stretched his arms over his head. Stella looked up at his hands, but could not see anything happening. She looked back at the Dragons. Alethia was still clinging to him as he thrashed. Helios recovered from his fall and was trying to jump on Onyxus again.

Stella and Rikenzia screamed. Fire was coming from Onyxus. Stella heard the thundering of Horses' hooves fleeing behind her and she wanted to flee with them. Onyxus was aiming at Alethia, who growled and let go as her front paws were burned.

Onyxus dodged Helios again, and in one humongous leap, was directly in front of where the humans were standing, all huddled together, Maximus' hands still in the air above them. Onyxus looked directly at the crystal, and Stella saw that for some inexplicable reason, Isaac was now holding it!

As Onyxus swiped his paw forward to snatch it from him, Isaac moved to shield it with his body. Stella gasped, fearing for her brother, but Isaac was unharmed. Onyxus' paw had stopped abruptly right above them like a bird that had just flown into a clear, glass window. Onyxus tried again, and again the invisible barrier stopped him. He looked quickly behind him and saw Helios and Alethia lunging toward him. He leapt out of the way, and then spread his enormous bat-like wings and jumped from the ground, taking flight.

Alethia made to take off after him, but stopped when she

heard Maximus shouting at her, "Let him go, Queen! We will catch him later!"

Maximus dropped his hands. Again, to Stella, it looked as if nothing had changed by his movement, but she knew whatever protective barrier he had put up around them was released. Stella stood up straight, along with Isaac and Rikenzia, and she placed a hand on Isaac's shoulder to restrain him.

Maximus said, "Stay here," in a tone they not dare disobey. Then he walked over to the older white matriarch mare. He placed his hand on her neck and was speaking to her and to Sarge. Stella could not hear what he was saying because of the distance the Horses had given the scene. She looked at all of the Horses properly now, especially the two to whom Maximus was speaking. The white mare was stunning. Her neck was so beautifully arched, like a swan's. Sarge's presence was bold and strong — intimidating, yet inspiring.

Maximus turned back to the kids and Dragons and said loud enough for them to hear, "All the Horses you see standing here are all of those who live on this particular Star. We will leave the black Dragon be for now until we figure out what to do next. Nobody," Maximus paused to look behind him and raised his voice, "is to leave the safety of being in this group," he looked back at the young people, "for anything. We don't know what Gershon knows, or if he'll send any of his other eleven Minion here . . . or if Dreold will come back."

Maximus started walking back toward the group and the two Horses Stella took to be the leaders of the Winged Horses followed him. When they were all gathered together, Arrow stepped forward, to make the necessary introductions, "This is my sister, Zordosa, and her son, Sargeant, who we affectionately call 'Sarge'.

Then, he introduced the Dragons to the Horses. "This is Alethia, the Queen of Gamma Draconis, and her son, Helios, the Prince." Arrow turned to the humans, "And, you know

Maximus. This is Rikenzia, from . . . ?"

"Capricornus," said Rikenzia.

"Capricornus. And here," he paused for a moment, "are Stella and Isaac — Eli's children."

Zordosa stepped forward to Stella and Isaac. Stella felt a thrill of awe course through her as she came close enough to touch. In a voice that matched her beauty, she said, "It is a true honor to meet you both. Your father was very dear to me."

Something about the sincere emotion coming through Zordosa's voice brought out the always close to the surface emotions in Stella. She let go of Isaac's shoulder and reached out to touch the white mare's forehead. Zordosa stepped into the pressure of her hand.

Isaac stepped forward too and reached out to touch her neck. There really wasn't that much to be said. It was quiet while Stella, Isaac and Zordosa stood around each other. Stella felt more connected to her father in Zordosa's presence.

Then, Maximus kindly broke the silence. "We need to decide what we will do next."

Isaac turned to Maximus and gave Stella a huge shock by bluntly saying, "I want to use the crystal to return to the Lair and free the prisoners."

There was shocked silence from everybody. Stella looked at Maximus and was relieved to see he looked as incredulous as she felt at this statement. Rikenzia was the first to recover and said, "But, Isaac — we just got out of there. Surely you don't want to do this right NOW."

Isaac was looking at Rikenzia, and Stella saw a more mature side of him than she had ever seen before. There was a protective tenderness in his expression as he said, "I know it is awful there, and I don't expect, or even want you to go with me. But, I've already thought this all through, and I know that I have to do this."

Rikenzia stood up straighter and said, "Well, if you're

going, I'm going!"

"Nobody is going anywhere!" said Maximus.

Isaac faced Maximus full on. He looked more like a man than he ever had before as he said, "Maximus, please listen to my plan. We already decided that we are united in defeating Gershon and his Minion. The first step I see is to free those prisoners."

"Isaac, I don't think you need to go straight to Gershon's stronghold to start this fight against him."

Isaac retorted, "It is awful there, Maximus! The prisoners get shocked with electricity at the whim of the guards' tempers. And what more loyal people do we need than the ones who will not give in to Gershon?"

Maximus had no reply to this but Stella did. "Isaac. I just got you back. You're not going!"

He turned to her, looking tender, but still sympathetic, "Stella, this is what we were born for. This is what we have been *saved* by our parents for. Those people are loyal, and those people need us the most."

Stella said, "You don't think it's slightly reckless going directly back to Gershon's Lair?"

"Maybe, Stella, but it's the only thing I can think of to do for the Zodiacs that is any sort of useful. Plus—Gershon won't kill me. He . . . well . . . he's using me. Or wants to anyway."

"What do you mean?" asked Maximus.

Stella listened as Isaac told them of Gershon's Telescope, and how Gershon had transmitted to the other Constellations about how he had found the son of Eli, and how Isaac was 'on his side'.

When he was done explaining, nobody looked reassured.

Maximus said, "Well, Isaac, he could still change his mind at any moment and decide to kill you. Even if he didn't change his mind, do you really want to risk letting yourself get used like that?"

"Maximus, I've told you I thought this all through already."

Rikenzia piped in before Maximus, "Let's hear your plan then!"

Isaac looked at Rikenzia and with excited tension said, "When Onyxus bit the crystal last time, it transported us to the throne room, where Gershon spends most of his time."

"Don't you think this crystal will do the same?" she asked.

"Yes, I do. That is why we will have to draw Gershon out before we get there."

Stella was exasperated. "And how in the blazes do you expect to do that?"

Isaac looked at her and said, "I think Gershon, now more than ever, will keep to his promise to start killing Zodians if you do not show yourself. His anger is probably very dangerous right now because of our escape."

Stella's breath was caught in her chest. He went on, "His Telescope is not in the throne room, but out on a ledge outside of the cave. I want to use the time when he will be talking to you as my cover to get there and get into the prison."

"Isaac," Rikenzia said before Stella could respond, "What about the guards?"

"I don't know. We'll just try to get around them, and fight them if we have to. Hopefully most of them will be out on the ledge with Gershon watching Stella."

Stella jumped back in, "And you expect me to be able to talk to Gershon while I know you're there, within his reach and risking your life?"

"Stella," he said, maddeningly calm and mature, "do you want to save those people?"

"Honestly, Isaac, when it comes to risking my brother to do so, then I don't know."

"But, I can do it. I will be back soon."

Rikenzia said, "You mean, we will be back soon."

Maximus stepped forward in between them and loudly

said, "Nobody is going anywhere! Isaac, you have never used any powers to fight, you don't know how to shield yourself, and as far as I heard, you only have an entrance plan — not an exit plan."

Stella was thankful Maximus was going to put a stop to all this nonsense.

Isaac deflated. "That's because I haven't really figured that part out yet. How do I get dozens of people out, and where do they even go? Can they all come to the island? But, Maximus, I *know* it is the right thing to do, and when are we going to have a chance like this? We have the crystal and the opportunity to have him distracted."

They were all silent, staring at each other while they contemplated the meaning of Isaac's words. Stella already knew Isaac was going to win this argument, and it made her stomach ache.

Helios stepped forward, "Isaac, if you are set on going, then I want to return with you."

Maximus said, "No, Helios. If anybody is going with him, it is me."

Rikenzia argued, "He's not going back without me either."

Helios said, "I will not let Isaac burn himself on that crystal. I will be the one to touch it."

Stella's anxiety was bursting. "Wait!" she blurted, "So, is this really happening then? And you're ALL going?"

She looked at Isaac and Maximus with a pleading in her eyes. "Does all of this have to happen right now?" she asked.

No one had to speak any words to answer her. She knew the answer, as did they all.

Maximus came over to her and hugged her again. Then he said, "Let's work out our plan."

CHAPTER 41

"Take the first step in faith. You don't have to see the whole
staircase. Just take the first step."

Isaac

Isaac felt relieved when Maximus said he was going to
come with him. He was one hundred percent convinced he
was going to go back no matter what, but the enormity of the
task was daunting.

"Wait, Maximus! Doesn't Dreold know you are alive,
now that you have fought him?"

Maximus, who had been talking quietly with Stella,
looked over at him. Isaac saw a flicker of a grin. "He did not
see me at all."

"But—then—you *still* can't go with me! They might see
you!"

"That is a risk we'll have to take, because you are not
going without me."

"But, Onyxus! He might know about you, and he might
have already told."

"Dreold seemed pretty confused when we were fighting.
I don't think Onyxus told."

Sarge stepped forward, "Yes, about the Dragon, Maximus.
Dragons are carnivores, correct?"

"Yes, they are."

"Well, we Winged Horses are only herbivores, and no
other creature lives on this Star with us. So, either the Dragon
must starve to death, or we will be hunted by him."

"That is not an option," said Maximus. "We do not want
any of you harmed. Alethia? Helios? Any ideas?"

Helios asked, "Can you transport him somewhere else?"

Maximus said, "I cannot transport him unless he
consents."

Isaac said, "Well, we'll explain his options, and one of

those can be to take him to a place where he can hunt without causing harm."

Stella asked, "Isn't there some sort of enclosure or something we can put him in? I don't like the idea of putting any other Constellation in danger, or involving them in this yet. I think that we should keep our known enemies in close proximity — especially ones that can do us so much damage."

Maximus put an arm around her shoulder. "This is why you two were meant for this. You spoke like a true leader just now, Stella."

Isaac thought the same thing. She did sound very dignified, and of course, what she said was true. They shouldn't subject anybody else to the danger Onyxus could bring.

Stella went on, "What about the crater that Helios left on our beach? I shudder to have him so close, but I think we could subdue him there, and we can feed him."

"That's..." Maximus paused, "...not a bad idea. But still getting him to consent will be the trick."

Zordosa interrupted, "In my opinion, from what Sarge and I heard, Onyxus is very afraid of Gershon, and he was afraid of being stuck here. I think he might go with you willingly — if it means hiding from Gershon."

Isaac thought about what Zordosa said. He thought about Dreold and Gershon knowing they were on Pegasus, and he became frightened. "Maximus?"

"Yes, Isaac."

"Remember those 'ripples' we were talking about?"

"Yes."

"Don't you think, with everything that has gone on here that those ripples will get us found again, and here?"

"That is a possibility. However, the thing about ripples is, to find them you have to be very, very in tune, and also looking very, very hard. Hopefully, it has been such a short time frame since this has all happened, that Gershon is either too angry to be in tune, or too busy with other things to be looking too deeply for them."

"But, we don't know for sure."

"No, I guess we don't."

"I think we should go now—just to make sure our plan doesn't get interrupted."

Isaac looked at Stella and saw she looked a little wide-eyed and scared.

Maximus said, "We're not going to the Lair right this second."

Isaac opened his mouth to protest, but Maximus cut him off, "No. We are going back to the lighthouse to work on a couple things before we go. Stella wants us all to return there before going our separate ways."

"Yes," said Stella, "Let's go now."

"And what of Onyxus?" Sarge implored.

Alethia answered, "You all go. I will stay here and discuss his options with him—and will make sure he does not harm these Horses." She looked at Stella. "I am sorry I cannot accompany you like I said I would."

Isaac saw that Stella was shaking her head. "No," she said, "Onyxus needs to come with us now. Right, Isaac?"

Isaac felt strongly about this, too. "Right. Dreold and Onyxus should not be reunited. Dreold could come back at any moment—with reinforcements."

"Alright," Maximus said addressing Isaac and Stella, "Why don't you two take Rikenzia, Arrow, and Helios back now to the lighthouse. I will get Onyxus and Alethia and I will be behind you shortly."

Isaac felt anxious about taking more time, but he nodded his head in agreement, knowing full well that he would not win the argument in this matter.

Stella was getting on Arrow's back. Rikenzia was walking up to Isaac. It felt good to have her close to him again. They had not had any time to talk since leaving the Lair. Somewhat awkwardly, he reached out to take her hand, then he said, "Go ahead and use your Star Charm that Maximus gave you to go back. I'll get Helios and come right along."

"Promise?" she said, eyes looking tired, but still twinkling.

"Promise."

Rikenzia and Isaac looked over at Stella. She brought her hand up to her chest where the Star Charm hung on a leather string around her neck. She closed her hand around it, and Isaac could see it glowing through the cracks in her fingers. In the time it took for Isaac to breathe in and breathe out, his sister and her Winged Horse had transformed and were gone.

"Your turn," he said to Rikenzia.

"Why not you next?"

"Because, ladies go first."

He let go of her hand. She smiled at him, and just like Stella, gripped her Star Charm and in just a breath, was transformed and gone.

Maximus moved in to stand directly next to Isaac. He said, "You good to get back then?"

"You good to get Onyxus back?" Isaac asked in return.

Maximus laughed a little and pushed Isaac's head playfully. "Get out of here," he said.

Isaac was smiling. He always felt good when he brought some humor into a dark situation. But then he got serious again. "Hurry, alright? It's not long now until Stella needs to show herself to Gershon."

"I know," said Maximus, "Now, take Helios and go. Try to land softly this time now that you are conscious. I don't want the beach looking like Swiss cheese with all the craters."

Isaac smiled. "I'll do my best."

"Do not . . . I repeat, do *not* open that glass or touch that crystal."

Isaac looked down at it. "Can I transform it, too?"

"I would think so. Dreold did. However, such dark

objects might be unyielding to be affected by anybody other than its maker, or for the use it was intended for. I guess all you can do is try. Do it now."

Isaac carried the glass cylinder in his hands and went to Helios. Helios dropped his head almost all the way to the ground so it was level with Isaac's torso. Isaac touched his head, and then began saying his affirmations to himself in his mind. He was getting really fast at transforming himself, and immediately felt that he was an energy field. Then, just as immediately, he felt a very familiar electric shock radiate up the atoms where his arm would be.

"Stop!" he heard Maximus yell. Isaac returned to form, which he immediately realized was a mistake. The crystal inside of it was spinning and vibrating—clearly resisting Isaac's transformation. The glass cylinder had grown so hot that it burned the flesh on Isaac's hand. Isaac yelled in pain and dropped the cylinder. It did not break, but landed painfully on his foot.

Helios grabbed the back of Isaac's shirt in his teeth, hoisted him up off the ground and moved him away from the cylinder. When Helios set him down, Isaac cradled his burned hand next to his chest. Maximus came over to him quickly. "Let me see," he said.

Isaac reluctantly gave Maximus his hand.

"I think since it was just the glass cylinder that burned you and not the crystal itself, you should be scar free. Stella should be able to heal you right away," Maximus said.

"Why wouldn't she be able to heal it if it was the crystal I touched?"

Maximus looked grave and serious as he said, "Isaac, you can never touch or be touched by something made by such dark forces without it leaving its mark on you. Do you understand?"

Isaac nodded.

Maximus let go of Isaac's hand and said, "Leave without

this," he pointed to the crystal, "go back to the lighthouse and have Stella heal your hand."

"And leave it here around Onyxus? No way."

"Do you think I am not capable of protecting it?"

"I didn't mean that, Maximus. And plus, if Stella sees me, she'll never let me go free those prisoners."

"Perhaps she would be right."

"No, she wouldn't. Take Rikenzia for example. She was there! You won't meet a more loyal person to us. Those people need out, and this is our only chance."

"You win," said Maximus. "Though, you still need be healed before we go."

"You can do it, right Maximus?"

"I . . . I haven't done it in a very long time, and I don't have as much of the gift running through my blood as Stella does."

"But, you can still."

They locked eyes. Isaac saw a hint of doubt in Maximus' eyes which unsettled him. He prompted, "Well, you can, can't you?"

"Y . . . yes. Here, give me your hand."

Isaac saw for the first time what this gift of healing was all about. Maximus held his hands around Isaac's hand. In just a moment, an orb of light formed there and it grew so hot, Isaac almost pulled his hand free from it. But then, a wonderful cool came over his hand as the orb of light turned blue. Maximus withdrew his hands as the light disappeared.

Isaac looked at his hand. The pain was gone and it looked and felt better than new. He looked up at Maximus and was surprised by what met his eyes. Maximus was curled over on the floor, looking like he was holding in a yell of pain. "Maximus? Maximus! What's wrong?" Isaac was starting to panic when Maximus didn't answer him after a moment then finally sat up.

Isaac let out his breath and with a confused expression

asked, "What happened?"

"When the pain left you, it had to go somewhere, and it usually transfers into the healer, and is usually much stronger."

"You didn't tell me that would happen. I wouldn't have let you."

"Old news," said Maximus, "Let's get moving. Stella is probably having a fit by now." He got to his feet. Isaac stood up as well.

"How are Stella and Rikenzia going to know we're not coming back, and to go on without us? And, do you really think Stella will be fine going there alone? I don't really think she will."

Maximus answered him, "Frankly, Isaac, I don't know what to do right now, because it seems like you both need me a whole lot."

"Go with Stella," Isaac said.

Maximus answered, "She'll be even more distracted and vulnerable with worry about you if I am not with you."

Isaac knew that was true.

"Excuse me," said a soft voice. It was Zordosa. "Why don't you send me back to where Stella is, and I will tell her what has happened. And I can accompany her in your place, if she'll have me."

Sarge stepped forward. "But, it could be dangerous, and I need you here with me."

"Sarge, you can manage here quite well without me. I haven't ever done much here anyway. I want to do this for Stella."

Sarge was silent. Isaac thought it was a perfect idea, but waited for Maximus' response. Maximus was silent in his response for several long moments and Isaac's anxiety was at the bursting point.

"Yes," Maximus said finally, "that is a good idea."

Isaac exhaled as if he had been holding his breath for too

long and was practically bouncing on his feet now. The deadline for Stella's appearance was close. "Alright," he said, "let's send her and get going."

Sarge looked surprised and he said, "The Dragon?"

Alethia said, "I will stay until they return to take him away."

Helios walked over to her and Isaac felt a pang as he realized the danger her only son was going through, and that Helios probably feared for her safety too. It made Isaac miss his own mother again. Alethia and Helios were talking in low voices and Isaac turned back to Maximus and the Horses to give them privacy.

Maximus had his hands tenderly on either side of Zordosa's cheeks and was speaking to her. He was giving her directions to give Stella.

Sarge interrupted again, "What about the Star Charm? What if I need to call you again?"

Maximus let go of Zordosa's face. "You are right, Sarge, I am sorry. Just remember, I won't be at the Telescope for a while." He moved quickly to Zordosa's mane and squeezed the Star Charm out of the braid he had placed it in, then moved swiftly over to Sarge and braided it into his mane, down by the wither. "Say goodbye quickly Sarge, we all need to go."

Sarge went to his mother and nudged her muzzle. They said their quick good byes and last minute words of encouragement. Then, Maximus placed his hands on her face again, and in another moment, the form of Zordosa was glistening like thousands of diamonds. Maximus shoved his hands forward like he was pushing her away and just like that, she was gone.

Maximus turned immediately to Isaac and said, "We have only a little bit of time. It's hard to say exactly when Stella will appear to Gershon and we should leave, but I should teach you how to shield yourself, at least."

Isaac was ignoring the river of multiple emotions racing through him. "Let's do it," he said determinately.

CHAPTER 42

"We want supporters who will help us grow, who will tell us the truth even when it is difficult to hear. We want those who will keep us focused on the vision . . . Once you have your team, let them help you strategize the steps of your mission, reminding you who you are, nudging you back on course when you begin to stray and holding your vision for you when you become discouraged."

Stella

When Stella, Rikenzia, and Arrow were pulled back through the Telescope they all moved over to the windows and looked out on the beach. Stella did not want to be down there when they brought Onyxus back.

They watched and waited, then watched and waited some more. Stella walked around the perimeter of the top most room, looking on all sides for any sign of them. Finally, she burst out, "Where are they?"

She looked at Rikenzia who looked equally as worried. Rikenzia said, "Maybe they're having trouble with Onyxus?"

Stella had flashes of Onyxus injuring somebody and tried to push those images out. "Maybe," she answered, "but Isaac and Helios were supposed to come immediately after us while Maximus and Alethia dealt with Onyxus."

Rikenzia shrugged, eyes worried.

Stella had an awful thought, and she felt angry. "They tricked us! They wanted me out of there!" She darted over to the Telescope. "I'm going back."

Arrow spoke up. "My lady, they have no reason to trick you. I don't think that is what they did. Please just stay here and wait."

"But, my brother!"

"I am sure he is well protected," said Arrow.

Stella looked at the time, and she looked at the sun beginning its rise on the horizon. Her stomach knotted again.

She'd have to go soon, whether it meant Maximus and Isaac got back or not. She knew how to get to the Star she intended, but she had not a clue what to do once she got there. The knots in her stomach turned rancid and she thought she was going to be sick.

"Stella," said Arrow and he came to stand next to her, "I know that when you are faced with something unpleasant to do, you must not think of all the negatives. I think for us to be successful on this journey, we must try and find some joy. What are some positive things we can think about?"

Stella tried to think about what she was about to do and where she was about to go. Vega — in the Constellation, Lyra. In the Summer Triangle. She was a princess there. She said in a soft voice, "Maximus said I might have family on Vega, and that they will love me there . . . like they loved my mother."

"Good," said Arrow, "I am excited to meet them, too. I suppose I can share you with them." He nudged her lightly in the stomach.

She smiled at him.

"Should I just stay here then?" Stella heard Rikenzia say from where the Telescope stood. Stella looked at her and was conflicted about what to do for a moment. She wanted all the support she could get, but she also thought that she wanted someone to wait in case anybody came back.

Rikenzia jumped back from the Telescope and Stella could immediately see why. Both lenses had started glowing bright and looked hot to touch. Stella and Arrow walked slowly to it and stood next to Rikenzia who was staring at it wide-eyed. A mass of light — billions of specs — came out of the eye piece and then formed themselves into a Winged Horse. The specs of light turned into their mass and then Zordosa stood in front of them.

Stella and Arrow rushed up to her. Before they could ask her any questions, she said, "That was the best sensation!"

"What are you doing here, Zorri? What is wrong?" asked

Arrow.

"Where are Maximus and Isaac?" prompted Stella.

"Everybody is unharmed, child. Isaac tried to transform and come back here with the crystal. But, it would not transform, and it burned his hand."

Stella and Rikenzia both gasped.

"Maximus was able to heal him. Because time is running very short, and because they did not want to leave the crystal alone near the black Dragon, they decided to stay, work on some new skills for Isaac, and then go directly to the Lair."

Stella felt hurt, but didn't interrupt Zordosa.

"I volunteered to come to you, Stella, to tell you all of this, and . . . well . . . and to accompany you on your journey if you will have me."

All of this information was a lot to process and Stella did not answer Zordosa right away. It was a slightly awkward pause, and Zordosa said, "I have instructions from Maximus. I can give them to you now, and then stay here if you'd like."

Stella felt relieved that Maximus had sent a message for her. "I want you to come, Zordosa," she said, "definitely. You as well, Rikenzia. Please, come with me too."

"Of course, Stella," Rikenzia answered.

"Alright," she said and looked at Zordosa, "What did Maximus tell you?"

"He told me to tell you what to visualize to arrive on Vega. He said to picture a glass castle, as large as ten houses put together. Inside the castle is a room that is heavily decorated in flowers, with a throne in the front which has a picture of your mother and you when you were a baby."

Stella could picture it, and she longed to be there. She wanted to see that picture. She didn't know if she could talk without revealing her emotions, so she nodded to indicate she understood.

"Are we ready, then?" asked Arrow.

"Yes," said Stella, "everybody stay close to me when we

get there — until I get in front of the Telescope. Wait, Zordosa, did Maximus say how to work the Telescope?"

"Yes, child, he did."

"Good. We all need to be touching to transform and go together."

Without another word, they all turned to face the eye piece of the Telescope. Stella had a lot of things she felt were powering her forward: keeping her brother safe, the support of her friends, and returning to the place where her mother had lived.

"Anything else, Zorri?" she asked one more time.

"He said good luck, and he knows you can do this, and he loves you."

Stella nodded her head. This didn't sound weird to her. Now that she knew he was her Uncle, a lot of things made sense. She knew she loved him, too.

"Ready?" she asked.

"Ready," they all said together.

She reached out for Rikenzia's hand. Rikenzia took it, then reached out and touched Zordosa's neck. Stella touched Arrow's. Arrow and Zordosa lifted up their inside wings up high so that they touched together at the tips over the girls' heads.

"Everybody think of that room. You know everything else you need to think of by now. Light and energy. Let's go."

She closed her eyes and pictured them all going as one. It worked.

CHAPTER 43

"One way to master your mind is to learn to quiet your mind."

Isaac

Isaac and Maximus moved more into the open, far away from the tree line. Alethia paced a circle around them looking all directions for a reappearance of Onyxus. The Winged Horses had returned to their hiding place.

Isaac was listening intently to Maximus as he told him about creating a shield. He was saying, "If atoms are everywhere, that means the air is thick with them, right?"

"Right," said Isaac.

"So, if you want to protect yourself from unwanted outside forces, you can cause the atoms around you to 'meld' together and create an invisible barrier."

"How do I do that?"

"The barrier starts at your heart, and all the atoms in and around it will be affected as it radiates outwards—melding together until it completely surrounds you."

"Yes, but how?"

"Isaac, you know how. It's in your blood. You have the capability to affect the matter and atoms around you—change them, mix them, un-mix them. You've done it many times already."

"Visualization and affirmations."

"Yes. The atoms will listen to you. Visualize them protecting you. It's not easy Isaac. To protect yourself with a barrier properly, you have to be very internally focused. You have to be aware of what is going on outside your barrier, but if you are not focusing on you—the beating of your heart, your breathing, and about keeping yourself guarded—whatever you are trying to keep out will be able to get in."

"That doesn't sound too hard," said Isaac.

"Well, it is hard. Gershon and Dreold know this one,

don't they? They will know if they can break your concentration, they can get through. They'll do anything Isaac. And . . ." he faltered, "well, Dreold killed your parents. He has a lot he could say to get through to you."

Isaac's stomach gave a painful twinge. For the first time since deciding to use the crystal, he thought maybe he wasn't up for the task after all.

Maximus said, "Do you know what you *can* do?"

"What," said Isaac in a monotone and barely audible voice.

"More than I can," answered Maximus.

Isaac looked at him, puzzled. "What do you mean? You know way more than I do."

"For now, maybe that is true. But, my mother was not the Princess of Vega, born with amazing powers of her own."

Isaac didn't answer.

Maximus went on, "With her blood running through your veins who knows what else your barrier can do? It's an intriguing thought."

"Are you sure we should do this?" he asked.

"Are you kidding me Isaac? After all of this, now you want to back out?"

Isaac felt ashamed. "No, you're right. I don't." He decided to be honest and added, "You just made me nervous talking about how I might not be able to hold my shield because they'll use my parents death to get to me."

Maximus didn't answer right away. He looked solemn when he said, "I'm sorry, Isaac. Like I said before, you are bound to have more powers than me, and I don't doubt that you can do anything you put your mind to. I just wanted you to understand that it was not in fact easy — that a lot of your effort will be needed."

"I understand," said Isaac.

"Are you ready to practice now?"

"Yes."

"I want you to look straight at me, the person who wants to slap you, while you put up your barrier. You have to be able to focus internally without closing your eyes because for this exercise you need to keep your eyes on what you are protecting yourself from. Do you think you can do that?"

"I'll try my best."

Isaac became stunned for a moment, because something just smacked him in the face. It took him a second to understand that it had been Maximus' open hand.

"Guard yourself," Maximus said, "I'm going to hit you again."

"You don't have to —" SMACK.

"Ow!"

"You can keep me out!" Maximus shouted. "Do it now."

Maximus hooked Isaac behind the knee with his foot and pulled his leg out from underneath him. Isaac fell to the ground.

"Isaac!"

Isaac saw Maximus' foot moving toward his fingers and he jumped off the ground and spun away from Maximus, keeping him in sight.

They started walking a circle around each other. Isaac was having a hard time focusing on what he needed to do without being able to stop and think properly. But, he tried. He focused on the breath going in and out of his lungs. He envisioned his heart, guarded by the atoms around it forming together to become impenetrable.

A monologue began running in his mind. *I can see Maximus, but I feel my own breath. He's getting ready to hit me again. My heart feels strong. He cannot hurt me. I have control. I am guarded. The atoms around me can meld and protect me.*

Isaac and Maximus stopped and faced each other square. Isaac willed the atoms around him to form together and protect him from outside forces. At that moment, Maximus ran at Isaac and for a moment Isaac was shocked because

Maximus looked mean and crazed. Maximus hit something invisible right in front of Isaac, and looked frustrated, but only briefly. Isaac lost his focus and Maximus broke through and grabbed Isaac around the neck.

He said, "Isaac, your barrier didn't hold."

Isaac just stared back up at Maximus. Maximus let go. "I knew you were accomplishing it, so I tried to distract you by looking like I truly wanted to hurt you. Do it again. This time—no matter what—hold your barrier. Be aware of me, but focus on you and your shield. Alright?"

Isaac nodded. He felt a little dumb. Of course Maximus wasn't really going to hurt him. Maximus paced around him again. Isaac watched him—aware of his movements, but concentrating internally and going through his monologue again. This time, as he asked the atoms to form together around him, he could feel a sense of solidity. It was like he was a figurine in the middle of a thick glass snow globe. He focused on that image.

He heard Maximus running up behind him, but Isaac knew he would not get through because his barrier would not let him down. Isaac felt a small push from behind, but nothing else had changed. Then, he saw Maximus walk around to face him. He was rubbing his arm. Maximus stopped and smiled at Isaac. "Ow," he said. He reached his finger forward and poked Isaac's shield. His finger looked like it was pressed up against glass. "It's a good one Isaac. I'm impressed."

Isaac returned the smile. Maximus' praise was something he highly valued.

Maximus looked around at the Dragons and Horses. "Well, I suppose we need to use that crystal and go soon. Stella should be in her mother's castle by now. You can take your shield down."

Dropping his shield was actually the last thing Isaac wanted to do. He liked how it made him feel. But, it was time to go, so he released the atoms. He and Maximus walked over to Helios, who stood with the glass cylinder containing the crystal between his front legs.

Isaac looked up at his golden companion, "Are you sure you want to do this?"

Helios looked down at him and held his gaze for a moment. Then he said, "Am I sure I want to go back to that place? No, I don't. But am I sure I want to keep you from touching the crystal? Yes."

"Thank you, Helios," said Isaac.

Maximus said, "Well, let's make sure Stella does not do her part in vain. Helios — when you're ready."

Helios got down on one knee to allow Maximus and Isaac to climb onto his back. Isaac was careful to avoid touching spots which were burned from those awful electrical spears. He wondered briefly if Helios' damaged scales would grow back as golden and shiny as the other, unharmed ones.

"Grip tight," said Helios, "I am going to rear up and stomp on this case to break it."

Before Isaac could protest to this plan because he knew it would slice open the Dragon's paw, Helios reared up and Isaac caught hold of Helios' scaly neck and Maximus was gripping the back of Isaac. Helios went down with a lot of force. Isaac cringed as he heard the glass shatter. All was a whirlwind as he felt a rip forward. There was no turning back.

CHAPTER 44

*"Pure energy — that's all fear is. Fear has no intelligence . . .
Like any energy . . . it can paralyze us. When harnessed to our
dreams, it is converted into useable energy, into excitement . . . it
supplies us with the fuel to accomplish [our mission]."*

Stella

When Stella materialized and looked at the picture in
front of her of her mom and herself, she saw it was the same
picture that was in their house on the mountains. She missed
looking at it and couldn't peel her eyes away.

Looking at the picture made her miss her mother with
renewed pain—like a scab being ripped off a wound that
wasn't ready. As she was struggling to keep the tears from
escaping, she heard a soft 'clip-clop' come up behind her. It
was Zordosa.

Almost in a whisper, she said, "Maximus told me to keep
you moving darling. The Telescope is up those stairs over
there."

Stella looked to where Zordosa had indicated with a nod
of her head. She saw big, glass blocks formed together as
stairs that spiraled to the right and out of sight. Stella found
herself unable to move toward them. "What am I going to say
to him?" she asked in a hushed voice. "What am I supposed
to do?"

Zordosa answered her, "Maximus said to follow your
heart, and don't let Gershon bully you. He said to tell you
that Gershon can't physically hurt you through the
Telescopes. Stand your ground, and remember how many
people love and will love you."

"Wow, Zorri," Stella said, "You have a great memory."

"A Horse's blessing and a curse."

Stella looked at Rikenzia, who had been very silent so far,
and reached out her hand for her. Rikenzia walked forward

and took it. Stella wondered if Rikenzia felt awkward, but Stella needed the comfort and support. Together, they walked up the glass stairs and the Winged Horses followed them.

When they neared the top of the stairs, Stella's heart was marching a fast rhythm. Rikenzia squeezed her hand.

The top of the tower was like a large gazebo—made of glass. There was a railing, a roof that was at least twenty feet tall and held up by glass pillars. Stella then saw the Telescope and it too was made of glass. Stella stepped to it and ran her fingers over it tenderly. "Zorri," she said, "Did Maximus tell you how to work this?"

"Yes. He said to point it to the sky, and also to stand in front of it. We want to put it up close to the edge, so all Gershon will see is your face and the sky."

Arrow nudged Stella toward the edge and said, "Sit down." She leaned against the edge. Rikenzia was gently sliding the Telescope over to be directly in front of Stella and positioned it as Zordosa had said.

"Now," said Zordosa, "Reach out and touch both sides of it."

Stella obeyed. She felt like she was holding somebody's face in her hands. She could see her own face reflected back at her from the magnifying glass, upside down. She looked terrified. Instantly she resolved to try and look a little less like an animal facing slaughter. Stella had expected additional instructions from Zordosa, but the Telescope had begun glowing with a purplish blue light.

Stella heard Zordosa say, "Excellent. Maximus said it should recognize you. Now, tell it, "Broadcast to Gershon's Telescope."

Stella's eyes flickered over to them, anxiety coursing through her.

"You can do it my lady," said Arrow. "You can save many lives."

Stella nodded, trying to look more reassured than she felt.

She turned back to look at her reflection in the glowing telescope and said, "Broadcast to Gershon's telescope."

A clear white sheet of light came out of the lens and scanned her up and down. Stella felt a little tingly. The light went back in. Then the magnifying glass changed so it looked liquid. It cleared and Stella saw the image of a man so foul, it could be no other than Gershon.

He leered at her. His voice came out through the Telescope, "Well, well, well. If you aren't the spitting image of Eli's unfortunate bride. I'll tell you princess, you sure like to wait until the last minute. I have a line of prisoners here, all waiting for you to betray them like Orel and Eli did."

Stella's courage came to her like a wave meeting the shore. She measured her voice and said, "The betrayal is not on their end, Gershon."

"Hoo hoo hoooo," he said, eyes widening for a second, "Don't you sound like the princess the Zodians have been *dying* to meet."

Stella heard a distant scream come through the Telescope and felt her breath pick up speed. But again, with a measured voice, she said, "Now, Gershon, are you so cowardly as to not hold to your word? You said if I showed myself their lives would be spared."

"Actually," he said, pointing his finger at her mockingly, "I said if you didn't show up, I'd kill them. I didn't say anything about what would happen if you did."

She said, "I think relinquishing your word would be a very childish thing to do."

He flared his nostrils and said maniacally, "Childish? There is only one child here darling, and that is you."

She answered him back, "I am prepared to talk with you as an adult."

He laughed and said, "Isn't that cute," which made her feel childish again, but she kept her back straight and her chin held high. She wondered briefly if Maximus, Isaac and Helios were making it through their mission, but didn't allow herself to dwell on it, because she needed to focus on herself and Gershon.

"Alright then!" he said, rather louder than necessary. "If you want to converse as *adults*, we'll converse as adults. Now, tell me, where are you?"

Stella glanced over the Telescope at Rikenzia and the Horses who were standing close.

"Ah," Gershon said, "I see you have supporters there with you."

"Yes, I do," she said, "Many of them. And they are willing to fight for me."

"No need to get all violent now princess! We're not talking about war here! Your mother would not approve. Tsk, tsk."

"My mother taught me to protect my family."

Gershon's voice took on an edge of hostility. "Speaking of your family—where is your brother?"

Stella felt a flush come to her face and she hoped Gershon could not see it. She answered, "He is protected."

Gershon did not say anything for a moment, he just stared at her. As much as she wanted to look away from him, she didn't. It was very awkward for several long moments.

Finally, he said, "I suppose you are as adamant as your mother, and will protect that little whelp no matter what I do?"

She swallowed, hoping he would not test his theory, "That is correct."

He stared strangely at her for a little longer. For a moment, Stella thought he was going to threaten something terrible, but to her surprise, he said, his annoyance thinly masked, "Very well, we'll deal with Isaac later. You do, however, need to tell me where *you* are."

She was thinking quickly of what to say, but Gershon interrupted her, "Actually, I don't need you to tell me. I can figure it out. See, I already know that you aren't on any of the Zodiacs—because I know when those Telescopes are being used. So, you are either using Orel's own Telescope, which I lost track of, or you're using your mother's—both of which make sense."

Stella was worried she had just given her mother's people more danger than they wanted. She thought quick. "How do you know there hasn't been more made?"

Gershon gritted his teeth and flared his nostrils, looking like a pit bull about to bite. "I would know about it. If Orel comes anywhere near the Zodiacs, I would know."

"How do you know that it is only he who can make them?"

Gershon's lip curled. "You're trying my mercy and patience Stella."

To Stella's surprise, she almost laughed at Gershon saying he had mercy and patience. But she knew better than to goad him by laughing. She was still fighting herself not to tremble in front of him and she did not want to provoke him more.

"Now," he said with a slight growl in his voice, "let's talk business. There is no point for you and your brother to fight against me. YOUR PARENTS ARE GONE," he shouted, "And I killed them. The Zodians follow me. They worship me and what I have done for them. They will never follow you."

"There are still those who resist you and wait for Orel."

"Oh, you mean the ones who are shackled and bound here and in little hidey-holes on the Zodiacs?"

"Have they ever agreed to join you and abandon Orel?"

Gershon paused for a moment and looked to his side. He turned back to look at her and with a curl in his lip said, "No, pretty little princess. Actually, they haven't. Thank you for waking me up to the fact that they are useless to me and I should dispose of them immediately."

Stella felt sick. Of course that is not what she meant at all. She felt like a foreigner in her own body because she kept saying such grown-up and 'queenly' things. She said, "You can break your promises to your Minions, but you will not break your promises with me, or I can never trust you to negotiate with you."

Gershon turned a violent shade of puce-red. Through gritted teeth he said, "You and your brother have a terrible habit of thinking you can order me around. I refuse to be bossed around by anybody—especially CHILDREN who are descendent of my greatest enemy!"

"You were the one who made yourself my grandfather's enemy," Stella thought she might be pushing her luck—but she had to keep him there and talking. To her horror, she knew she had indeed pushed her luck too far when he put his face closer to the Telescope so Stella could see the veins in his eyes and said, "What you don't know is I have groups of Zodians gathered for 'assemblies'. Large groups. Ten-thousand in number each—at least. For each prisoner I have shackled here that dies, ten-thousand from the Constellation they are from die as well."

Then he turned to his side and said, "This one is a Gemini. Servant! I don't want to see that stupid Gemini traitor in my face anymore!"

Stella heard a scuffle and a distant scream that kept getting further and further away—like it was falling. Stella felt her face lose its color as her body became weak.

"Say good-bye to ten-thousand-and-one Gemini's!" Then he laughed like he had just told an amusing joke.

She saw Arrow, Zordosa and Rikenzia take a step toward her but she shook her head quickly at them. She was fighting back tears.

She and Gershon were looking at each other again—Gershon with a crazed and eerily happy look. "That's better, princess," he said, being mockingly kind.

Stella wondered how much longer she must keep this up for Maximus and Isaac, and if she'd be able to get through it without getting anybody else killed.

CHAPTER 45

"Decisions are constantly before us. To make them wisely,
courage is needed — the courage to say no, the courage to
say yes. Decisions do *determine destiny."*

Isaac

The moment after Isaac had felt the rip forward from Helios stomping on the crystal, he fell off the Dragon and was thrown onto some familiar cold and damp slate floor. He scrambled up quickly and was more relieved than he cared to admit that they were alone in the throne room. The green, snake-like reflections from the pool of water brought back unpleasant memories that made him want to get away from there as quickly as possible.

He looked behind him and saw Maximus kneeling on the ground, already attending to Helios' paw, which was leaving a small pool of blood on the slate floor. "I'm going to need your help with this Isaac," Maximus said, "Just hold your hands around him and I'll teach you how to heal him."

"No!" said Helios, "I will not have this pain pass into him."

"Shh," Isaac said.

Maximus said quietly, "Helios, we can get rid of this injury, and the pain. Yes, it will hurt, but we can get rid of it."

"No," he said with a great amount of force, "it can wait. We're in a hurry."

"What about the blood?" asked Isaac.

Helios said, "Wrap something around it."

Isaac looked frantically around for something. He saw a large fur draped over Gershon's throne. Did he dare? He ran to it, paused for a second, and then ripped it down. He hauled it back to Helios, laid it on the floor in front of him and told him to step on it. Once he did, Isaac and Maximus folded it up around his paw. Maximus ripped a piece off his shirt and tied it around Helios ankle to keep the fur on, pulling and tugging on it as tight as he could—Helios trying not to groan.

"Thank you," said Helios. "What do we do now, Isaac?"

"We go through that door," he pointed, "and get to the prison."

Looking at the door, they all realized the same problem at the same time. "I can't fit through there Isaac," said Helios.

"Uh," Isaac said, searching for what he wanted to do about this. Maximus saved him and said, "We can short-distance travel directly into the prison."

"Really?" Isaac asked.

"Yes, really. For short distance travel, you need to have been there before—which you have. You need to visualize with exactness right where you want to appear. Since you have been the only one to be in there, you must take *us* with *you*."

Isaac didn't exactly feel relieved by this. First, he'd never done it before, and this was kind of important. Secondly, Helios wouldn't fit in there either. When Isaac told Helios this, he said, "You two go, and I will stay here and fight Gershon if he should become wise to your presence."

Maximus and Isaac looked at each other. Isaac said, "But Helios, he hurt you so bad last time."

Helios did not look concerned. "Last time, he caught me unaware. Last time, I did not get to see you and Maximus prepare to shield yourself. Dragons have abilities and powers of our own you know."

Isaac started to respond, but Helios cut him off, "Go. Quickly."

Isaac reached out and touched Helios's wing briefly, trying to convey that he thought Helios was noble and brave. Helios nodded his head.

Maximus said, "Alright, everything is pretty much the same for short-distance travel, but *no crash landings*. You must concentrate on keeping yourself together—light as air, tight into yourself. Does that make sense?"

Isaac nodded.

"Then visualize the exact place you want to appear, and tell yourself to go there — think as if you are already there. See the sights, smell the smells, etcetera. Good?"

"Yes," said Isaac. Maximus was talking rushed, but Isaac had the idea. He was pretty sure he could do it. He decided to appear right at the switch for the electricity and could see it perfectly. "Ready to go?" he asked Maximus.

In response, Maximus stood arm in arm with him.

"There is probably going to be a guard or two standing directly where I am putting us," added Isaac.

"Thanks for the warning. Let's go."

They transformed and Isaac thought "go" and their mass of light and energy flashed away.

Isaac managed to stay upright and landed precisely where he meant to. Exactly as Isaac had suspected, the guards were standing there. Luckily, the shock of seeing people materialize right before them stunned them long enough for Maximus to jump into action and restrain one of them. He grabbed his arm and twisted it up behind his back and put his other arm around the guards neck. The other guard panicked and jumped toward the switch that would shock all the prisoners.

Isaac jumped deftly in between the man and the switch, grabbed his wrist and slammed it against the wall. He pushed against the man's arm with both hands, but this guard was a lot stronger than the pathetic one that was there before. He was pushing back against Isaac and with his free arm grabbed Isaac's shirt and was pulling him up into the air. Isaac could think of only one thing to do. Shield himself.

He wasn't sure how it would work with somebody already grabbing onto him, but it was his first instinct, so he did it. He could feel the guard's violent intent, but Isaac was more aware of himself. The atoms and molecules around his heart formed together and radiated outward. When the shield reached the guard's hand, it seemed to have zapped him. He yelled and let go of Isaac. The guard stood stunned, just staring at Isaac.

Isaac ran fast at the guard and slammed into his belly with his shoulder. The guard stumbled backward, hit his head on the stone wall, and was still.

Isaac was horrified rather than triumphant. Did he just kill him? He didn't see any blood but he looked as lifeless as ever.

He turned around at the sound of scuffling. Maximus stood strong while the guard he was holding flailed around. In just another moment, the guard went limp and Maximus laid him on the ground. He must have seen Isaac's horrified expression, because he knelt down and felt for a pulse on the guard who had hit the stone wall. Isaac held his breath and after a moment, Maximus said, "He's alive—just unconscious."

Isaac nodded then they moved the guards together and Isaac started searching for something to bind them up with. All he could find were some loose chains. He brought them over and they wrapped them around the two guards. Maximus quickly tightened the chain and then wrapped his hands around them. Isaac saw a quick flash of light and when Maximus removed his hands, the chains were melded together. He looked at Isaac and said, "Now what?"

Isaac turned and looked down the aisle. He could see a few faces trying to peer up out of their cave cells without touching the bars. A low murmur started and people were now putting their hands on the bars.

Isaac said quickly to Maximus, "When I broke out of here before, I transformed the bars by touching them. We could do that to let everyone out."

"Perfect. Talk to them—tell them what is going on."

He walked down the aisle and said, "I am Isaac—son of

Eli. This man and I are here to set you free. When your bars transform into light, step into the aisle."

In a hurry now, Isaac and Maximus got to work. Isaac glanced to see if there was somebody inside—there were many empty—and then transformed the bars, then moved on to the next. Those who were set free were moving down the aisle behind them and helping everybody step through the lights. The specs of light just dissolved and the bars did not return.

When they got to the end of the detention passageway, Isaac turned around to see about two dozen faces looking back at him. They were all varying in ages from a young kid, to the elderly.

Isaac noticed how battered and extremely skinny they were. They looked physically weak and Isaac hoped they'd be able to withstand the escape. But although they looked physically weak, their countenances were bright and hopeful, even though a little frightened.

Somebody moved their way up through the prisoners. When the person reached the front of the crowd, Isaac saw a woman, about the same age as Maximus. Her dark hair was tattered and matted to her head, and although she was thin beyond belief, Isaac could see that she had probably been very nice looking.

Maximus walked up to her looking stunned. "Chantelle?" he asked.

She answered with a voice so quiet Isaac could barely hear her, "Maximus? We thought you were dead."

"I know. I'm sorry. Cecily knew I was alive—but she was sworn to secrecy." He faltered for a moment and then asked, "How . . . how is she?"

Chantelle looked grave. "Last I knew, she was still in hiding and still safe. It is more difficult than ever to remain hidden."

Maximus turned back to Isaac and Isaac saw him make an

effort to erase the concern off his face. He said, "We must hurry."

Isaac nodded. He knew they must hurry but he hadn't a clue how to get them all out quickly from here. He didn't think he could transport so many different beings at the same time. If only they had a Telescope they could use.

Wait, Isaac thought, *there IS a Telescope we can use!*

"Maximus," Isaac said, "What about using the Telescope that is here?"

Maximus did not answer right away. After a moment he said, "Remember what I told you about the crystal? How you can't use or touch something so evil without being scarred forever by it?"

Isaac nodded.

"That Telescope was not made by Orel so I can only guess Gershon made it himself. So using it could scar these people permanently."

No one spoke for a moment. Chantelle asked, "Is there another way?"

Isaac looked at Maximus for an answer because he could not think of another way.

Maximus said, "I cannot think of another way. We do not know where we are in the Universe and it is protected from being found so we couldn't get back if we tried to take you one by one. We were only able to get here with a crystal transporter that was not meant for us."

Isaac added, "You do not have to risk using the Telescope. I understand if any of you do not want to come."

Chantelle said, "Isaac, you and Maximus have come to save us. We are loyal to Orel which means we are loyal to you. We are getting out of here with you no matter how we have to do it."

He looked behind her to the other prisoners. Through the dirt and weariness on their faces, he saw hope. As he looked at them, they nodded their heads in agreement with her.

Feeling bolstered by them, Isaac said, "There should be a way outside of this cave to get around to the ledge where the Telescope is."

"Out the door by the front?" asked Maximus.

"Yes, we'll try to find a way outside." Isaac answered.

"Wait!" a young voice at the back of the crowd shouted.

"What is it?" Isaac asked.

"We want to get outside?" the young voice asked back, now a little closer.

"Yes," said Isaac.

A young boy emerged from the crowd, very pale and very little. "Then we should go up!" he said, the confidence in his voice not matching how meager he looked. "The ground above is not very far above our heads."

Maximus and Isaac again exchanged glances. Isaac asked, "Can we do that?"

The young boy answered, "I've already started to make a hole in the cell I was in."

"What is your name, young man?" Maximus asked.

"Cael."

"Ok Cael, take us there!"

CHAPTER 46

*"The only way anything has ever been invented or
created is because one person saw a picture in his mind.
He saw it clearly, and by holding that picture of the end
result in his mind, all the forces of the Universe brought his
invention into [reality] through him."*

Maximus

Maximus was more impressed by Isaac than he could ever explain to anyone—he was so gifted for having so little instruction. Even though he was the son of Eli and Isolde and this was to be expected, Maximus still found it extraordinary. Without the natural-born leader in Isaac, Maximus would not be there, in the very lair of the man his entire family had fled from. Without Isaac, Cecily's sister Chantelle would still be here being tortured.

Isaac and Maximus were working their way through the people following this little boy to his cell.

Isaac asked Maximus, "What are we doing exactly?"

"We are going to heat a spot in the stone ceiling until it becomes molten rock and comes down. Then we will cool it very fast and it will harden like the sand on our beach where you landed the first time. Then we'll have something to step onto to climb out."

"How do we heat things?"

"Again," Maximus said, "it is about concentrating on molecules. We want the molecules inside the cave ceiling to shake together rapidly, like they would do to create fire. They will heat up and the rock will melt."

Isaac looked thoughtful for a moment then asked, "How do we cool it?"

Maximus said, "Leave that to me this time and I'll teach you later."

They had arrived at the cell Cael was in. Looking inside,

Maximus could not see anything — it was complete darkness. The little boy said, "Now you can see how nobody saw me."

Maximus felt a surge of affection for this little boy. He was always thrilled when he met someone from the Zodiacs who had broken past limitations and began discovering what they could do. And for this boy to do it in such dismal circumstances, especially for one so young was incredible.

"Follow me slowly," said Cael.

They took six or seven steps in and then Cael said, "Stop." They stopped, and couldn't see anything. "The hole I started is right above us, if you step forward a little, you can feel the mound that has hardened there."

Maximus pushed his foot forward until he found it. Without wasting any time, he grabbed the boys' shoulders and positioned them on opposite sides of the mound. He said to them, "Hold your hands up and arms wide and face your palms in towards each other. Then, rotate your arms back and forth so you are creating a large circle above your head. Start small and as it starts to melt and come down, back up until our hole is about three feet wide. Shake the atoms together to get them hot. It will work."

He could hear their feet shifting on the ground as they rotated their arms through the air. A few long moments passed. Maximus could feel his every heartbeat. The room became a little brighter. Maximus looked up and saw a spot in the ceiling begin to glow red hot. Then, a drip of molten rock fell down onto the mound. A few more drops fell until it became a thin stream, like out of a faucet.

"Excellent boys. Keep it going and start backing up a little."

The stream of molten rock became wider. Maximus focused on his part of the job — cooling and hardening the rock after it fell.

Maximus had to step backward as the boys' stream of molten rock had now turned into a hollow circle about a foot wide.

"Almost done!" Maximus said, crouched down and circling around the boys, cooling and hardening the rock all the way around. The circle kept getting wider and then after a moment, the molten rock stopped falling down. Maximus stopped when he was done and stood up straight.

Through the hole in the ceiling, they could now see the sky. Maximus looked toward the opening of Cael's cell, and in the dim light, he could see Chantelle standing there, with many other faces trying to peer inside. Maximus turned back to the mound and tested it with his foot. When it stayed solid, he stepped on it lightly at first and then firmly until it was holding all his weight.

Then Maximus saw Isaac kneel down next to the mound and touch it with his fingers.

"Can you move please?" Isaac asked him.

Maximus got down. "What are you doing?" he asked.

Isaac didn't answer.

After a moment, a small hole opened in the mound and out pushed a thick vine. That vine was followed by a few more next to it and as they rose up toward the hole above they wove themselves together, splitting in different directions and winding together again. Maximus noticed the ends were getting very pointed and sharp. He wondered what Isaac had in mind but his question was quickly answered when the vines cleared the outside of the hole. They curved back around and to Maximus' disbelief he saw that they were cutting back through the ground above their heads.

Little rock debris fell onto Maximus and Cael as the vines pushed through the bottom of the stone ceiling. They kept growing and weaving themselves back to the mound. Isaac removed his hand and Maximus looked up to view the final effect. It was like a large ladder made with extremely strong and thick rope.

Maximus was speechless when Isaac stood up next to him.

After a pause, Isaac asked, "Do you think it's not good? Should I test it myself?"

Maximus looked him in the eye and said, "No, Isaac — it's perfect — just what we need." They turned to Chantelle who looked awe-struck.

"We're ready," said Maximus.

One by one the prisoners climbed the vines until it was just Chantelle and Cael standing with Maximus and Isaac.

Maximus took Chantelle gently by the wrist and pulled her up onto the mound. She gave them a grateful look and then climbed the vines.

Cael went next, looking like he was so excited it was finally his turn to use Isaac's vines. Isaac followed him after shrugging his shoulders. Maximus took one last look around and then placed his hands and feet on the vines and climbed out.

It was cold outside. Very cold. The prisoners were huddled together and trembling. They kept glancing around nervously, looking for anybody who might catch them. But there were none.

"Which way?" Maximus asked Isaac, hugging himself against the cold.

Isaac walked past the huddled people then said, "Follow me, quietly. Be careful."

Maximus helped get the group moving.

The terrain was dangerous. The black rock was sharp, jagged and slippery. The light from the Stars was somewhat helpful, but it also created shadows that made it even more difficult to know where to place your feet. Maximus, at the rear, often heard a foot slipping and then a gasp of pain that was quickly masked.

Their incline was becoming steep. They had to use their hands as they climbed. The group stopped and Maximus tried to look ahead of them. He saw Isaac looking back at them, motioning to be very quiet. He motioned 'wait' and then turned and pulled his head up over the top.

Maximus began to climb past the people who were gripping the rocks and trembling. He motioned for them to stay where they were as he made his way up to Isaac.

When he made it to the top, the first thing he saw was the pale look of terror on Isaac's face. He looked over the ledge and saw Gershon, with a dark metal Telescope which had the tiny image of Stella in the lens of it. Beyond the Telescope stood more prisoners being restrained by a line of Gershon's guards. They were standing at the edge of a drop off.

He tried to listen above the thudding of his heart to what Gershon was saying to Stella. Maximus could not completely make out his words, nor did he hear Stella's response, but what she said infuriated Gershon. Gershon yelled, "You just cost yourself more deaths princess!" Maximus and Isaac both jerked in shock when they saw a guard throw a prisoner over the edge.

When Gershon turned back to Stella, Maximus could tell he was more pleased with what he saw there. "I like these tears better than fake courage, princess," he said, "Now, join me . . . or they all die."

Maximus' head was scrambling. What could they do? Revealing themselves would mean the death of all the prisoners. *Hold on Stella*, he thought, feeling more helpless than ever.

"Maximus," Isaac said frantically and they both dropped their heads back behind the ledge, "stay here and get them out when Gershon goes away from the Telescope."

"No!" Maximus answered as heatedly as he could without drawing attention. He knew what he was planning. "You could die."

"I have to go. Stella can't come here, and she probably will come to try and save lives."

Isaac transformed and disappeared faster than Maximus had ever seen. He felt sick. Something was going to go terribly wrong.

CHAPTER 47

". . . we must take the raw product of fear and turn it into an energy that will serve us."

Stella

Stella stood transfixed with horror. Gershon had just murdered a person and ten-thousand more on Gemini. At first, the look of insane glee on Gershon's face had frightened her. But as he spoke to her again, she found her fright turning into fury. Anger. How could he stand there, after what he had just done and look happy about it? He was sick. Stella felt dirty just to be looking at him.

He spoke to her, "You can stop more of this happening — you know — people dying."

"I know I can," she answered hotly, but offered no further explanation.

Gershon raised his eyebrows. "Now," he said, "I don't know what you mean by that — but let me explain to you your ONLY wise option."

"Only one?"

Her lack of fear seemed to be infuriating him. "Yes, princess, only one that will not lead to more deaths — like yours and your brother's. Join me."

"Never," she said in an even, but firm tone.

Instantly, Gershon swelled with fury. "You just cost yourself more deaths princess!"

He waved his hand and Stella heard the horrifying scuffle and scream that kept getting farther away.

Her anger was instantly gone and she felt helpless. The scream now gone still echoed in her head. She tried not to imagine the sounds of thousands more dying along with that voice. She was doing everything wrong. No one else could die.

She was tasting her salty tears and she knew she looked

pathetic and weak, but she didn't care anymore. She was completely lost as to what to do next. Gershon looked eerily happy again. "I like these tears better than fake courage princess," he said, "Join me, or they *all* die."

How could she choose between two things that she could not do? She did know one thing . . . she could barely stand in her own body knowing so many people died because of her. She couldn't let it happen again.

As she opened her mouth to respond to Gershon, he whipped his head to the side alarmingly. When he looked back at Stella it was only for a split second and he looked scared. He said, "Don't you dare go anywhere." Then he swooped off out of her line of vision.

Had he just seen Isaac? She wanted to hear something . . . anything . . . or to see Gershon come back, but everything was eerily silent.

Then she saw bursts of different colors and then nothing. She jumped up and started pacing, biting her fingernails. Arrow stepped in front of her to stop her pacing and just as he did, an entire new situation presented itself.

There was an elderly woman in a soft white robe with a crown on her head standing at the stairway entrance.

CHAPTER 48

"Though my dictionary defines courage as having the ability to face danger without fear, I see courage as being willing to harness fear's energy to my mission. Big risks take big courage which is why fear is stronger – to give us more energy."

Isaac

The second that Isaac materialized in Gershon's throne room, Helios was upon him, badgering him with questions. "Helios!" Isaac shouted above his voice. When Helios stopped talking, Isaac glanced quickly at his paw. The fur was soaked through with blood and marks of blood were all over the slate floor. Isaac said to him, "I am sending you away from here now."

"What? No you're not."

"Listen," Isaac said as patiently as he could in his hurried panic, "my sister is in trouble. I am about to lure Gershon in here away from the Telescope so Maximus can use it to get everyone out. I do not want Gershon trapping you again. I don't think I can make a shield big enough for both of us."

Helios had lifted his head to its full height and was contemplating what Isaac had said. "What if I refuse?" he asked.

"I beg you *not* to Helios. If I am focused on protecting you too, I can't protect myself fully."

Isaac reached into his pocket and felt the scale. As his fingertips touched it, they tingled like it was electrically charged and Helios responded like Isaac touched him directly.

"You can feel when I touch your scale, can't you?" Isaac asked.

"I guess I can!"

All at once, Isaac knew how to compromise with Helios. "What if I send you to where Maximus is hiding outside with the prisoners? You can help Maximus fight off the guards.

Then, if I get in too much trouble, I will touch your scale and we'll both leave this place immediately like we did before. Until then, I need to concentrate and shield myself from Gershon until all the prisoners escape."

Helios nodded his head once. Isaac hadn't sent any creature a short, or even a long distance—but there was absolutely no time for self-doubt. He put the scale back in his pocket, then pictured Maximus sending Zordosa. Isaac saw the spot in his mind just below where all the prisoners were crouching and did it—he hoped. After a moment of immense concentration, Helios was transformed and gone. There was nothing that could be done if he HAD done it wrong, so Isaac dashed to the opening that would lead to the ledge outside.

He stopped just outside the opening and yelled Gershon's name. He let Gershon get a good look at him, saw him get frenzied, and then Isaac moved back inside.

Once there, he tried his best to calm down and form his shield. He braced himself for the sight of Gershon when he heard him rushing through the passageway. Isaac focused on all the people he was there to protect. When Gershon finally burst through into the throne room, Isaac felt his shield grow even stronger instead of weaken.

Gershon slid to a halt as he caught sight of Isaac. Isaac could not identify Gershon's expression. It was everything from shocked to angry, triumphant to . . . fearful.

Focused on guarding his heart, Isaac said, "My sister will not join you."

"Don't start off with that bossy tone, boy. If you had seen her face right before you interrupted us, you would have seen she was about to agree."

Gershon started walking up to Isaac and Isaac had the inclination to start backing up, but he didn't know if he could coax the atoms to meld fast enough as he moved, so he stood his ground and kept his eyes on Gershon. "I'm here so that she will *not* join you—and neither will I."

Suddenly, Gershon's eyes widened, his lips curled and he lunged forward with hands outstretched for Isaac's neck. Isaac knew he wasn't supposed to close his eyes, but he did anyway and flexed his body, visualizing his shield holding strong and pushing Gershon back.

Gershon's howl of pain was like a victory trumpet to Isaac. He had done it. His shield had not broken. But the howl of pain was also a warning bell. Yes, it had worked, but Gershon had not even tried close to his worst yet. And now he was even angrier.

CHAPTER 49

"The virtue lies in the struggle, not in the prize."

Maximus

Gershon had disappeared inside the cave after he saw Isaac without a backward glance at his guards—who looked fearful to make a move without instruction.

Maximus thought of Stella and didn't want her to see anything that might cause her to do something rash, so he lifted a rock without touching it, raised himself up on the ledge and forced the rock down at the Telescope. The impact made the Telescope spark a little and Stella's image disappeared.

Maximus turned around quickly and looked down at the prisoners who were making a commotion. Immediately, he saw the glistening orange scales of Helios. At first he didn't understand why Helios was suddenly there, and then he quickly realized what Isaac had done. He was slightly irritated at Isaac for sending away somebody that could have helped protect him. Then he remembered Helios would have had to agree, so Isaac's reasons must have been solid.

As Helios got closer to Maximus, he could see the Dragon was in bad shape. The only thing the blood-soaked fur was doing was keeping out the rocks.

Maximus said as loud as he dared to the prisoners, "Calm down! It's alright. He's with us."

Helios asked him, "What is your strategy?"

"I don't have one yet."

"Well," Helios said as quietly as a deep voiced Dragon could speak, "We have to hurry. Isaac wants to distract Gershon long enough to get these people and us out, and then he'll leave again."

Maximus tried to suppress his panic that Isaac might not get out at all. He looked over the ledge again. "I'm not sure what those guards will do with the prisoners they're holding when they see us. Maybe you should go down first and see if you can scare the guards into letting them loose."

In answer, Helios heaved himself up over the ledge, no longer caring how much noise he made. With his injured wing, Helios just slid down the steep incline, using his claws to control his speed. Somehow, he was managing to ignore his injured paw. Maximus watched the guards long enough to see the appearance of Helios was causing the desired effect. Helios was roaring, blowing fire and his scales were taking on a strange glow. "Let the prisoners go!" he growled and thrashed his tail, knocking bits of stone off the wall. The guards who hadn't already run when he was coming down the incline screamed and ran without their prisoners as the bizarrely glowing Helios blew more fire.

Maximus turned around to the people behind him and yelled, "Let's go! You're going to have to slide down this ledge to get to the Telescope."

Luckily, the incline on the other side was smooth like a slide, apart from Helios' gouge marks. Maximus went first and climbed over the ledge and positioned himself to slide down feet first. It was steep and he dreaded the landing. He took a deep breath and pushed himself off. To his relief, it was not nearly as slippery and fast as Helios had made it look. Still, there was no stopping. Upon impact with the flat ground, he absorbed the shock by bending his knees and rolling to his side. He jumped up to his feet immediately and motioned for the rest to follow then turned around and ran to the Telescope.

Herein lied most of his worries. What would it do to him? What would it do to *them*? He didn't know exactly how Gershon built it, but he guessed it was mostly like the ones Orel built. It had to be able to work as a transporter for those of Gershon's Minion who couldn't travel without the Telescopes.

So, Maximus simply turned it around to point to the sky. When he did, he was standing in front of the eye piece. He could feel its powerful abilities pulling at him and he stepped away from it. Most of the Minion must not be very quick at transforming if this Telescope was powerful enough to aid the process that strongly.

Still, Maximus' stomach was in knots worrying about what it would do to the people who were about to go through it. He turned around and saw that he was surrounded by most of the people, including the ones Helios just freed. Only a few remained up top, Chantelle and Cael among them. Helios was keeping the guards from both coming over to the Telescope or from going to retrieve Gershon. Maximus saw a few of them throw their spears at him, but they just bounced off.

Focusing on the Telescope again, Maximus needed to decide where to send the prisoners. There was only one choice for a secure location and soft landing, but it meant he'd have to link the two Telescopes—Orel's and Gershon's.

That thought sent a shiver through Maximus. No doubt he would have to stay behind and destroy the Telescope so that Gershon could never discover where Orel's Telescope was—because it was at their lighthouse—their home.

To set up the connection, he had to offer Gershon's Telescope an object to that was associated with Orel's. He reached in his pant pocket and let out a breath of relief to find he still had one Star Charm left.

He stepped around to the front of it and pressed the tip of the Star Charm to the glass. Instantly, it turned a softer consistency and pulled it in like a hungry frog. Before Maximus had completely released the Charm, the Telescope sent out a zap to his fingers. The pain shot up through his arm. Maximus rubbed it and watched the Telescope, hoping against hope that it would work. After a second, which seemed like an eternity, the Telescope turned and pointed a different direction in the sky. It had found the location of Orel's Telescope. The glass on both ends of it emitted an eerie glow. It was ready.

With trepidation pouring through him, Maximus turned to the prisoners, now all joined around him and said, "One by one, step in front of the eye-piece. It will do most of the work. But you need to know you have the capabilities as Zodians to transform into pure light and energy. It's what atoms are made of, and you are a mass of atoms. Repeat that to yourself.

He spoke to the prisoners who had just joined them, "We don't know what this Telescope might do to you physically or mentally. You do not have to take the risk." He looked back at the others, implying again that they did not have to do it either.

They all stood straighter and no one backed down. "Yes we do," Chantelle answered. "Staying here is not an option and we want to be with you and Eli's children."

They all nodded. A different adult male said, "Are you sure there isn't a different way for the children? They shouldn't have to suffer this."

Sadly, Maximus looked around as if searching for another option—not expecting to find one. As his eyes turned back to Helios, his hopes jumped. He knew he could probably transform and send Helios back because he was a creature with whom he had a connection. Maybe if the children sat on him, they would all transform together. It would be faster than going one by one through the Telescope. But still, there were risks.

He turned to the adult whom had asked the question and said, "They could sit on Helios and I could try and send them all together, but there are risks. For one, it might not work. Two, if it does work, I can't guarantee a soft landing, and that could cause injury. Third, it will leave those guards unattended by the Dragon."

Maximus didn't realize Helios could hear him, but Helios

yelled from the distance, "Though I want to be of the most assistance possible, I must be available for Isaac. He is going to call me to him with my scale when he needs me so we can leave together."

Maximus asked, "How can he do that with your scale?"

"I am unsure, but that is how he got me out of here the first time. We can feel each other when he touches it."

"Well, then you must remain—we cannot send the children with you."

"But they cannot go through the Telescope either," said Helios. "You know, Isaac was able to bring Rikenzia at the same time as us last time without touching her as well."

"What are you saying?" asked Maximus.

"I'm saying it is incredibly risky, but maybe the children can be transformed and transported with me."

Maximus looked at the children and he saw one of them shrinking back, shivering and curling up. Maximus swept over to him and knelt in front of him. "It's alright," Maximus said. What had Gershon done to him to make him so afraid and withered away?

The boy lifted his chin slightly and with a shaky voice said, "I'd rather go through the Telescope, and I want to go soon. I need . . . to get out . . ." and he curled back up.

The adult who had spoken up for the children said, "I will go first—try to take the sting out of the machine a little." He stepped toward the eye piece. Maximus could hear him talking to himself. The Telescope's glowing eye piece became a beam of light that scanned the body up and down. The man's face contorted with pain, but no sound escaped his lips.

Faster than the blink of an eye, the man seemingly dissolved like a poof of dust and was sucked through the eye piece. The speed was so instantaneous that all they could do was sense that something had left the other end, but there was nothing to see for it. The other people looked scared, but still determined.

"Orel will appear to you all once you are through his Telescope, which is where it is sending you," said Maximus. He didn't know how he knew this—he just did.

This seemed to give them strength and add to their commitment to go through with the escape.

"You next, young man, let's get you out before things get worse here," said Maximus.

Cael and the other children who were staying, quickly hugged him and then he stepped to the eye piece. When the Telescope scanned him, the boy screamed, and Maximus felt pain course through his own body. Then, they all stood there looking at the empty space where the boy had been. Maximus felt anguish and a new fury pulsed through him. They needed to stop the evil that surrounded Gershon.

The next person stepped forward. It was a woman, classy looking even with being malnourished and un-bathed. She went like the adult before her, also holding in her cry of pain. Steadily, the people started stepping in front of the eye piece and then disappearing, some crying out in pain, others holding it in. Maximus ached with anxiety over what was happening to them. His eyes glanced toward the cave entrance. He wondered how Isaac was keeping Gershon from running out to the sounds of the shouting guards. Maximus worried for Isaac, but knew it was a good sign Gershon did not emerge. If he did, that would mean Isaac was captured... or dead.

CHAPTER 50

"That a man can change himself . . . and master his own destiny is the conclusion of every mind who is wide-awake to the power of right thought."

Isaac

"So," said Gershon through gritted teeth, "you know how to shield yourself. That's . . . 'cute'. What else can you do?" asked Gershon demandingly.

"Enough to fight you," Isaac answered bravely—still holding his shield ever stronger.

Gershon laughed and started pacing a circle around him. Isaac kept his feet in one spot and only turned his head to keep him in view as much as possible. "How did you escape, and more importantly, how did you get BACK?"

"I used the talents that were born to me," Isaac answered maturely.

"So . . . you got out of there as a Shooting Star—without a Telescope. And took the Dragon and a girl with you? Maybe I indeed have met someone worthy enough to challenge me. But that still doesn't explain how you got back. This place cannot be found."

Isaac answered, "Unless it is by something made to transport somebody here."

Gershon scowled and stopped in front of Isaac. "How did you get another crystal?"

"Your pals Dreold and Onyxus."

Gershon's eyes widened so much the veins inside of them were popping, making his eyes blood shot. "Do you know where they are?" Gershon asked, his lips barely moving he was pursing them so tight.

"We're holding Onyxus. Dreold ran like a scared little puppy. He could be anywhere."

Gershon glanced at Isaac's hands and arms. "The crystal

didn't burn you," he stated.

Isaac could tell the confusion Gershon was suffering was causing him pain—pain of being out of control—and it could backfire on Isaac at any time. Isaac double checked with his shield and it still felt solid. Then he answered Gershon simply, "I had someone else touch it for me."

"Then, there is someone else here?"

That did it—his anger and frustration burst out like a child throwing a temper tantrum. He beat his fists on Isaac's shield and screamed. He had the most threatening look on his face that Isaac had ever seen. "Who else is here with you? WHY DID YOU COME BACK?"

Almost on cue, they could hear shouts and yells from the ledge outside the cave. Gershon stopped his tantrum and stood erect to listen. He took a step toward the noise.

Isaac said, "Go out there and I'll leave. You'll miss your chance to capture me."

Gershon actually started shaking violently with his rage. Isaac was admittedly scared. He'd never seen such anger contained in a human body, and he didn't know what to expect.

"WHAT IS GOING ON OUT THERE?" Gershon shouted. Then he held out his hands in front of him, but did not make contact with Isaac's shield. But for the first time, Isaac could feel something penetrating his shield. He started to feel it tighten on him like a boa constrictor snake.

Isaac knew if he let it continue, he'd be suffocated by his own shield, or he would lose hold of it. It felt like a fist was closing around his heart and it was becoming harder and harder to breathe. He struggled with what to do . . . let the shield drop or try and push Gershon off? He thought about the scale in his pocket—but knew it wasn't time yet. There was still too much noise out there which meant not many of the prisoners had escaped yet.

Anticipating something awful if he dropped his shield,

Isaac made the decision to fight it off—even if he was afraid he'd suffocate in the meantime. Again going against what Maximus told him not to do, Isaac closed his eyes and pushed back. His shield might have other powers, right?

Then he had a thought as he tried to breathe and push back the atoms squeezing him. *If things made by evil forces could cause permanent scarring to good people, then could good things cause as deep of an effect on something evil? Could anything good even touch Gershon, who was so far gone to the other side?*

Gershon could obviously feel Isaac pushing back, because he started fighting with his words, trying to get Isaac to let go. "Dreold told me the state your mother was left in. Want to hear?"

No, Isaac did not want to hear, and thinking about his mother caused his shield to weaken. He gasped in pain as Gershon's grip became tighter. *Focus,* Isaac screamed at himself in his head, *Maximus said this would happen. Maximus. Stella. Rikenzia. Helios.* He thought of everything he had to live for.

Gershon did his insanely gleeful laugh when he felt Isaac's shield weaken slightly. But, far from weakening him further, Gershon's joy at his pain made Isaac stronger. Isaac did not want to give Gershon that sort of satisfaction but then Gershon started talking about Isaac's mother again and try as he might not to, he couldn't help but listen. He told himself he could listen and still push the shield back. He tried. Gershon was saying, "You see Isaac—her head is no longer a part of her body. Remember how beautiful she was? Well . . . zip! No more. That pretty little neck—burned in half."

A sob escaped Isaac, but he did not drop his shield. It was the only thing he had and he was only allowing room for one kind of pain, and that pain was sympathy and love for his mother. Through eyes now wet, he forced himself to look at Gershon. Isaac again saw fear in Gershon's eyes. Gershon had probably expected Isaac to drop his shield, but the contrary was happening. The shield was growing. Isaac's feelings for his mother were leaving no room for anything else.

Sympathy. Compassion.

Isaac looked at Gershon with new eyes. He tried to find things to pity instead of fear. Isaac could feel some pressure relieving off of him. Gershon screamed, "WHAT ARE YOU DOING?"

Isaac didn't answer, he just continued to stare at him. He wondered what had happened in his life to create such hate and malice toward other people. Could he have faced some tragedy that he suppressed while he served Orel? As Isaac looked at him, he knew how lonely Gershon must be, even if he'd never admit he needed other people. Who could truly love somebody like him? Gershon made it fully impossible.

Gershon widened his stance and looked like he was trying to push harder against whatever Isaac was doing. Frantically, he started talking about Isaac's father. "And your dad? Guess what happened to that failure?"

"No, Gershon," Isaac said quietly.

"No?" he asked incredulously.

Isaac ignored him again and just expanded his shield more. It reached Gershon's foot and pushed it back. Gershon growled in frustration.

Isaac knew someone that might possibly love Gershon . . . Orel. Orel had undoubtedly once loved Gershon, probably even as a brother. In fact, he probably still did in some way. Disappointed in him? Yes. Hurt by his actions? Yes. But, hate him? No. Isaac remembered it wasn't only his parents Gershon had killed—Eli and Isolde were Orel's son and daughter-in-law. Orel was as much of a victim as Isaac was. And yet he could sense that even though Gershon might never regain Orel's full fellowship and affection, Orel would never say he hated anyone. Isaac felt he had no right to hate him either. It didn't mean he loved Gershon by any means—but realizing he didn't hate him was a revelation.

But it was more than a revelation — it was a power surge. Isaac could feel it bursting forth from him, and he could even see it — like a wave. Isaac watched in disbelief as his shield, now visible, travelled through Gershon and knocked him to the ground — unconscious.

Isaac was stunned and even confused by what had happened. He felt his mind going black and his body going weak. He wanted to be home more than anything at that moment — home at the lighthouse. He put his hand in his pocket and felt a comforting energy from it. *Let's go home, Helios,* he thought. And that is the last thing he remembered thinking.

CHAPTER 51

"When you are challenged, as you will be . . .
you must constantly think of yourself as the 'new you'
and not let the old you make your decisions."

Stella

The older lady was staring avidly at Stella with a somewhat frightened expression. Then she said, "Isolde? It... it can't be."

Stella cleared her throat and answered softly, "No, I'm Stella."

The woman's expression changed slightly. It looked more joyful. She walked through the doorway and over to her. "Stella," she said.

"Yes," Stella said, feeling slightly like she was being x-rayed.

"My granddaughter!"

Stella's insides leapt and she and her grandmother embraced and both wept.

Stella could hear Arrow let out a relieved and joyful whinny-laugh. Stella and her grandmother held on to each other for another moment, Stella noting how small and fragile her grandmother felt, then they let go and wiped their eyes.

"What is your name?" Stella asked her.

"I am called Soryl. You, my granddaughter, can call me anything you'd like—just don't call me old."

"Soryl," Stella repeated with a contented sigh. "Grandma Soryl."

Stella turned to the Horses and Rikenzia and introduced them.

"Incredible," her grandmother said, "Isolde had told me she met these amazing creatures with Eli."

Stella wondered briefly how her grandmother felt about

Eli for taking away Isolde and the chance to know her grandchildren. She didn't seem like a bitter person. Her grandmother looked at Rikenzia and said, "So wonderful to meet a daughter of the Zodiacs."

Rikenzia smiled charmingly, showing no shyness or fear, "And it is wonderful to meet you, your majesty."

Her grandmother looked back at Stella, "So, tell me all about it! How and why are you here? And you know how to use the Telescope! When I came in, you looked frightened. Are you in danger?"

Stella smiled briefly at her ability to rapid-fire questions just like Isaac. Then, because she felt like her grandmother was so much like her mother, she broke down in tears. They moved to the railing.

"Do you—do you know about my mother?" Stella asked almost not able to speak.

Soryl dropped her head and nodded. "Yes, we received the news and have been grieving."

Then Stella broke down in tears and told her everything— even about being responsible for the deaths of tens of thousands of Zodians.

CHAPTER 52

"Every noble acquisition is attended with risks; he who fears to encounter the one must not expect to obtain the other."

Maximus

All the adults but Chantelle had gone and now she went to stand in front of the eye-piece. "Chantelle—" Maximus started, but she interrupted him. "I have to Maximus. I was a leader among these people. I can't put them through that without knowing what they're going through myself. I'll see you back there." She stepped in front of the eye-piece. She closed her eyes, tightened her face, bracing for whatever was to come, and then went just like the others.

The Telescope looked sinisterly hot—like it would burn anyone who touched it. Maximus looked at Cael and the other three kids. There were another two boys and a girl between Cael and Isaac's age.

"Maximus!" shouted Helios. "I can feel Isaac touching the scale. I can feel he wants to leave. We must go!"

Maximus saw him instantly start dissolving into light and energy and the children darted to Helios and stepped into his specs of light. It was working—they were dissolving too. The specs of light gathered into a ball and shot upward. Maximus happened to see another very bright ball of light leave Gershon's Lair. It joined with the Dragon and children, then it was gone faster than Maximus could follow with his eyes. *They left.*

The Telescope. How could he destroy it? And where was Gershon now?

"How will we destroy it?" asked a small voice.

Maximus whirled around. "Cael! Why didn't you go with the others?"

"Because you weren't moving—and I thought you might

need help."

Maximus wanted to scold him for such a ridiculous choice, but didn't get the chance. They both heard a shout and turned to see a manic looking Gershon emerge from the cave entrance.

"WHAT IN OREL'S FALLEN UNIVERSE HAPPENED OUT HERE?"

It was pandemonium inside Maximus' head. He felt as if he were running in many different directions at once even though he was just standing there. The guards were scattering like cockroaches.

"What do we do?" Cael asked, sounding panicked.

Maximus jumped into action. "We must destroy the Telescope—but I don't know how!"

An electric spear came whizzing toward them and landed a short distance away. Maximus saw Gershon picking up spears without touching them, igniting their electric power and hurling them at him and Cael.

Maximus ran to and grabbed the spear that had been thrown at them and tried to bash the Telescope but it was ridiculous. The spear just broke without making so much as a scratch on it.

"Over the ledge!" Cael yelled. Then he yelled again, but this time it sounded different—it was a scream of pain. A spear hit his arm by his shoulder and the electricity was burning him and starting to spread. Maximus pulled it away as quick as he could and Cael crumpled to the ground, unconscious. An injury from an object made by dark forces—Maximus feared the worst for him.

Gershon was sprinting toward them now, so fast it was unnatural. Maximus grabbed Cael up under one arm like he was a football and started pushing the Telescope to the edge of the vast opening that possibly had no bottom. Maximus strength was powered by adrenaline, so the heavy Telescope, which was luckily on a stand and not bolted down, moved over the ground. As they approached the edge, Gershon screamed—and it sounded very close to Maximus, almost right behind him. Maximus knew at once that he was going to hurl himself over the ledge with the Telescope. He'd have to transform he and Cael while they were falling.

At the last second, he shoved the Telescope as hard as he could, then dove off the ledge to the side of where he had pushed the Telescope over. He could hear the Telescope banging against the sides of the ledge and then he caught sight of it bouncing away from the ledge and falling fast. There was a strong gravity that was pulling all of them down with an irregular speed and force.

Maximus was hugging Cael with both arms as they were spinning and hurtling downward. It was disorienting. It could go on forever but Maximus had to get them out of there. He just wanted to be wherever Isaac and Helios were. He strained his mind to focus on them and not on the sensation of falling. *Transform! Light and energy! Go to Isaac and Helios!*

Familiar warmth started through him and he knew soon, he and Cael would be with Isaac. He kept his mind on them as long as he could. He felt a pull and then impact. He couldn't feel Cael in his arms anymore, but hoped he was there with him somewhere, and he wanted to know if they were with Isaac—but all his strength left him and his mind went blank.

CHAPTER 53

"The emotions are an incredible gift that we have to let us know what we're thinking."

Stella

"You must go then! Go back to Orel's Telescope and wait for your brother there," Soryl said.

"Yes. But, can . . ." she stuttered a little, "can I come back?"

"Stella. You are the Princess of Vega. This is your home—please DO come back, and bring your brother."

Stella's eyes filled up with tears again. She felt comforted but still incredibly sad.

"Listen, Stella darling—those Zodian deaths were not your fault. Not even close. Gershon is the demented human being, not you. He made it so I couldn't watch my daughter grow in her marriage, or get to know you and your brother, whom I didn't even know about. He is the one who is doing all of this. You are not to blame for his choices to kill those people. Listen to me," she said, waiting for Stella to look at her, "It is not your fault, and you do not need to feel guilty. People make unbelievably cruel choices sometimes, but you do not need to suffer for that. Alright?"

Stella wanted to believe her but she could still hear their screams.

"Oh, dear Stella, you are so sweet to mourn for them. Surely you are a true leader. You have to go on now though, remember it is evil you are fighting. Be strong, angel girl. There are hundreds of thousands and millions more who still need you."

This thought was not necessarily comforting to Stella. She felt like an enormous failure already and all she could see was that she might let these people down as well—in ways she could not fix. Tears were blurring her vision as she looked down at her feet.

"Listen, Stella," her grandmother said and gently turned Stella's face to look at her with a hand on her cheek, "every great leader feels just as you are feeling now. The fact that you feel for your people and do not feel adequate enough means that you are most assuredly the right person for the job. Now, get back to your brother then come back here with him for some rest."

Stella nodded and her grandmother dropped her hand from her face. Stella freely let the tears run down her cheeks. She hugged her grandmother one more time then turned to Rikenzia and the Horses, "Ready?"

"Ready," they said.

They each bowed to the queen then they stood together in the same way they did to travel to the Glass Castle. The girls held hands and each touched a Horse. The Horses wings touched over their heads.

Stella took one last look at her grandmother, who looked awe-inspired. "We'll be back soon," said Stella. Then she and Rikenzia gripped their Star Charms, became warm and tingly and then left the glass floor of her mother's castle.

When they landed in the top most room of the lighthouse, it was utter chaos. There was hardly an inch to spare and it was noisy. People filled the room. Most crying—some laying quite motionless.

"Stella!" said Rikenzia, "These are prisoners from Gershon's Lair!"

Rikenzia began moving through them, touching them and talking to them. Stella did not know what to do next, and the Horses were not moving a muscle for fear of stepping on someone. Stella scanned the room for Maximus and Isaac, but just as she feared, they were not there.

The person closest to Stella, a woman who was about the

age of Maximus and looked like she couldn't move her legs spoke to her with pain in her voice, "Maximus will be coming back with Isaac, the Dragon and four other children — not through the Telescope."

"Thank you," Stella said and immediately stood up to leave out the door so she could go to the beach.

"Wait," the woman said, "Maximus said . . ." she took a breath, "Maximus said Orel would appear to us when we were all here."

"And so he shall," Stella said and turned back to the Telescope and pointed it toward the shimmering wall of thick liquid. She didn't wait to see Orel, but instead stepped her way carefully to the door and called the Horses after her. Arrow and Zordosa carefully made their way through the people, wings spread out above the ones laying down to keep their balance, and tucking their wings in to move by standing people. These people did not look good. Stella knew she should stay and help, but she needed to find Maximus and Isaac.

She and the Horses squeezed through the door and then Stella mounted Arrow. Arrow dove off the landing to the center of the lighthouse, then leveled himself out and started pumping air with his wings so that he landed gently. Stella turned around to see Zordosa was going down the stairs gently but swiftly.

Just as they went outside, they saw an enormous Star land on the beach. The horses flew over and touched down just outside the crater. "Just go straight down there Arrow," Stella said. "Don't touch the sides, they still look hot. Stay here Zorri, please. Just wait for us to call."

Arrow lifted off again and lowered himself into the crater, being careful.

Stella could see the glittering scales of Helios and she saw people on top of him and on the floor. When Arrow touched down, Stella slid off him and went to the first body she saw. It was a young boy, and not Isaac. He looked like he had a severe burn from his arm up the side of his neck but was alive.

Helios was beginning to stir and Stella went to the front of him. She saw blood pooling on the ground then she saw Isaac and Maximus on the other side of the Dragon's head and neck.

Maximus was unconscious, but Isaac was pushing himself to a sitting position. She hurried to him.

"Stella!" he said as he stood up.

They hugged and then Isaac asked, "Where is Maximus?"

Stella moved aside so he could see Maximus. He looked like he was sleeping peacefully.

Stella saw Isaac look over at the boy with the burn and he ran to him. "Cael! Are you alright?" Isaac nudged him, trying to wake him up.

"I wouldn't do that Isaac, he is going to be in a lot of pain when he wakes up."

Isaac stopped and looked extremely sad.

Stella told him, "There are more people up on top of Helios. Three more I think."

Helios spoke, the lack of volume and power in his voice surprised Stella. He said, "They're alright I think. I can feel them."

"How did they get here with us?" Isaac asked Helios.

"Three children joined me as you were transforming me by touching the scale. They came too. I am not sure how Maximus and this young one got here."

Stella told him, "There are a lot of people up in the lighthouse. One of them told me that Maximus said Orel was going to speak to them. They don't look well, Isaac."

Isaac stood to his feet in a hurry and Stella stood after him. "We should get up there now," Isaac said.

"What about Helios, Maximus and these kids?"

"Go," said Helios, "Maximus is not physically harmed. He should awaken soon."

"But, you are hurt Helios," said Stella, "and so is this boy. I'll stay here until Maximus wakes up. You can go to the lighthouse, Isaac."

CHAPTER 54

"What do we live for, if it is not to make life less difficult to each other?"

Isaac

Isaac felt torn about which way to go. Helios needed healing soon . . . very soon. But he didn't know how to do it. Isaac wished Alethia was there to be with Helios and help him. Thinking of Alethia sent a new pang of worry through him about Onyxus on Pegasus. There was so much that was urgent business, but Isaac felt strongly that he needed to get up to the lighthouse to check on the escaped prisoners.

"I'll be quick," he said to Helios and Stella. "I'm going to short distance travel into the lighthouse."

"Uh . . ." Stella said. In a hurry he transformed. He had to admit, he was getting good. He thought about landing just outside the doorway at the top of the stairs. A pull forward and he was instantaneously at the door to the top most room.

He stepped in cautiously. The sight of the people startled him even though Stella warned him. Some people's arms had crippled up beyond use. Some people looked like they were lost in their own minds and scared. All of them looked affected in some way or another.

Isaac spotted Rikenzia moving among the people and checking on them. He felt an amazing sort of gladness and appreciation surge through him at the sight of her.

Then, he looked back toward the Telescope and saw Chantelle was there on the ground. She didn't look right and Isaac decided he would go to her first. When he got to her, she looked at him and started crying. "Oh, I'm sorry Isaac, I don't mean to be such a mess. It's just . . . you're alright. What a relief. Maximus and the others?"

"They're on the beach and they're fine. Cael is burned badly though. What happened to you?"

"I'm not sure," she answered, "I can't move my legs but it doesn't hurt."

Isaac didn't know what to say. He turned and looked at Orel's projection and he was surprised to see he also had tears wetting his cheeks as he looked at his people in pain. Orel found Isaac's eyes and Isaac stood up.

"Thank you, Isaac," he said, "These are some of my most loyal people."

Isaac didn't feel accomplished however. He felt guilty. He cleared his throat and said, "There probably was a different way to get them out—but I didn't know of any."

"You and Maximus did what you had to do, and these people made the decision for themselves. They will be rewarded for facing this pain to escape Gershon. No doubt they were offered many chances to join him to escape such pain, but they didn't. They are valiant and noble."

Isaac looked around at them. As he did, he had a feeling that although they were physically suffering, on the inside, it's like they knew something Isaac did not—like they could see something more than what the average person could see, and it gave them happiness.

"Can you heal them?" Isaac asked.

"Has Maximus told you the risks of using anything that has been made by evil forces?"

"Yes. He said it will forever leave its mark on a person."

Orel nodded. "Through this life, these people will always have traces of the sacrifice they made. When you look at any one of them, you will be reminded of what they did."

Isaac asked, "You can't heal them then?"

"Not fully. Not when they are still there."

"What will happen with them then?"

Orel looked around at the people. "I'm going to offer them the chance to come live with me here.

"Is that possible?"

"For these people it is. They have done all they need to

do. If they are with me, I can heal them."

"How will they get to where you are?"

"With my Telescope. Go and bring Maximus and Stella here."

Isaac nodded and left to do as he was asked. He gave one last glance to Rikenzia who was still tending to the people. He walked out and closed the door, then transported himself back to the crater where everyone was.

CHAPTER 55

"Once you begin to understand and truly master your thoughts and feelings, that's when you see how you create your own reality, that's where your freedom is, that's where all your power is."

Stella

Helios' blood was starting to get to Stella. Not in a pass-out sort of way, but a worried-for-his-life sort of way. His scales were starting to look pale and dull. She decided to heal the gash. She didn't know how much it would hurt being a Dragon size wound instead of a human size wound, but she wasn't afraid anymore. She thought she could handle the pain a little better now as she wasn't as worried or sad as she had been before.

She glanced at the boy Isaac had called Cael. She must send him up and out of here with Arrow, and call Zordosa down to help get the other three. Just on cue, she heard voices from on top of Helios.

"It's alright," she called to them, "Slide down off the Dragon and we'll get you out of here. You're safe."

Then she called to Arrow and he came to her as the people came down — three kids.

She said to Arrow, "I want to get Cael and the other children out of the crater so we can take them to the lighthouse. Can I lift Cael onto you and have you take him and another one up and bring Zordosa back down to get the others?"

"Anything to help," he answered.

It was difficult work to lift even such a small boy and balance him on Arrow with the help of the others, but they did it. Stella elected the smaller of the other two boys to ride behind Cael and hold him on.

"Be as steady as you can," she instructed Arrow, a little nervous but also trusting Arrow. He stood in one spot and pumped his wings until he went straight up. *Poor Horse,* she thought. She watched for a moment to see that the kids were holding steady on Arrow's broad back and then she anxiously waited for them to come back.

Arrow came back and was followed by Zordosa who made the descent into the crater look effortless. She landed gently, and then Stella helped the girl climb onto her back. The girl looked as star-struck as Stella must have been the first time she climbed on Arrow. The other boy was up on Arrow, and again, up the Horses went, straining and pushing with all their might. Stella didn't wait to watch this time, but hurried to the front of Helios.

She looked one more time at Maximus. He still looked like he was sleeping peacefully. Then, she asked Helios if she could see his paw. He offered it to her and she removed with difficulty the soaked whatever-it-was from around it. The smell of his blood was strong and metallic. For all of Stella's weaknesses however, she was surprised to find out she didn't react negatively to blood.

She revealed the gash below and saw just how deep it was. "Don't move," she said and held her hands up to the wound to begin to heal it, but Helios pulled his paw away.

"What's wrong?" she asked.

"I can't let you do that—the pain is strong even for me."

"You don't really have a choice, Helios. You're dying from loss of blood, I can tell. *You* don't, or *I* don't want Isaac having to deal with the pain of healing it, OR the pain of losing you. I can handle it, alright? Now give it back."

He considered her for just a second, and then he offered his paw again.

She again held her hands out in front of her and willed the cells in the Dragon's paw to regenerate at an extremely fast rate and heal. She envisioned his paw healed. She did not know *how* the two sides of flesh were supposed to come together, but she knew they could. She focused her thoughts on it being perfect again.

She felt the heat and saw the globe of hot energy forming from her hands and on around the Dragon's massive paw—and it was spreading up toward his wing. She didn't know for sure that she had it in her—and seeing it working gave her a much needed boost to her confidence. What an amazing gift she would forever be thankful she was born with.

After another moment, the massive orb turned ice blue and cold, then she dropped her hands. Helios let out a comforted sigh of relief and a second afterward, the pain that he had felt in his paw was in her. It stabbed and ached and burned. But she stayed standing. She wasn't going to let it take her down. She grimaced as the pain coursed through her, but it was just pain. Pain is something only the bearer of it can keep alive. She wanted none of it and she thought of reasons why she was happy. She counted her blessings. Although every inch of her was screaming and wanted to collapse on the floor, she did not allow that. Then, with relief that actually *did* make her fall to her knees, it left her.

She had done something good, and she had done it without prompting or coaching from anyone. She looked up with a smile on her face and was surprised to see Isaac standing there next to Helios, his mouth agape. "Are you alright?" he asked her.

"Of course I am," she said, still enjoying her feeling of accomplishment. "I healed your Dragon's cut."

"I know, I saw." He sounded happy.

"And my wing!" Helios said.

Stella looked around and saw Arrow and Zordosa standing behind her, staring at her and looking amazed as well. "How did you not crumble in pain like you did when you healed Isaac?" Arrow asked.

"I don't know really," she answered, "I just feel stronger—and happier."

They all continued to stare at her.

"What?" she asked.

Isaac answered, "It's just not what we were expecting after what you have just been through."

So, Isaac knew about those people. Stella became solemn for a moment again. "I know—but someone helped me understand. Isaac, we have a grandmother! I met her."

"We . . . we do?"

She nodded with a smile.

"On Vega?"

She nodded again.

"Why didn't Maximus mention her?"

"Because . . ." they heard a tired and scratchy voice from Helios' other side, "I didn't know if she was still alive, and I didn't want to get your hopes up."

Helios scooted back and Isaac and Stella ran to Maximus. He was starting to sit up and they knelt down next to him and helped him. They started to ask questions about how he felt, but he just grabbed them both to him and hugged them. They were in an awkward position in his tight arms, but he wasn't letting go . . . and he was crying.

"What's wrong Maximus?" Stella asked a little worried.

"Oh, nothing anymore," he said and let go of them. They sat back and then got to their feet, helping Maximus up. "You're both here and safe!"

Stella was touched by his emotion over them. She knew how much of his life he'd given up protecting them.

"How did you get out Maximus?" asked Isaac.

"Stories later," he answered, then he asked, "Has anybody seen if there are people in the lighthouse yet?"

"Yes, we've both seen them," Stella answered.

"And?" Maximus prompted.

Isaac answered, "And they're not in great shape, but they're going to be fine. Orel is on the projection right now. He wanted me to take you and Stella there."

"Let's go then," said Maximus, "I have no energy for

transforming anymore though."

"I'll carry you out," said Arrow.

"And I'll take you, Princess," said the sweet voice of Zordosa.

"I'll take you out Isaac, said Helios."

Maximus looked at Helios. "You're healed!"

Helios nodded toward Stella. "The healer here did it. It was incredible."

Maximus looked at her with wonder and she smiled back at him.

Then they all climbed onto the animals. They strained to fly and climb out, but Stella could tell they were happy to be serving. It was Stella's first time on the back of the Horse that had carried her father, and she felt privileged to be riding on her.

Stella didn't know what Orel had in store when they were all there, but she didn't feel apprehension like she would have before. She was starting to trust Orel. *After all,* she reminded herself, *he's family, too.*

CHAPTER 56

"Help thy brother's boat to yonder shore, and lo, your boat arrives also."

Isaac

Helios, Arrow and Zordosa stayed outside the light house while the humans went inside and climbed the stairs to the top most room. Arrow told them that the children had already gone up there, carrying Cael, who hadn't awakened yet.

Isaac was nervous about Maximus seeing Chantelle. He knew she was important to him. When they got to the landing, Stella and Isaac stepped back to let Maximus through first. He had slowed on the climb up the stairs, his energy still spent.

"It's a tight squeeze in there," Isaac told him, "And the people are not the same."

Maximus nodded then opened the door and they followed him in.

The sight was slightly different now. There were the four children, Cael now awake and looking in definite pain, and three adults grouped over to one side, Chantelle among them. She was lying on the floor on her side and propped up on her hands with straight arms like a mermaid would sit.

The rest of the people had been moved and helped so that they were forming a circular line which started at the Telescope. Isaac knew what the line was for, but he knew Maximus and Stella did not know yet.

Isaac tried to spot Rikenzia, and he finally saw her holding up a boy who was about their age. He looked like an infant in an adolescent body—he couldn't support his weight and he looked glassy eyed and was drooling with his head over on his shoulder. She was being so kind and gentle with him. Isaac was about to go help her but heard Orel call them up to him.

They went, moving through the people to get there.

Orel told Maximus and Stella, "These people have proven their loyalty to me, and to our family. Because of what they were injured from, they will forever be this way while they live here, or on the Zodiacs. But I can give them relief and comfort if they were here with me."

Maximus interrupted, "They're going to come live with you? No one even knows where you are."

Orel answered him, "No one needs to know where I physically am. Do you think that bringing them to me is the right thing to do?"

"Of course! I couldn't think of anything better for them. I just . . . you just haven't done anything like this before."

"No one has ever needed, wanted or deserved it more."

Maximus nodded and Isaac saw him searching the room. He knew he was looking for Chantelle, but from where they were standing, he couldn't see her on the floor.

Orel said, "I gave them each the choice. There are three adults who have chosen to stay, plus four young people. They feel they still have work to do."

Isaac now knew what the group standing off to the side was doing—they were staying—which included Chantelle.

"Really?" Maximus asked, "Who? Are they sure?"

"They are sure," said Orel. "We need to start. Maximus, I'd like you to move the eye piece of the Telescope into this sheet of liquid. My image will disappear. Then, help them one by one place their hands into the magnifying lens. I will transform them and bring them to me.

Isaac was completely confused as to how he would do this. Even Maximus asked, "How will that work?"

Orel smiled lovingly, "I made that Telescope, remember? I still have a few 'tricks' you don't know about, son."

Stella asked Orel quietly, "And we still can't know where you are?"

"One day, precious. For now, we can still talk, but over a distance."

She nodded.

Orel was looking at Isaac now. He said, "I'll be back after this is done. I'd like to hear how you escaped Gershon none the worse for wear."

"Yes, sir," Isaac answered.

Orel took one last look at them, said, "I'm proud of you all," then he told Maximus to proceed.

Maximus did what he was told with the Telescope, then guided the first person forward by her hands. She was mumbling to herself incoherently. She shuffled her feet forward at Maximus' gentle pressure. He placed her hands toward the lens, and it softened like the liquid sheet Orel's image had just been on. Her hands sunk in and her demeanor changed. She giggled as her arms were transformed into billions of microscopic lights that spread until her entire body was consumed.

Gently and slowly, not instantaneously fast as normal, the lights were pulled through the Telescope. Maximus got the next person, a man whose skin looked burned and raw. The man sighed when his hands moved into it like it was cooling and soothing his burns. His transformation and departure happened faster than the first woman. Isaac wondered if Orel somehow knew that that man needed the instant relief.

Maximus looked at Stella and Isaac and they instantly jumped into action. They helped move the line forward and escort people to the Telescope. They were each damaged either physically or mentally, and sometimes it looked like both. But they each moved willingly forward and each received relief the moment their hands moved into the liquid-like surface of the Telescope's lens.

In not too long of time, they had moved almost all of them forward and through the Telescope. Isaac noticed Maximus wasn't helping for a moment. He looked and saw him talking to Chantelle. By their body language, he could tell Maximus thought she should go so she didn't have to suffer without the use of her legs. She was reassuring him she wanted to stay.

Isaac turned back to his work. It was now time to help Rikenzia carry the boy whose weight she was supporting to the Telescope. As Isaac wrapped his arm around his waist he could feel a special presence from him. He didn't know why, but he wanted to cry with sympathy and love for this boy. Isaac thought about how this boy had been whole just a short time ago, and who knows what he had been through even before this? He never gave into Gershon. While Isaac supported his weight, Rikenzia lifted his hands to the Telescope. As his hands entered, the boy became very still, like he was listening to something. As his arms transformed, he actually lifted his head off his shoulders. He became lighter in Isaac's arms. Isaac let go and the boy stood unsupported as the transformation spread over his whole body. The boy turned and looked at them and Isaac saw gratitude in his eyes.

Orel pulled this boy slowly through as well. When he was gone, both Isaac and Rikenzia were wiping their eyes. It was a miracle and Isaac felt so blessed to have known someone so pure, even for a small moment.

CHAPTER 57

"Action will sometimes be required, but if you're really doing it in line with what the Universe is trying to bring you, it's going to feel joyous. You're going to feel so alive. Time will just stop."

Maximus

Everyone that was leaving to live with Orel had now departed. Maximus was so exhausted he didn't know if his body could keep functioning. But he didn't want to stop yet, so he kept pushing forward. There were still people to take care of. Cael was the most pressing matter. The boy was pale with pain.

Maximus was planning to heal him if he could conjure the strength, but Stella stepped over. "I can do it," she said.

Maximus liked this improvement to her confidence and decided to let her do it. Healing must be her true calling. He told her, "This one might be different to heal. Remember, it was given to him by an object made by Gershon. It will probably never look completely normal again. I'm not sure if healing it will do anything different to you than what you're used to."

He saw a shadow of fear come into her eyes, but she didn't say anything.

She knelt next to Cael and explained what she was going to do. He nodded his approval and she set to work, the orb of light growing in her hands. Maximus was still marveling at her. He felt like a proud father might, even though he knew he had little to do with her gifts.

When the orb cooled and disappeared, Stella instantly grabbed her head. Cael stood up and tried to touch her. "No Cael — leave her," Maximus said.

Stella sank to her knees and continued to grip her head. A

tear slid down her cheek. She started rocking her body back and forth. Maximus didn't know how to help because he didn't know what she was dealing with. He knelt down next to her and reached his hand forward. "Stella?"

Lightning fast she slapped his hand away and rotated away from him. Isaac tried next. Her eyes were still closed and more tears ran down her cheeks. She rocked and shook, but no sound escaped her. When Isaac touched her she jerked away from him like he had shocked her. They all watched helpless for a moment longer. When nothing changed, Maximus went to a window and yelled for Arrow to come up. It didn't take long before he was entering through the door.

Maximus told him briefly what happened. The Winged Horse went straight up to her and dropped his head and neck down so his eyes were level with her head. He moved himself in the way of her rocking motions. She bumped into him once and didn't react. After another couple bumps she started slapping at him too. He did not move away from her flailing arms — not even an inch. She stopped after a moment and leaned her head against the Horse's forehead. Their closely matched hair fell forward and blended together. She looked like she was taking deep breaths.

She sat back on her heels and opened her eyes to the sight of Arrow's face inches from hers. She threw her arms around his head and hugged his face. He kept very still for her. She sat back again, let go of him and wiped her eyes.

She looked up and Maximus and Isaac. "That was awful," she said.

"What happened?" asked Maximus and Isaac in unison.

"Not physical pain. It was emotional pain. I could hear Gershon's voice in my head telling me how useless I was. All my mistakes kept replaying in my head. His voice was telling me how unworthy and dirty I was . . . and that's how I felt . . . so dirty. I didn't want anyone touching me or talking to me so that nobody had to be infected by my filthiness.

"Then I could smell Arrow, and I could feel he wasn't moving away from me. I remembered about love and forgiving, and how he said he'd never leave my side for anything. Then my head became clear."

She wiped her face again. She stood up and hugged Arrow around his neck, then came to hug Maximus and Isaac.

"But, did it work?" she asked and she looked around for Cael.

He was feeling his neck.

"The pain is gone," he said, "but it feels like it probably still looks bad."

And it did, but not as bad as it had. The raw redness of it had vanished, but the skin still looked wrinkly and scarred.

"It's alright!" said Cael, not waiting for anybody's answer, "I'll just switch my wardrobe up a bit and nobody will know."

"I'm glad the pain is gone," Stella said.

Now that Cael was as healed as he could be, Maximus wanted to talk to the three adults who stayed behind. Maximus still didn't understand why they wanted to stay when they had the chance to be pain free and live with Orel.

Maximus asked the names of the other middle-aged woman and man. The woman said, "I am Gemma, from Virgo." She didn't look physically harmed, but Maximus noticed it looked like she could never hold completely still. Some part of her was always moving or twitching. But, she looked Maximus in the eye, and seemed of sound mind. Maximus greeted her, and thanked her.

Maximus looked at the man. He didn't know how he hadn't noticed until now — the man definitely could not see. Maximus asked anyway, kindly and softly, "Sir, can you see?"

"No," he answered, "I am blind. But I seem to be otherwise unharmed."

"I am sorry," Maximus said.

"No need," he said, "I am Tevech, from Sagittarius."

"Our young Cael is from Sagittarius as well. And

everyone knows Chantelle? She is from Libra." Maximus knelt down next to her. Oh, what would Cecily say? Isaac moved over to them with a chair. Maximus lifted her into it. Once seated, Maximus asked them, "What is it you three would like to do?"

Chantelle answered, "Well, is the plan to get the Zodiacs back now that Stella and Isaac are back?"

Maximus looked at his niece and nephew and they nodded.

Chantelle saw them nod, then she said, "Then, I think we should return to our own Zodiacs, tell our story, and start building a resistance like we never have before.

Stella asked, "Won't you get caught again?"

Chantelle asked, "Maximus, is Gershon's Telescope destroyed?"

"I think so. I hurled it over the ledge and it fell. I don't know if Gershon will be able to recover it or not. The strength of the gravity was like nothing I have ever felt before."

Chantelle looked worried but said, "It's going to take a while for him to try and recover it, make a new one, or to travel from Zodiac to Zodiac and instruct his Minion members to get his war together. We might have a little time before anyone is the wiser. The Zodians need to feel hope. Yes, we are damaged, but we are strong in spirit. They will see we defied him. Right, children?"

The girl said, "Right. Plus, they will know Orel's family is back and that they helped us, we'll make sure of that."

The older of the two boys said, "The love of Gershon is dying off. People know they made a mistake. When they see another way, they'll follow! Even if it's a difficult path. Well—most will, hopefully."

The younger boy said, "That's what we want to do, too. We want to go back to the Zodiacs and start turning people around."

Maximus was blown away by the maturity and strong

personality of these Zodian youth. They were so advanced and untainted with the doubts of Gershon-affected adults. He looked at Stella and Isaac who were standing together next to Arrow and Rikenzia. They looked impressed as well.

Maximus said to the three children, "Well, how about you three introduce yourselves first, and then we'll go eat a warm meal before going our separate ways." They all smiled and nodded.

The girl introduced herself as Vespius from Aries. She was thirteen years old. The older boy was Nevicis from Gemini, and he was fifteen. The younger boy was Ethan, from Leo. He was ten years old. Cael introduced himself to the others . . . from Sagittarius, only eight years old.

Though they looked confident in their own right, when Stella and Isaac came forward to greet them, Vespius, Ethan and Nevicis acted shy, like they were meeting celebrities. Cael was acting like nothing bad had ever happened to him.

Maximus had Rikenzia introduce herself, and he learned she was from Capricorn and was fifteen years old. Same age as Isaac. And yes, he could see the sparks between the two already and resolved to talk to them later.

"Alright," he said, "let's go get some food, and maybe some rest."

CHAPTER 58

"Nothing is limited — not resources or anything else. It is only limited in the human mind. When we open our minds to the unlimited creative powers we will call forth abundance and see and experience a whole new world."

Isaac

Isaac was with Maximus and Stella in the top room of the lighthouse speaking with Orel. Orel told them the people had all arrived safely, and he was working with each one individually and they were recovering well.

Isaac didn't know exactly how to explain what happened in the throne room, but he did his best attempt. He glanced at Stella when he got to the part about Gershon trying to break him by talking about how his parent's died.

His pause gave Maximus the chance to guess what had happened next. "Did he try to use your parents' deaths against you like we thought he might?"

Isaac nodded. He was trying not to think of the images of his mother that Gershon had put there. But it wasn't working, and it made him feel sick. The more he resisted the thoughts, the stronger they came into his mind.

"Did Gershon succeed?"

Isaac sighed, "No, my shield never dropped. In fact, it kept getting bigger. I . . . this . . . I know this is . . . I mean, I know this might be hard to understand, but I started to feel sorry for him. And, I thought of you, Orel — and how it wasn't just my parents, but your family too that he had killed. And, I thought . . . well, I guessed that you don't actually hate him . . . do you?"

Orel's expression was affectionate. "I am definitely disappointed and deeply saddened by him and even angry.

He will never regain what he once had, but you're right, I do not hate him."

Isaac nodded. "When I thought of that, I thought, maybe I don't hate him either. Then, my shield kind of . . . well, I don't really know what it did."

Orel said, "My guess is it did what your mother can do — send her feelings out as an actual, physical force."

"Must have," said Isaac, "I could actually see it burst out from me. It went through Gershon and he fell to the floor. I saw it all, and then started feeling weak, so I touched the Helios' scale and I just wanted to come home."

"And then he did," Maximus said, taking over the story. I saw Helios transform in front of my eyes. The kids, minus Cael went to him and transformed as well. Then up they went. They were joined by another ball of light, which was Isaac and they were gone.

"Then it was me and the stowaway, Cael, and all too suddenly, Gershon emerged and was coming after us."

He recounted the rest of the story of Cael getting hit and hurling the Telescope and themselves out into the great space with unknown depth.

They all sat in silence for a moment then Rikenzia said, "Gershon is probably dangerously angry right now."

Orel said, "No doubt he is. I think he knows now that Stella and Isaac are working whole heartedly against him. He will become more extreme than he ever has been before. Especially because he will be afraid now — afraid of the escaped prisoners, afraid of Isaac's abilities, and we're not sure if he recognized Maximus or not — but no matter if he did, he'll know there are many actively fighting against him. He'll be getting ready to fight by enormous force."

"And we will do the same," Maximus said.

"Yes, it is time to end Gershon's dictatorship and get Isaac crowned the King of the Zodiacs."

"M . . . me?" This really threw Isaac off. "I thought we

were going to get the Zodiacs back for *you*?"

"I feel my time has passed. It is time for you, Eli's son, to lead the Zodiacs."

Isaac looked at Maximus, "But, you're Orel's son just like my dad was. Why not you?"

Maximus put a hand on his shoulder and said, "I've never wanted that, Isaac. It's just not for me. I like supporting the leader, not actually being the leader—and I'll support you with everything I have. Is that going to work for you?"

Isaac looked at Stella. What did she think of all this? She looked deeply into Isaac's eyes as if trying to read his thoughts. She looked away from him after a moment and back to Orel. "I believe Isaac can do this," she said, "but will Zodians follow such a young person?"

Orel answered, "I believe they will change their ways and follow Isaac more readily than they would any of us. There is something about the innocence of youth, and something in particular about Isaac that inspires people."

"What about Stella?" Isaac asked. "She is first born and has the same heritage as me. Shouldn't she be the leader?"

Orel answered, "Stella has another calling, and I think she knows what it is. See, Isaac, on the Summer Triangle, women inherit the crown."

Isaac looked at Stella and saw excitement on her face. Finally, she found where she was happy. Isaac wondered why he didn't feel as happy about inheriting the Zodiacs.

"Is this something you can accept, Isaac?" asked Orel.

Isaac thought about all he had accomplished so far. He thought about his initial joy of finding out he wasn't some sort of 'freak'. He thought about the grateful looks from people he helped free. He thought about Rikenzia and her support, even if she was a little bossy. He smiled.

"Is that a yes?" Orel asked.

"Honestly," Isaac answered, "I am scared."

"You will have much support," said Orel.

Isaac nodded. He knew that was true.

"In fact, I will show you just how much support you have. Maximus, can you please bring Rikenzia, Nevicis, Ethan, Vespius and Cael here, please?"

Maximus nodded and went to go get them. When they came back in with Maximus, they were very reverent in front of Orel. They looked overwhelmed to be standing there in front of his image.

Orel talked to them about Gershon, and about what had to be done next. He praised their loyalty and strength. He told them he wanted to pick a new twelve to be Stewards of the Zodiacs and he wanted the Stewards to be youth. "The plan is to stop hiding and start turning things back to us. Isaac will be named Zodiac Prince, and when the time is right, King."

They looked over at Isaac and looked happy for him which made Isaac feel awkward.

"Now," Orel continued, "because of the turmoil Gershon has brought to the Zodiacs, you each might not know about your unique gifts. Or if you know about them, you have not had the opportunity to develop them."

They all stood with backs a little straighter—anticipating the excitement of what Orel was about to share with them.

"Ethan, from Leo—our Lion Constellation."

Ethan looked back at Orel and Orel told him, "Leos are positive thinkers and adventurers. Zodians from Leo have the ability to affect moods and feelings in others, and with this ability, you also have the ability to create energy fields. You must be aware that you do not let pride or ego ever block you from using these powers unwisely, or for your own gain."

Ethan nodded.

"Nevicis," Orel said. "You are from Gemini, the Constellation of the twins. Gemini's enjoy knowing a little bit of everything. They are multi-dimensionally talented. Because of this, Gemini's have the ability to take on other forms as shape-shifters. You must be careful though that your craving for excitement and ever changing focus does not drive away those closest to you."

Nevicis nodded and shifted his weight back to his heals — looking humbled.

"Vespius."

Vespius looked steadily back at Orel with confidence and affection.

"You are from Aries — the Ram."

She nodded.

"Aries are not afraid of challenges. You are a doer — not a talker. Our Aries Zodians have the ability to accelerate and/or slow the growth of things, both physical and intangible. Going forward, you need to be aware of your competitiveness. And also be willing to accept when a challenge might be too much for you to handle alone."

She nodded too, like they all had, looking both happy and humble.

"Cael," said Orel. Cael still looked nervous, but he stood up straighter and looked like he was trying not to smile.

"Sagittarius. Our Archer — the Constellation of the Centaur. These Zodians are very generous and honest. They are very intellectually advanced. Cael, as a Sagittarius, you have the potential for powers of accuracy and matter manipulation. And with these powers, as accurate as you will be, you need to be aware of what you set your sights on. Does that make sense?"

It didn't make sense to Isaac, but Cael nodded energetically.

"Good," said Orel with a smile. "And now Rikenzia. You are from Capricornus, the Constellation of the Goat. Capricorns are persevering people and you always rise to the challenge, no matter the opposition that comes your way. You are a hard worker — sometimes a little too much."

Rikenzia nodded knowingly and glanced down at her

feet. She looked back up when Orel continued, "You have the potential as a Capricorn to perfect the art of transforming and transporting. You will be able to go where not too many others can—and this because you are not afraid to take the first step in an unknown direction. Use caution though Rikenzia, and know when to not go somewhere you shouldn't."

"Of course," she answered him, "I'll do my best."

Orel looked pleased and asked the group of them, "Will you five be willing to be the leader, or the Stewards of the Constellation you come from?"

They looked stunned. When none of them said anything, Orel said, "I don't think I could think of anyone better for the task. You are all loyal, smart and will not falter under pressure as you have already proven. Please, will you serve as Isaac's Stewards?"

Rikenzia answered, "For you, and for Isaac and Stella, we will do anything."

The other four added their affirmations. Cael looked frightened for the first time Isaac could remember seeing him. Vespius had a tear in her eye, but was staring unblinking at Orel. Nevicis looked ready to jump into action right there and Ethan stared wide-eyed. Rikenzia beamed over at Isaac.

"Thank you," said Orel. He looked at Maximus, Stella and Isaac and said, "May I present your first five of twelve Zodiac Stewards!"

Rikenzia piped in before they could respond, "Can we call ourselves something else, though? 'Stewards' does not have a very good ring with the Zodians anymore if you know what I mean."

"What would you suggest?" Orel asked.

"Are we going to learn skills like the last Stewards did?"

"Yes, you will need to learn a lot."

"Then, can we be called the Shooting Stars?"

Orel looked at Isaac. Isaac nodded. It was perfect.

"Alright then," Orel said, "May I present your first five of twelve Shooting Stars!"

Everyone smiled, including Isaac. He did indeed feel stronger already knowing he had people like these around him.

"Now," Orel said, "It will be up to all of you to find who the other seven Shooting Stars will be from Taurus, Cancer, Virgo, Libra, Scorpius, Aquarius, and Pisces. Also, Gershon will turn this into a universal battle. Each of you should gain the alliance and companionship of a creature Constellation as Stella has paired with Pegasus and Isaac has paired with Draco."

The five Shooting Stars looked excited about getting their own companion as well.

Orel gave some instructions to Maximus on getting the Zodiac Leaders set up with Star Charms and to not wait too long before starting their training.

Orel looked at the anxious group and gave them an edict. "Maximus is your official trainer now. Respect and honor him."

Everyone said their good-byes and good-lucks then Orel's image disappeared. For a moment, they all stayed staring at where it had been. Characteristically, Rikenzia was the first to break the silence. She came over to Isaac and Stella and asked, "I've been thinking I'd love to try and have a Phoenix as my companion."

Isaac could not think of a more noble and beautiful creature that matched Rikenzia more perfectly. He looked at Maximus who nodded his approval.

"Looks like we're going to Phoenix next." Isaac said.

Rikenzia clapped her hands, threw her arms around Isaac's neck and hugged him.

ABOUT THE AUTHOR:

Leslie Hodgson (pronounced with a silent "g", Hod-son) currently resides in the Seattle, Washington area with her husband and three young daughters. Leslie has always had a fascination with the night sky and has lived with horses her entire life. Her nickname growing up was "barn girl" as she was never far from her horses. She started a business combining two of her three favorite things: kids and horses. Her other favorite thing is writing, and she hopes to share the magic of the night sky, animal companionship and endless possibilities with you!

QUOTE REFERENCES:

Chapter 2: Charles Haanel, *The Secret*
Chapter 3: Terence
Chapter 4: Prentice Mulford, *The Secret*
Chapter 5: Dr. Fred Alan Wolf, *The Secret*
Chapter 6: Michael Bernard Beckwith, *The Secret*
Chapter 7: Madame Swetchie
Chapter 8: Wade Cook, *Treasure Thinking*
Chapter 9: Prentice Mulford, *The Secret*
Chapter 10: W. Clement Stone
Chapter 11: James Allen
Chapter 12: Rhonda Byrne, *The Secret*
Chapter 13: Bob Procter, *The Secret*
Chapter 14: Rhonda Byrne, *The Secret*
Chapter 15: Rhonda Byrne, *The Secret*
Chapter 16: Prentice Mulford, *The Secret*
Chapter 17: Robert Collier, *The Secret*
Chapter 18: James Ray, *The Secret*
Chapter 19: Jack Canfield, *The Secret*
Chapter 20: Wade Cook, *Treasure Thinking*
Chapter 21: Bob Trask, *Romancing the Soul*
Chapter 22: *The Secret*
Chapter 23: Jeremy Collier
Chapter 24: Dr. Denis Waitley, *The Secret*
Chapter 25: Richard Cumberland
Chapter 26: Neale Donald Walsch, *The Secret*
Chapter 27: Proverbs 3:5
Chapter 28: Wade Cook, *Treasure Thinking*
Chapter 29: Lisa Nichols, *The Secret*
Chapter 30: Aldous Huxley
Chapter 31: William Gilmore Simms
Chapter 32: Carl Jung (1875-1961), *The Secret*
Chapter 33: Michael Bernard Beckwith, *The Secret*
Chapter 34: Michael Bernard Beckwith, *The Secret*

Chapter 35: Genevieve Behrend (1881-1960), *The Secret*
Chapter 36: Jack Canfield, *The Secret*
Chapter 37: Marci Shimoff, *The Secret*
Chapter 38: Madame Dorothee Deluzy
Chapter 39: Vernon Law
Chapter 40: Bob Trask, *Romancing the Soul*
Chapter 41: Dr. Martin Luther King, Jr. (1929-1968), *The Secret*
Chapter 42: Bob Trask, *Romancing the Soul*
Chapter 43: Rhonda Byrne, *The Secret*
Chapter 44: Bob Trask, *Romancing the Soul*
Chapter 45: Thomas S. Monson, *November 2010 Ensign*
Chapter 46: Rhonda Byrne, *The Secret*
Chapter 47: Bob Trask, *Romancing the Soul*
Chapter 48: Bob Trask, *Romancing the Soul*
Chapter 49: Richard M. Milnes
Chapter 50: Christian D. Larson (1866-1954), *The Secret*
Chapter 51: Bob Trask, *Romancing the Soul*
Chapter 52: Pietro Metastiasio
Chapter 53: Marci Shimoff, *The Secret*
Chapter 54: Chinese Proverb
Chapter 55: Michael Bernard Beckwith, *The Secret*
Chapter 56: Bob Doyle, *The Secret*
Chapter 57: Rhonda Byrne, *The Secret*
Chapter 58: John Assaraf, *The Secret*

96244618R00170

Made in the USA
Columbia, SC
23 May 2018